CHAPTER ONE

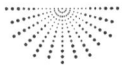

"Miss, stop! The bridge is about to open."

I ignored the toll bridge operator's screams and sprinted ahead. This drawbridge took forever to open and close. If I got stuck waiting for the ancient thing to run its cycle, the interview would be over before I got there. The bridge was just starting to creak open, barely a foot gap. The toll bridge guy was hot on my heels as I leapt to the other side. Or tried to.

I tripped over my own feet, flying forward. I skidded to a stop on my hands and knees.

That was when it all changed. The sun was gone. The breeze was gone and the air grew—flat. The world was gone. All the things Gram had said right before I left the house came rushing back to me. What the hell had she done?

Two hours before the world as I knew it ended...

. . .

1

Jeannie: *Did you watch?*
  Me: *You know I didn't. I never do.*
  Jeannie: *Good. He doesn't deserve your attention.*
  Me: *Talk later. Leaving for the interview soon.*

I took a last look in the mirror, smoothing down some stray auburn hairs and straightening the suit my friend Jeannie had lent me. Today I would get the job I'd gone into debt for. The day I stopped worrying about every dime as the beginning of the month came again, along with the bills. It would be the day I hung up my waitress apron, gave up walking in between the tables like an invisible ghost until someone's food was too cold or a meal took too long.

I opened the door to leave my room, and my mother was headed toward me, letter crumpled in her hand, anger roiling off her.

"He's saying he's going to raise our rent again," she said, thrusting the piece of paper at me.

I took it, scanning the words while trying to keep a calm exterior. My mother was quick to temper, and my getting worked up as well would only fuel the issue. As it was, I'd taken over all communication with the landlord. It was the only way he'd allowed us to stay after she threw a pot at him when he raised the rent last time.

My stomach dropped. He was hiking the rent on our small house by five hundred dollars. The rents in South-west Florida were so bad that we'd have to pay it. There was nowhere else to go.

"Can you believe what he wants for this dump? He's just like all the rest of them, trying to screw us. Take every-

A BRIDGE TO NOWHERELAND

GOING NOWHERE #1

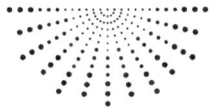

DONNA AUGUSTINE

thing we have." Her voice was shrill as she headed toward her cabinet, the one where she kept her vodka.

"I'll call him and talk to him. I'm sure we can work something out," I said in a soft monotone, knowing that what I'd be working out was a possible extension until I got a paycheck. When she was like this, giving her the slightest hint of your own fury was like handing her another magazine of bullets. After managing her moods for more than two decades, I'd gotten quite proficient at it, even as that tone of hers sometimes made me feel like that small, scared child again.

I tucked the letter into my purse on the kitchen table so she wouldn't be able to reread it another fifty times, working herself up until she was taking a sledgehammer to the bathroom.

Grammy walked out of her bedroom, took one look at her daughter, and rolled her eyes before taking a seat at the kitchen table. She patted the chair next to her.

"Billie, come sit and talk to me before you leave," she said, smiling. Gram was always smiling—even when she was being mean, she smiled. It was a mystery to many how she'd given birth to a woman who never smiled at all.

"Ma, she doesn't have time. She'll talk to you when she gets back." My mother paused to take a drink from her coffee mug filled with vodka. "Right now we need her to get to this interview if you want to have a place to live next week. God knows the tips she's making at the diner aren't cutting it."

"I've got a couple of minutes." It was quarter to eight. I could squeeze out fifteen minutes for the woman who'd been the most mothering female I'd had in my life.

"Yeah, sure. You've always got time to talk to her. You two know everything." Mom's eyes were glued to me as I sat next to Gram. "You know, I bet *his* new wife doesn't have to worry about anything. She gets everything she looks at. She doesn't have to concern herself with who's covering the bills. We'd still be getting money too if you weren't so proud and above it all."

My father must've won the award for her to be bristling this bad. I hadn't watched last night's ceremonies, but the sound of awards being given out had been coming from her room. As much as I tried to avoid all information regarding him, I'd seen snippets that he was up for best artist.

Knowing what a glutton for punishment she was, she'd probably watched the red carpet leading up to them as well, where he would've been posing with his wife and upgraded daughter. She would've watched every second as they stood there posing, lights shining on their glossy matching blond hair and tall, slender forms. She'd probably recorded it to watch repeatedly.

"You know, if you'd taken that college money then you wouldn't have all this student debt and—"

"Mom, we don't need him or his money. I'll get this job and it'll all be okay."

He'd been ordered by the court to pay for child support and then college. I didn't want a dime from him. I'd had no say over what Mom got before I was eighteen, but he'd get no credit for anything I had a say in. It was bad enough I saw his green eyes staring back at me every time I looked in the mirror.

She was glaring at both of us now as I tried to ignore her. The last thing I'd wanted this morning was a fight.

I sipped the last of my coffee while sitting next to my grandmother, who was looking a little sharper in the eyes than she had in a while. "What's going on, Gram?" I asked.

My grandmother might not know what day it was, but she was still the most pleasant person in the household.

She smiled at me, patting my hand while turning toward my mother. "Do you mind?"

My mother scowled, making the lines on her face even harsher. "Really? I'm getting kicked out of the kitchen?"

"There are things Billie and I need to discuss that require privacy."

Gram had never made it a secret that I was her favorite, even over her own daughter. She'd said many times she thanked the powers that be that my mother had me, so Gram having her hadn't been a complete waste of resources. I was never quite sure how to reply to that, so I'd usually just nod.

My mother shook her head, took her mug, and grabbed her pack of cigarettes. "I'll be outside if anyone needs me."

"Good. We're alone." Gram smiled as if oblivious to her daughter's glare. She might be. After you saw something enough times, it was easy to become blind to it.

"What's going on, Gram? I don't have too much time before I have to leave."

Two wrinkled, frail hands wrapped around mine. "I have some things I need to tell you before you go that are very important. When you get to the outpost, tell them you have a reservation or they'll toss you in the river."

"Gram, don't worry, the firm I have an appointment with won't throw me in a river." I smiled, patting her hands, hating how thin and fragile they felt. She was really losing it now, worse than usual. How much longer would we have before we couldn't have any kind of conversation?

"The firm? Of course they won't do that, but that's not where you're going. You aren't supposed to be an accountant. I keep telling you that, but you don't believe me. I understand why, but you need to listen to me now."

Those frail, bony hands were gripping mine with more strength than I'd thought she possessed.

"Gram, being an accountant is a good job."

"It's not what you're meant for. You're like me. You're *special.*" She grinned as her eyes lit up. "You know, if I hadn't loved your grandpa, I never would've quit. But it was all worth it for him, and now you."

Quit? Had she had a job she *could* quit? I'd never before heard her speak of any kind of career.

"Gram, I thought you were a housewife?"

"That's what I chose to be after I quit, but I couldn't tell anyone about my life before Grandpa. It would've caused issues." The last sentence was a mere whisper, as if she were afraid my mother was listening in and she'd find out her secrets.

My phone buzzed on the table, my boyfriend's name flashing on the screen.

"Is that Johnny?" Gram asked, forgetting about all else as she stared at the phone like she wanted to smash it to pieces.

"Gram, Johnny is a good person." I slipped my phone into my pocket, hoping she'd forget about him and let it go.

"What's he want?" Her tone dripped disdain. From the second he walked through our door, complete with a bouquet of daisies for her, she'd despised him on the spot for no apparent reason.

"He's wishing me luck."

She hmphed.

"Gram, I don't know why you dislike him so much. He's a good man." It wasn't actually that surprising. She hated almost everyone, and sometimes only seemed to tolerate my mother. Grandpa and I were the only two people she'd ever seemed to really love, and even I was no match for him. The sun had risen and set with that man until the day he died.

"He's a bad apple. Not to mention a man like that is going to curl into a ball and cry when the shit hits the fan. Do you really want to be with someone like that? Just like your father. Bad blood." She made a wiping motion with her hands, as if rubbing off the dirt he'd left behind.

"He's nothing like my father. And I don't need him to be some sort of protector. We aren't living in medieval times."

"You never know when you might need someone capable of fighting beside you. *He's* not it." She spoke of him like he was her mortal enemy instead of a nice guy that I'd met in my first year of accounting. He'd been grad-uating as I was just starting.

"You don't need to worry. There will be no fighting in my future."

"Sure," she said, nodding at me as if I were the one needing placating. "He doesn't matter anyway, and that's not what I needed to tell you." She took me in a hug. "You need to know I won't see you for a while after today. I'll be gone before you get back. I'll see what I can do after I get settled, and I'll get in touch with you."

"Gram, where are you going? Why do you say these things?" I glanced at the clock. Eight minutes before I had to leave for an interview and she had to do this now?

"I only speak the truth, Billie. I used up the last of my resources getting you the reservation. I'll be dying this afternoon, but you won't be back until after I'm gone."

"Gram, I'm going to go to the interview and I'll be back before dinner. Then maybe we'll go to the park, okay?"

She smiled serenely. "Sure."

She was really losing it. The doctors had told us the dementia would slowly get worse. But why was it that she always told *me* the craziest things? Did I bring out the cuckoo in her somehow? Did she build it up inside her and then I was the trigger?

"Gram, why don't you talk like this to Mom or my cousins?"

"Because they aren't like us. They're *boring.*" She sighed loudly, shrugging petite shoulders. "What can I say? Special skips a generation sometimes. I never liked to say anything bad about them, but I find them to be annoying."

She waved her left hand, her wedding ring still shining on her finger. She smirked and added softly, "Look, they aren't important. Never really were, to be totally frank." She shook her head, as if trying to shake off the rest of the family. "You go have your meeting and just remember to tell them you have a reservation and it'll be okay. Just make sure you tell them fast so you don't end up in the river and they box you up for an eternity." She finished that off with another smile and her arms out. "Now give me a hug and know I'll see you again at some point."

"Okay. I love you," I said, trying to get my wits about me. Gram was crazy, but this was a new low.

I gave her a kiss on the cheek, grabbed my purse, and headed to the door.

"You're going to do great. I'll be dead before you get home, so I just want you to know that." She waved from her seat.

"Bye, Gram."

My heart was racing and a feeling of dread filled every part of me, and why? Nobody knew when they were dying. She hadn't said anything about knowing Grandpa was going to die until *after* he was gone. A lot of people made great predictions in the past tense.

My mother was sitting on the front stoop, leaning against the corner of the house, the rage seeming to have worked its way out a bit. "Good luck on your interview. You'll do well. You always do well. You try too hard not to," she said.

"Thanks." I patted my pocket, making sure I had my phone, and dug through my purse for my car keys, which I dropped with shaky fingers.

"Is your grandmother telling you crazy stories again? You know she's got dementia, right?" My mother took a long drag from her cigarette as she watched me trying to orient myself.

"I know." Somehow admitting that Gram was nuts, even to my mother, felt like a betrayal.

"But she still gets to you anyway. I understand. She gets to me too, just in a different way," she said, and then sipped from her mug. "She is what she is."

"Okay, well, she's telling me she's dying today, so can you go sit with her?" I never asked my mother to do anything. I'd given up relying on her a long time ago, but even the farce of her possibly doing this might help me get through today.

She shrugged, which I was going to take as a tentative agreement.

"Did she mention what time she would be departing?" Mom asked.

"Sometime this afternoon."

"I guess she didn't want to go before she had her midmorning snack?" My mother raised her eyebrows, as if to say, *You can't possibly believe this.* She shook her head. "I'll go sit with her. Get going. You don't want to be late. And don't forget to call the landlord, since I'm not allowed to."

I nodded and took off, knowing I'd need the ride to the firm to calm my nerves, and talking to my mother any longer wouldn't help matters.

The accounting firm was one mile away when my car decided it didn't feel like moving anymore. The light changed, I hit the gas, but the thing wouldn't budge. I floored it, and it moved all of two inches. My transmission, which had been slipping on occasion, seemed to have decided that this was the moment it wanted to make its final stand. I tried again and again. It wouldn't move.

Cars were honking behind me, and I put my flashers on, rolled down the window, and waved my hand, signaling for them to go around.

I slammed the wheel and grabbed my purse. It was one mile. Just on the other side of the bridge. With ten minutes left until the interview, if I ran and their interviews before me went over a little bit, I might be okay.

I abandoned my car, waving at the people cursing. If I got the job, it would be more than worth the towing bill.

I sprinted toward the bridge; I sprinted into nowhere. I sprinted into what would be the end of my current life and a new one that was unimaginable.

CHAPTER TWO

I jumped across the small gap that had opened. The ground had been right there, but somehow I was stumbling into nothingness, surrounded by the kind of darkness that was so utterly complete, your eyes had nothing to adjust to, and then suddenly there was light again. The ground underneath my feet was a worn wood as I found myself in a room.

In front of me, lounging on a sofa, a woman with platinum-blond hair was sucking on a lollipop, glaring at the man sitting on the couch across from her.

"You're such an asshole, Dice. You take all the good colors and leave the lime," she said.

The guy wasn't paying attention to her complaints because he and another man were too busy staring at me as I stood.

The girl finally glanced over at me and then looked back at her friends. "I'm not cleaning that up specifically because you took all the good colors. I don't care if it's my turn. You toss her." She went back to sucking on her green lollipop, making noises of displeasure at the same time.

"Oh no, Cookie," Dice said. "I'll get you a bag of strawberry. I'm not cleaning this one up. The last one ripped my favorite shirt as I was tossing him."

Tossing him? Gram had said something about getting tossed in the river. This couldn't be real, could it?

No, I'd hit my head. I was dreaming. Now that I knew I was dreaming, I could wake myself up. Unless I was knocked out cold. What if I was in a coma?

"I did it last time. I'm not doing it," said the other guy, the one whose shirt looked like it was going to rip apart under the strain of his muscles.

No one was looking at me much. I glanced behind me, looking for the bridge. If I was dreaming, then whatever I wanted would happen and there *would* be a bridge. But all I saw was a door. I would've remembered coming through a door. I squeezed my eyes shut, telling myself that there was a bridge.

No bridge? Why was there no bridge? I'd been on a bridge. Then where was I? Had I fallen into some room attached to the underside of the bridge? Had I fallen and hit my head?

"Not only did I not eat the last of the good lollipops, I'm almost positive it's not my turn. You two figure it out," Cookie said.

"Fine. We'll draw straws for who does it," Dice said, looking at the muscleman.

They were *definitely* talking about throwing me into the river. What else could they be talking about? It *had* to be me. But that would be insane, right?

The room looked normal enough, with some couches and shelves. It looked like a random family room that was a little dated, more than a bit worn, but pretty comfortable.

And the people, the ones who were ignoring me as they

bickered, looked normal enough too. Well, sort of normal. The chick had a nasty-looking dagger strapped to her leg.

The guy she'd called Dice looked fairly normal too, with sandy brown hair and a friendly enough face. If it wasn't for the gun holstered on his waist, his shoulders— another one on his leg…

The guy holding the straws had forearms the size of redwoods and looked like he spent his day chugging protein shakes. He could probably break my bones with a snap of his fingers, let alone toss me into a river.

Yeah, these people weren't that normal.

"Fuck," Dice said, looking at the short straw in his hand.

"You have the worst luck of anyone I've ever met. I don't know who gave you the name Dice, because you shouldn't ever be let near a pair." Cookie was giggling.

Dice sneered. "Go screw, Cookie. Where'd you get your name? Not like there's anything sweet about you."

The insult didn't seem to put a dent in her laughter, or the muscleman's.

Dice walked over to me.

I stepped back.

"What's your name?" he asked, chewing on the end of his short straw.

"Wilhelmina Adelaide, but I'm called Billie." I answered before considering whether it was a good thing for this man to know my full name. I'd never had anything to hide before, though. When someone asked me my name, I *always* told them.

"Well, Wilhelmina Adelaide, Billie, whatever you want to call yourself, *you* are a trespasser. Unless you can offer a defense, you will be terminated, and your body will be thrown into the river. Do you have anything to say for yourself before this sentence is carried out?"

He went back to chewing on his straw as he glanced at his watch, the casualness of his demeanor not boding well for where I might end up. If this was some sort of sick joke, he would've tried to act scarier. This guy didn't care if he killed me.

And he'd said *terminated*. How many killers said terminated? They'd say something like "I'm going to kill you," right? Gram had used the word terminated, too. Holy shit, Gram, where the hell was I? Was he reading me some twisted version of my Miranda rights? What the hell was this?

No. This was all too crazy.

"What do you mean exactly by 'throw me in the river' and 'terminate'? Are you saying you're going to kill me?" This couldn't be for real. I hadn't even done anything to these people. I didn't know who they were, and they were going to toss me into a river? A river I couldn't even see anymore?

He looked at his watch again. "You have thirty more seconds. Do you wish to add anything else to your defense?"

"These trespassers are so annoying," Cookie said from across the room, where she settled back on the couch. Her boots dropped onto the table with a thud. "It isn't like anyone ever has a defense. Just more red tape for us." She motioned to the muscleman. "Connor, give me that magazine."

Connor tossed it to her and the two of them went back to what they'd been doing.

"Twenty seconds," Dice said, staring at his watch. "Nineteen." He cracked his neck.

My pulse was racing and it felt like there was no air in the room.

"Just toss her," Connor said.

What if this wasn't a dream? This didn't feel like a dream in the slightest. If this wasn't a dream…

"I have a reservation," I blurted out, following Gram's instructions.

Dice's head jerked up. Cookie and Connor turned to me, and Cookie's lollipop fell out of her mouth.

Connor said, "Huh?" as if he hadn't heard me right.

"I have a reservation." Another few seconds of silence ticked by. "A reservation?" I repeated, afraid they hadn't heard me. If there was a chance of getting thrown in the river, I'd repeat "reservation" as many times as needed. I'd skip and sing it too, if that helped.

Cookie got off the couch and walked over, looking me up and down. "*You* have a reservation?" She scoffed, shaking her head. "No way am I buying that."

"I do. I'm supposed to be here." I infused as much strength and confidence in my tone as possible, as if my life depended on it, which it probably did.

Dice ran his gaze over me again, as if he were truly paying attention now. "Who put a reservation in for *you*?"

The way they kept saying *you* in that tone was starting to get my hackles up, not that I was ready to make this situation worse. I had to focus on getting out of here alive first.

"Tessa Hendrick." *Gram, you got me into this. You better get me out.*

"Tessa Hendrick? Never heard of her," Dice scoffed. "Who is she?"

"My gram," I said. "I mean, my grandmother."

"Gram?" Cookie said, snickering. She turned to Connor, who was heading over. "Connor, you hear that? Her *gram* got her a reservation."

15

Dice turned to his friends. "Yeah, her *gram*." They all laughed some more.

"It's my grandmother. I call her Gram. It's not an unusual nickname."

They continued to snicker. I barely knew these people, but I was finding them very unlikable.

Dice stopped laughing, glancing at me before looking back at his friends. "What if she does have a reservation?" His voice was a little softer now, losing some of the arrogance.

"Gotta call the boss," Connor said, shrugging overly large shoulders.

"Nothing else to do," Cookie said, waving her lollipop around.

They were all staring at me.

I shrugged. "I've got a reservation. You have to call," I said, as if I had a clue about anything I was saying.

Dice shook his head, sighed, and then dug a phone from his pocket, dialing who could only be the "boss."

"We've got a trespasser who says she has a reservation." Dice kept his gaze on me as he listened. "I'll check, boss, but she doesn't look reservation-worthy." His nose crinkled, as if I smelled. "Okay, I'll get back to you."

"Well?" Cookie asked the second he took the phone from his ear.

"Says to put a call into the system." Dice raised his brows.

Cookie tilted her head a bit as Connor bobbed his. I was getting the distinct impression that reservations didn't happen very often.

Dice headed to the other side of the room, where a mustard-yellow phone was hanging on the wall. The thing was straight out of the sixties, with a spiral cord and rotary dial. The last time I'd seen anything like that was an estate sale down the street, when old man Harper passed and his kids tried to sell literally anything that wasn't nailed down.

Dice dialed only four numbers before putting the phone to his head. "I need to check a reservation for a..." Dice looked at me.

"Wilhelmina Adelaide," I said.

He repeated my name into the phone and then smiled a moment later, looking in my direction like a person who was about to say, *I told you so.* "No reservation? You're sure?"

"Billie Adelaide. Everyone calls me Billie," I said. Gram knew better than anyone how much I hated my given name.

He sighed, rolling his eyes. "What about *Billie* Adelaide?"

A couple of seconds later, his face scrunched, just like someone whose *I told you so* was about to get boomeranged right back at them.

"Yeah, thanks," he said, not sounding thankful at all, then hung up the phone a bit forcefully. "It looks like she does indeed have a reservation."

He walked over and stopped in between Cookie and Connor.

"It doesn't make sense. She seems so *flat*," Cookie said.

"Yeah, I know," Dice said.

Connor nodded.

Flat? That wasn't something I'd ever been called. He couldn't mean my physical appearance. I'd been told I was born with more curves than a roller coaster.

So what did he mean by flat? Yeah, I was going to be an accountant, and sometimes they got a bum rap, but that didn't mean I was humorless. I had a decent personality, or so I'd been told. No one should judge my personality based upon this situation. That wouldn't be fair.

Cookie was twirling a platinum-blond lock. "Are you sure we have to keep her? She doesn't look like much. Call the boss. Maybe we can throw her into the river anyway."

Dice was already digging his phone back out. "I'll ask, but if she's got a reservation, he's going to say we have to keep her."

His two friends were staring at him as he waited for an answer. I was trying to remain calm as I assessed all the different exits in case I had to run. There was a door across the room, a door behind me, and a hallway to the left. The door behind me might be my best bet, since that was the direction I'd come from.

"Yeah, she's got a reservation. Can we just—" His chest rose and fell. "Okay."

Dice ended his call. His friends were all ears while my muscles tensed. I was ready to sprint, punch, kick, bite. I wasn't taking anything off the table.

"He says we have to keep her," Dice said.

"But she's so *human*. This can't be right. I don't see why we get stuck with her," Cookie said.

Were these people *not* human? Where the hell was I? Had I been abducted? The yellow phone and plaid couch didn't scream cutting-edge technology, but maybe it was a decorating choice?

"Are you…aliens?" I asked.

Cookie threw back her head, laughing. "She thinks we're aliens. This is absurd. And *we're* supposed to keep her?"

Dice took a few steps toward the hall and then looked pointedly at me. "You need to follow me now," he said, as if I were an idiot for not reading his mind.

The other two didn't look like they were going to come, which meant wherever I was heading, the odds would improve. That was enough to get me following him down the hall.

"Where am—"

"Don't talk," Dice said. "I should've told you that one first. And don't touch anything. Don't look anywhere. If you do, I might still throw you in the river, reservation or not."

At least I knew that last threat was empty. Whoever the "boss" was, he'd laid down the law, and so far, that included not killing me.

There wasn't much to look at as we proceeded down a plain hall, not even a picture hanging. I wasn't sure what he was so worried about me touching.

"Could you just tell me where I am?" I asked.

"You're talk-*ing*," he said, almost singing the word.

It was done. There was no way I was changing my mind —ever. These people—aliens, whatever they were—were horrid, and I hated every one of them.

He opened a door to a room that was a cluttered mess.

"Go in there and wait. Don't touch anything, don't do anything until he gets here."

"Who's he?" I wasn't going to take another step until he told me.

He stared at me, as if he knew that I'd drawn a line. "Kaden. That's the boss." He pointed in the room. "Now in."

I walked in. Before I could ask another question, the door slammed shut. The footsteps retreated and I edged closer to the door, finding it locked.

CHAPTER THREE

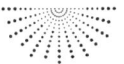

The window across the room was the first one I'd seen in this building, but nothing in the view made sense. We were high up in a mountain, but Florida *didn't have* mountains. There were more mountains to the left and an ocean off in the distance. There were glittering lights of a town below. Lights that sparkled in the *night*, except it was morning. If I did want to get out of this building, this window wasn't the way.

Nothing made any sense, and I'd never been prone to delusions. I could've tripped, passed out for a while, and they'd brought me here. It was the only logical answer, and would fit—except they hadn't wanted me here.

I dug my phone out because these psychos hadn't checked my pockets. My battery was on red and there were no bars to be had. I explored every corner of this room trying to get a signal on my phone. They must've known there was no service in here. That was probably why they'd stuck me in this stupid room.

Whatever this place was, or who these people were, Kaden had stopped them from killing me. He might be the voice of reason in this group, and it seemed what he said ruled. I'd talk to him, explain that I needed to be released, and that would be that. No harm done. It was all a big misunderstanding. So big I couldn't quite make heads or tails of it, but that was fine. We'd talk, they'd let me go. I'd call the firm and tell them I'd had an accident. It would all be okay.

I was pacing the room, trying to find a signal, when the man who had to be Kaden walked in.

Eyes the color of a blue glacier ran the length of me. They were startlingly bright against darkly tanned skin and black hair that made them appear almost cooler. Or maybe it was the clinical way in which he was scanning me.

I stood still, refusing to turn away or fidget. I purposefully let my gaze run the length of him in return.

He was tall, broad, and my chances of besting him in any kind of physical fight were nil. He'd have to be so clumsy as to trip over his own feet in order for me to have a shot.

As he walked in the room, there was a sleek grace to his movements that stripped away that last possibility. He moved like a predator, his features sharp, almost savage.

I swallowed, in spite of my determination to come off as cool as he did. The sound would've echoed through the room if it hadn't been drowned out by my raging heartbeat.

"So you're the reservation." He walked over and settled into the chair behind the desk. There was a slight citrus smell mixed with pine, like I'd wandered into a magical forest with a lemon grove. He stretched out long legs, continuing to eye me up like someone who was born having the upper hand, had never known anything but being on top of the food chain.

"Looks like it," I said, still attempting to play it cool even as my palms were about to drip sweat.

"Not exactly what I expected." He didn't bother expanding on whether that was better or worse, although I had my suspicions.

My spine stiffened. My chin notched up. It didn't matter how he looked at me. It wasn't like I *wanted* to be here. I still didn't know where *here was.*

"Where am I?"

He leaned back a little farther in his chair, crossing his arms over his chest. "You're saying you managed to get a reservation and you don't know?"

There was no way around it. It wasn't like I could do an internet search for "weird place under the bridge." I'd have to embrace the ignorance and hope it didn't land me in the river.

"Yes. That's why I asked," I replied, trying to sound as condescending as he looked.

He rubbed the shadow on his jaw. "And you got this reservation from your *gram?*"

I could practically hear the other three laughing as they informed him of *Gram's* reservation.

"Grandmother. Yes. But I'm wondering if whatever this reservation is for is not a good fit for me. Perhaps you should point me in the direction of where I came from and we can forget I was here." My heart thumped a little louder and a sheen of sweat broke out on my forehead.

"I'm not sure you understand the scope of the situation. That's not possible. You have a reservation. We can't simply call it a day." His voice grew even more condescending, which I hadn't imagined was possible.

This had to be some sort of illegal business. Between the look of his people and him? No way this was an up-and-up situation, and Gram had been nuts enough to think it might be a good fit for me? Whatever she'd arranged, this was *not* where I should be.

"Look, I don't want to know anything about your business. I'll never tell another soul I was here because I don't even know where *here* is. You just need to let me go. Blindfold me on the way out if you want. I don't care. It's fine."

He smiled now, and it softened his harshness just enough to make him devastatingly handsome. If I didn't suspect he was some sort of psychopath running a criminal operation, I would've found him attractive. Luckily, I hadn't been born yesterday, and I knew a predator when I saw one.

I glanced at the other chair in the room, deciding whether to sit or attempt a quick exit while he was across the room.

He jerked his head toward the door. "That idea won't work out well for you."

"Are you saying you won't let me leave?" It was hard to speak when your chest was so tight it felt like there was an iron grip around it.

"What would you do if I did? Would you call the police?" He waved his hand in a blasé motion.

I could feel a drop of sweat sliding down my temple. It was hard to play it cool when I looked like I was sitting in a sauna.

"No." Of course I'd call. I'd already tried, not that I'd tell him.

"Where would you tell them you were?" He disregarded my answer for the lie it was.

"They could ping the phone and find my location."

"You think so?" He reached into his pocket and tossed his phone at me. "Call them. Let's see how it works out for you."

It would be miserable to play poker against this guy. There was no sign of whether he was bluffing. Would he really have given me his phone if I were able to call the police? It must be a trick, and he assumed this would make me believe him, that I'd hand back his phone without bothering to try.

I dialed. He leaned back, stretching his neck as if he were killing time.

"Nine-one-one, what is your emergency?" the operator asked.

Kaden yawned. This wasn't looking like a bluff, but…

"I'm lost. Could you possibly ping my phone and come and get me?"

"Ma'am, it doesn't appear you are in our jurisdiction. I can forward you to the Antarctic authorities if you would like?"

Antarctic?

"You couldn't have pinged me already."

"No, but I can see on our calling data that you are in the Antarctic. As I said, I can help forward you to their authorities." She was losing her patience. Did she think this was a prank call?

He wasn't bluffing.

"That's okay. I'll call them." I gripped the phone for a few more seconds before I placed it on his desk. I bit my lower lip and then slowly looked up. "I'm not in Antarctica, right?"

"No, you're not." He smiled. "You are at an outpost between *Topside* and *Nowhere*. My outpost, to be precise."

"Topside and Nowhere?" Yeah, okay. The guy was

nuts. This place was nuts. Why was I even speaking to him, dragging this out? "Look, you agreed to let me leave. Can I go?" I'd figure out where I was after I left. I stood, ready to fight to the death to get out of this room, this building.

"You can walk out of here whenever you want and go back to wherever it is you came from. But you won't stay there because you have a reservation. That sets certain things in motion."

"What is a reservation? Can you tell me that?"

"It's something beyond my scope of control that says I have to honor your presence here and accept you into my crew," he said.

"What..." If this was a criminal enterprise, knowing anything else could cause me problems. "Look, your offer to let me stay is very generous and all, but I don't belong here. I need to leave. If you give me your contact information, I'll let you know if I change my mind. I appreciate your offer of...whatever. But I'm ready to go."

"Sure," he said, not so condescending, more placating.

He probably thought I'd want his nefarious kind of life. I'd chosen accounting for stability. I *liked* stability. My childhood had been chaotic enough to last me a lifetime, and this place reeked of upheaval.

I was getting out of here and *never. Coming. Back.*

He got up and walked to the door. I didn't hesitate to follow.

He paused, his hand on the door as I kept a few feet of distance between us.

"It will become very uncomfortable," he said.

This guy didn't quit, and I wasn't going to stand here listening to his threats. He was letting me go because he knew he couldn't keep me. That would be insane. He could say whatever he wanted about the cops not being able to help me.

"I'll manage," I said.

He looked at me and shook his head, like I was some stupid, wayward kid. He walked out the door, me on his tail. We were back in that lounge area where the other three were.

"Dice, have her sign a release and send her back. She thinks she can go back and stay."

"But…that *never* happens," Dice said.

Kaden's little crew of murderers were staring at him, and then me, with various degrees of gaping disbelief.

Kaden shrugged. "There's always a first. She wants to try, let her. Perhaps she's right and we know nothing."

He walked away without another look in my direction.

Dice rolled his eyes but walked over to a built-in on the other side of the room and grabbed a clipboard and pen out of a drawer.

He shoved it in my direction. "You'll need to sign this, and then you can leave."

"Sign for what?"

"For anything you see, hear, or do going forward with this organization, including what you have already seen, heard, or done."

I looked down at the paper, squinting as best I could, trying to decipher something on the sheet. It was absolutely impossible. There was fine print and then there was this. The type was so small that it didn't even appear to be letters, just lines and dots.

"I can't read this."

"Doesn't matter," Dice said.

"But you want me to sign it." I got so close my nose was practically touching the paper.

"Yes. If you don't, you void the reservation's protection and get thrown in the river."

That got Cookie's attention. She yelled from the couch, "If she doesn't sign, I'm still not tossing her. I'm not ruining my nails. I just got them done."

"I'm not either! She doesn't sign, you're still it. Short straw stands," Connor said.

"Fine. I'll toss her, but I call next one now. I'm not getting stuck doing all the dirty work around here," Dice yelled back, before turning and looking at the clipboard in my hand. "You signing or what?"

Dice was staring at me like he didn't care what I did, as if resigning himself to being the one to drag the garbage pail out to the corner.

Why was I dragging this out? I had no choice. This man would murder me and not miss a wink of sleep over it.

I signed, trying to make my name as legible as possible, and then handed it back.

"Great. Go." He pointed to a door in the back of the room with a lit green light above it. He waved me forward as if he were as happy to see me leave as I was to go.

I didn't waste any time and ran for the door. I opened it and the world went black, then suddenly, everything righted itself. I was standing on the bridge, where I'd fallen. Or started to fall? It was light out, and as I turned, there was no room, no building. There was a bridge with cars driving past, and I knew exactly where I was.

Shit. I'd had a psychotic break. I'd been under a lot of stress. I hadn't slept well. I'd been on edge all week, thinking of this interview. It happened to people all the time.

I looked at my phone. Two hours had passed. It was too late to go to the appointment, but I'd call and say I was sick. It wasn't exactly a lie. I'd beg for a new appointment. Right now, I'd go home. But everything would be fine. I'd eat better, sleep better. It would be good.

All I wanted to do was get home, see my grandmother, and hug her.

My phone had finally died. When I got back to where my car had been, it was gone, probably towed. It was okay. I wasn't that far. I could walk.

I hit my block a half an hour later, just as an ambulance was rolling out a body, completely covered in a blanket, including the head. The only thing that was visible was a stray lock of silver hair hanging from the too-still body.

I stopped walking, dropping to the ground a couple houses away, feeling utterly numb. They were taking my gram away. The only person who had ever loved me, no matter what I did, was gone.

CHAPTER FOUR

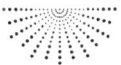

The casket was lowered into the ground. Inch by inch, Gram was disappearing from my life. The woman who'd been more of a mother to me than anyone was gone. She'd warned me she was leaving, and I hadn't believed her. I'd written the conversation off. What I'd do to get those last minutes with her back…

My boyfriend Johnny laid his arm around my shoulders, and I flinched. My skin had felt like it was on fire since I woke up this morning with some sort of stress-related rash. There wasn't a bump or spot to be seen, but even clothing grazing my flesh was nearly intolerable.

"Sorry," he said. "I forgot about the skin thing."

"It's all right." I took his hand in mine, looking up into his warm eyes, ignoring the discomfort that even that contact caused.

"I have to head out soon," he said softly. "I'm sorry, I just can't miss this meeting at work."

"It's okay. Go."

He gave me a kiss and then went to say goodbye to my mother.

A few more people were strolling over to the grave as he did. The turnout was bigger than I'd imagined. Besides Jeannie and a few of my friends that stopped by the service, there were so many people I'd never met. Who were they all?

My mother sidled up to me. "Are you looking for him?" she asked—even now, at her mother's funeral, her obsession with my father took top billing. "He's not coming. I called and left a message with his people, but he's too good to show up to support either of us," she said, her whisper doing nothing to disguise the acid in her tone.

My mother took every opportunity she could to find a reason to reach out to him. She'd done this my entire life, using any excuse she had, including me. I'd seen the disregard he had for us both when I was a child, and yet here she was, fifty-five and still clinging to some delusional hope.

For the sake of sending Gram off as she deserved, I'd feed into her delusions.

"His assistant might not have given him the message," I said, trying to manage the fury already brewing in her eyes. It was a lie. Any sane person knew that, but when someone refused to accept the truth, there weren't too many avenues left. I'd spent every last dime I could get my hands on, maxed out the last of my credit cards to pay for this service, and Gram's daughter was not going to ruin it with one of her episodes.

"You think?" she asked, ready to cling to any glimmer of hope, no matter how unbelievable.

"Definitely," I said, watching even more people I didn't know walking toward the grave. "Do you know any of these people?"

"Huh?" She glanced around as if not having noticed the

crowd. "Them? They're probably from that place where she played bingo."

I scanned the crowd again. These were Gram's bingo friends? There wasn't a senior in the group, and their clothes all looked designer "They're a little young for her crowd, don't you think?" I asked.

"Honey, I know Grams had hit ninety, but"—she nodded toward the group—"eighties isn't exactly a spring chicken."

Eighties? There wasn't a face over forty in this crowd. My mother was sipping from her to-go cup. Had she hit the booze hard enough to not see their faces clearly?

I shifted closer to one of my cousins. "Lizzie, what do you think of the turnout? I didn't realize Gram had so many friends."

"I'd hardly call a handful of seniors a crowd."

This was now the second person who didn't see what I saw. Was I having another break from reality?

I leaned closer to where my cousin Batina was. "What do you think of the turnout for Gram?"

"Considering most people her age are dead? I guess a handful isn't bad," Batina said. "By the way, nice service. I certainly wouldn't have spent the money, but Gram always did like you best."

"Thanks," I said, trying to ignore the dig as I meandered away, trying to dodge another potential scene. I had much more pressing issues, like figuring out if I was losing my mind.

I continued my way around the site until I was within five feet of a woman probably in her early thirties, who was standing alone. The closer I got, the more alarmed she looked.

"Thank you for coming. How did you know my grandmother?" I asked, pretending that she wasn't taking a step away from me.

"We worked together back in the day." She took another step away from me, nearly tripping.

Worked together back in the day? With Gram? This woman wasn't old enough to have that many days in the rearview.

She was gripping her purse, glancing at some of the other younger people there. I could see from the looks flying back and forth that at least some of these people knew each other.

"Really? That's great. How many years ago was that?" I tried to move slightly closer without her breaking into a run.

"Oh, must be about fifty years ago now."

Either I was going crazy, having another break from reality, or everyone else was insane. Could schizophrenia come on suddenly like this? With no warning signs? One day you're fine and the next you've lost your mind and are living in La La Land?

I wanted to press her further, but did I dare? Anything else might damn me to the insane asylum. I might already be standing on the threshold anyway. She might not even be real, so did it matter?

"Fifty years? You look as if you aren't a day over thirty-five," I said, couching my suspicion in flattery.

Her lips parted as her eyes narrowed. "You must be kidding, of course," she said, laughing in a brittle way.

It *wasn't* me. She was lying through her teeth. I was seeing reality and this woman wasn't happy about it. *At all.*

"Sure I am," I said in a tone that left my meaning ambiguous.

"Well, I must be going."

"Nice of you to come."

She stepped away, and then stopped beside a few other gatherers. They talked amongst themselves but kept glancing in my direction. Slowly, as if timing their departures, they started to drift off until none of the mysterious younger crowd were left.

Then there were just the few of us left, my cousins and my uncle, who left shortly after, giving my mother barely a glance before he did. No one knew the reason my mother and uncle didn't speak anymore, but knowing the two of them, it was safe to say the blame lay at both their doors.

I made my way back to my mother, waving her to follow me to the car. She stumbled off the tree she'd been leaning on and started walking.

We'd taken her car, since mine was sitting in an impound lot with a dead transmission. I got in the driver's seat, waiting for her to make her way over while still sipping from her travel mug.

She got in the car and let out a soft sigh. My mother had two gears: angry and bitter, and fuzzy and concerned. The angry and bitter tended to dominate, but usually somewhere in between being sober and passed-out drunk, her senses got a little fuzzy and she seemed to be genuinely concerned about others. Even to this day, I wasn't sure who was the real person and who was the booze.

She lifted her hand to touch my face, and I jerked back, every nerve in my body rebelling at being touched. Even sitting was bothering me.

"Sorry. My skin is still irritated."

She pulled her hand back, her attention growing sharper, or as sharp as it could be given the amount of alcohol she'd probably consumed.

"Are you okay? I know you were closer to Gram than

anyone else," she said, proving my gauge on her mood to be correct.

"I'm just a little rattled by everything."

"I know it's a lot. I'll pay you back for the service, too." She was looking out the window now, so calm. "As soon as I figure out where Gram had her accounts."

I nodded, not saying anything. So that was where the good mood came from. She'd always believed Gram had hidden money. If Gram *had* had money, she would've helped us more, or at least helped me. My mother, on the other hand, would never give me a dime, even if she did find some of this mysterious money.

"Although you won't need it once you start working."

"I don't have the job yet." The accounting firm that I missed the interview with had been more than accommodating, telling me to take a week off after I told them I'd had an accident and then a death in the family.

"I'm sure you'll get it."

Of course she did. Then that would be her rationale for keeping any money she found.

"Did Gram ever tell you any other secrets? Anything about having a job before she married Grandpa?" I kept my eyes on the road, trying to pretend the question had no weight.

"Gram never worked. Where did you get that from?" she asked, tilting her cup enough so she could drain the last few sips.

If I did ask, she probably wouldn't remember most of this conversation tomorrow anyway. There was really nothing to lose.

"You know how Gram used to talk about all sorts of crazy stuff? I think maybe..." Mom was leaning on the headrest, tilting her head to the side. She'd have zero recollection. "Maybe she wasn't so crazy. Some of what she said might be true." If it wasn't, then I was crazy too. It was one or the other. It looked like my mental health would sink or swim with Gram's.

"I know, honey. Of course she was crazy, but she's in a better place now." She yawned.

Why did I bother? She barely listened to me anyway.

"No, I'm saying that she might *not* have been crazy," I said, my voice a little louder so she'd have to hear me.

"I know, she was crazy. I'm agreeing with you." She turned to look at me, as if she didn't know why I was picking a fight.

"But she *wasn't* crazy."

She was staring right at me. There was no way she hadn't heard me this time.

She looked at me as if I were completely baffling her. "Billie, I'm not arguing with you. Everyone knows Gram was crazy. Do we have to keep talking about this?"

I wasn't crazy. She couldn't hear me. Or she heard something completely different than what I was saying. Or maybe what I *thought* I was saying wasn't what was coming out of my mouth? I didn't know, but if I weren't crazy, I'd signed a nondisclosure.

I pulled up in front of our house. She got out and stumbled toward the door as I sat there, wondering if I was crazy and dreading walking into that house again. Gram wouldn't be sitting at the table, playing solitaire and drinking a coffee, smiling at me as I came in.

"Billie?" my mother called, wobbling her way back to the car. "Until I do get that money settled, have you talked to the landlord yet?"

With all the things going on, the rent raise had been

completely eclipsed. It had been buried under the avalanche of other worries.

"No, but I'll call him tomorrow. I promise."

"Just because Gram is gone doesn't mean we can afford to be homeless."

"Mom, I swear, I'll handle it. I've got to go somewhere right now. I'll be back soon."

"Where are you taking my car?"

"I'll be back," I said, afraid to leave her car at the house when no one was there to hide her keys.

My mind felt like a quarter horse on a race track that had no end. It was sweaty, foaming at the mouth, and about to keel over from exhaustion.

I glanced around the park, making sure no one was within hearing distance.

"Gram? You out there somewhere?" I whispered. No one answered, which was probably to be expected. Except if I wasn't going crazy, and what I'd been seeing weren't delusions, then her telling me we'd talk again had to be true too. I'd even come to her favorite spot, under the big old oak tree with all the Spanish moss.

Unless I was indeed crazy. If I was, then talking to her wasn't going to be the straw that broke the camel's back on my diagnosis. The delusions would be.

Maybe one more time? I had a few minutes to kill while I waited for Johnny to meet me here after work anyway. If I concentrated hard enough, maybe Gram would hear me from wherever she was. I checked the area again and realized Johnny was already here, getting out of his car with two coffee cups. At least I had a good boyfriend. Would he stay with me if I was crazy? That was a lot to ask of anyone.

He walked down the path toward me and then past me.

"Johnny, where are you going?" I yelled before he got too far.

He spun around, as if he hadn't noticed me. "Oh shit. I don't know how I didn't see you sitting there. Lots going on at work. I guess I just spaced out."

He gave me a kiss hello before sitting down on the bench beside me and handing me a latte.

"How was everything after the service?" he asked. "I feel like I should've stayed." He reached out, rubbing my shoulder.

"I told you to go back," I said, leaning away, my skin feeling like it was actually on fire now.

"See? I should've insisted," he said, looking at where I'd edged away from him. "Obviously you're annoyed."

"No, I'm not. I think I might be allergic to the detergent I'm using or something. My skin feels worse than it did earlier."

He nodded, looking as if he were going to take my word for it. He then continued to talk, except I was having trouble concentrating on his words as the breeze kicked up. Everywhere my clothes touched me, it felt like sand-paper rubbing. I looked up at the sky and around. If Gram was here, this was something she'd do, make it almost unbearable to sit here with Johnny.

"Billie?" Johnny asked, his voice louder, as if this wasn't the first time he'd said my name.

I forced my attention away from the chafing and back to him.

"Are you okay? Did you hear anything I said?" he asked, looking at me like I was acting odd.

If he thought this was weird, the delusions were really going to be too much for him.

"I'm sorry," I said, getting up. "I have to go home and change. It's not you, I swear. My skin just feels horrible."

He nodded, standing with his coffee. "You want me to come with you?"

He'd seen my mother drunk plenty of times, but tonight might be a real bender. Handling that situation on top of how I was feeling would take more energy than I had left.

"No. I'm pretty tired after today. I'll talk to you later," I said, already taking off.

He took a step to follow me but then stopped and watched me leave, a sort of hopeless look on his face. I waved again as I got in the car, forcing a smile. He waved back, looking a little better.

My mother was passed out on the couch when I got back and headed right for the shower. The drops of water felt like little bullets against my skin until I had to stand out from underneath the direct flow and try to soap up like that.

The pain seemed to be intensifying by the minute. I was getting sick. That was all. I'd been running and stressed. It would go away.

Except it didn't.

I drove myself to the emergency room an hour later, knowing that this bill might do me in financially but not having another option. There was something *very* wrong. I couldn't sit—couldn't even stand. The feeling of irritation all over my body was getting worse, as if it were seeping deeper into my flesh, which felt like it was chafing from the inside.

It took five hours for a doctor to pronounce me

perfectly healthy and suggest I was having a panic attack. There was only one place left to try before I was positive I'd die of pain.

When Kaden had said I'd be back, that I wouldn't last long, I wrote him off as an arrogant asshole, thinking he knew it all. Then I decided he was a figment of my fractured mind.

It was time to find out which one was the truth.

CHAPTER FIVE

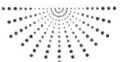

"Stop here," I told the driver as we got to the base of the toll bridge.

"Here?" the driver asked, looking around as if I were crazy. My gut was telling me I'd better get used to these reactions, because I might indeed be as insane as he seemed to think.

"Yes." I grabbed my bag and was out and staring at the place. I might really have cracked up. There was no hidden building here. I peeked over the side, looking for something underneath.

Maybe the pain was making me finally crack, but I was here now. I'd go the final distance.

I'd made it about a quarter of the way up when the feeling of my insides being shredded seemed to ease. I stopped walking, trying to evaluate it. Yes, it was definitely a little better. Another few steps and it diminished a bit more. The pain wasn't gone, far from it, but it was definitely more bearable, as if some of the pressure was being released the closer I got to where I'd fallen. Did this mean I was crazy? Maybe, but I didn't care if it was all in my head and a delusion helped it. I'd take anything I could get.

The same guy who had been operating the toll bridge the other day was here again. Would he remember me?

I froze, panic immobilizing me as the toll bridge man stepped out of his booth and headed toward me. Was he going to tell me to leave? Threaten to call the cops? This was the most peace I'd had all day. I couldn't go. I'd chain myself to a pole if I had to.

He continued toward me, tapping his watch.

"We have a schedule, you know. I don't open up whenever you want." He put his hands on his hips. "That stunt you pulled last time? Running past me? No more of those. This time you wait until *I* say it's okay, and then you get to go into the outpost."

The toll guy was one of *them*? Or was I just completely gone? Some schizophrenics saw people and things that didn't exist. Were they real, or was I crazy?

I looked him over, his uniform, his slightly mussed salt-and-pepper hair. If I'd made him up, I was doing a very good job. I reached out a hand and touched his shirt. It *felt* solid.

"What are you doing?" he asked, growing more agitated as he swatted my hand away.

"You're really here, right? You're not, like, some weird figment of my imagination?" If he was in my head, would I be honest with myself after I'd gone through all this trouble of making him up?

"This is why I hate newbies. Thankfully for the rest of us, you're rare. You have no idea how annoying your self-centered questions are, as if I wouldn't exist if *you* hadn't thought me up." He did a little jazz-hand motion, with a mocking face to match.

Okay, if I was crazy, my psychotic delusions were also telling me I was an egomaniac. This was not a good day by anyone's standards. Couldn't I have nicer imaginary people? Would I really make all of them such assholes?

Yeah, I might.

"And now you just stroll up, not caring that I have a schedule," he said. "I can't just open and close at your whim every time you want to come and go, so let's clear that up right now." He was pointing at me.

He looked so real that I couldn't stop myself. I grabbed his finger.

He smacked my hand, so hard it burned a bit.

"Stop. Touching. Me." He took a step back, as if I'd touch him again if he wasn't on guard.

There was a mark on my hand, complete with a little dent from his ring. I wasn't wearing rings. I couldn't have made that dent if I'd hit myself.

This was real, but I wasn't sure if that was better than being insane. It wasn't in my head, and some really crazy shit *was* happening, I felt like I might die if I didn't do something.

I reached out a hand, and the toll bridge guy jerked back. I pulled my hand back quickly. "I just wanted to say I'm sorry. I don't mean to keep touching you. I won't do it again. I just really need to get to the outpost."

He eyed me, keeping his distance like I was a feral dog with fleas. I'd been called worse.

"Can I wait? I'll wait until you're ready." If he said no, I wasn't above getting on my knees and begging.

The stench of my desperation seemed to soften him a little.

"I didn't tell you to go away. I just said we don't open and close on a whim. But as it happens, I was going to open soon anyway. Go over there and I'll let you know when it's ready." He pointed to a spot a good bit away from any risk of accidental touching.

"Do you have a copy of the schedule so I know in the future?" I had a bad feeling I'd be coming back again.

"We don't keep copies of the schedule lying around, and we certainly don't hand them out to just *anyone*." He looked me up and down, making it very clear I was one of those vague *anyones* that were deemed unimportant.

"How will I know when I can come?" I wasn't leaving here without some definitive answers now that I knew just how bad it could get.

"When you want to cross, you come here and I'll tell you when I'm ready." He tilted his chin up, giving me an *I'm the boss* look.

"Do you have a phone number I can call or text instead of having to make the drive?"

"I don't give out my number, and your questions are giving me a headache."

Of *course* he didn't. I had student loans; my car was dead. I didn't have a job, and at this rate, odds weren't looking good for getting one. I couldn't tell my boyfriend any of this or he'd dump me based on my lack of sanity. The only person that would've listened to me, who'd loved me in spite of all my faults, was dead, and even thinking of that made me want to crumble where I stood, so I forced that out of my mind. My life was falling apart quicker than cheap toilet paper in a rainstorm. So in spite of the toll guy hating me, I nodded.

"Sorry again about the touching. I promise I won't do it again."

The only sign that he'd heard was the slightest nod of

his head. I walked to the spot he'd pointed to because he was the only way to get to the outpost.

I found a spot on the sidewalk and sat, getting as comfortable as possible. As if on cue, it began to rain.

The toll guy went into his little house as the rain began to pour down, plastering my hair to my face. I didn't budge. I'd sit on that cement as long as I had to because this was the most peace I'd had in hours. I'd sleep here if I could.

Ten minutes went by, and he kept watching me through the window of his booth, making sure I hadn't moved. Another minute, another check. This went on for about twenty minutes before he stepped out of his house with an umbrella and waved to me.

I walked over, stopping quite a bit short of him, afraid that an accidental brush of the hand that would send him into a rage. The two of us were already treading rough waters.

He stared at me in silence for a second as the rain made rivulets down my face. "It's time for the bridge to open. You can go through as soon as it starts."

"Thank you," I said, as if I didn't suspect he could've opened it as soon as I got here. I ignored the fact that he'd had an umbrella and had sat in his booth dry, not offering to lend it to me.

He nodded. I walked to the seam in the bridge, my entire being soaked, my bag dripping, and waited for it to start separating.

I'd thought I'd panic. Maybe I would've if I wasn't in so much pain. Now cold and wet on top of it, I felt utterly defeated by life. At that moment, I might've leapt into the abyss if someone said it would help.

The bridge began to creak open, just an inch apart, and I took a step. For less than a second, I was in that all-obliterating black, and then I was standing in that strange lounge again, the pain completely gone. I sagged, taking a minute to appreciate the relief before I bothered to see if I was alone.

I wasn't. Dice glanced up from where he'd been lounging on the couch, reading a gun magazine. He took one look at me and let out a short laugh.

"You actually lasted longer than I thought." He looked at the clock. "Shit. Cookie won this one. Her ego is going to be bigger than this outpost soon."

"You bet on when I'd come back?" I asked, dripping onto the floor while this guy laughed at me.

"Yeah, of course. Why wouldn't we?"

I didn't get a chance to answer, as Kaden walked in, holding a mug. He leaned on the back of the other couch, sipping his coffee or whatever it was, while taking me in with a slow perusal.

"Things not working out the way you planned?" There were a thousand I-told-you-sos wrapped up in that one sentence.

"No." I stiffened so much my back cracked.

"You were so confident that you might be the first, I thought maybe you'd pull it off."

Bullshit. He didn't think I had a chance in hell. I bristled at his pokes and prods.

"Would you mind telling me what this place is and what is going on? Why am I getting sick?"

"You want to know now?" He sipped his coffee, making me say it.

"I just asked, did I not?"

Even when he smiled, he looked like a predator. I

wasn't sure if the chill that shot through me was from my being sopping wet or him.

"Your chemistry is changing. Until it's completely transitioned, this is the only space you'll be comfortable."

"What do you mean, my chemistry?"

"Imagine you're water." He pointed to the door I'd come through. "There you freeze." He pointed to another door on the other side of the lounge. "Go through that one and you boil. This is the only place that you can exist without doing either until you've transitioned into…something different —stronger, which neither boils or freezes. This is sort of a gray area, a buffer between Topside and Nowhere."

He watched me as I absorbed it all, or as much as I could. Every time I came to grips with one situation, things seemed to get worse.

"Topside and Nowhere?" I asked. I dropped my dripping bag on the floor so I could use both hands to shove my wet hair out of my face and try to grasp what was going on.

Kaden glanced at the puddle forming under my feet as he continued. "Topside is the world as you know. Nowhere, well, that's something completely different."

"And that door leads to Nowhere?" I pointed in the direction of the other door he'd mentioned.

"Yes." He took a sip of his coffee, waiting for me to ask my next question.

"And that's what, exactly?"

"Have you ever heard of the dark web? The part of the internet devoted to anonymous dealings? Take that basic idea and transfer it to the universe, and that's Nowhere. It's the universe's equivalent of the dark web, where there is no law, no oversight, no rules."

Nothing about that sounded good. I'd known it the first time I came here. This place was not for me. A shiver shot through me, and it had nothing to do with my wet clothes.

"Look, can you just fix me up and let me go back home —or Topside, as you call it?"

"If it were only that simple." He shook his head, his thoughts broadcast by his expression. I was already a pain in his ass that wasn't going to listen.

Kaden looked over to Dice, who was getting up.

"I'm on it," he said, as if he'd gotten a silent order.

"I'll be back in a little while to see how things are going," Kaden said, walking toward the door that led to Nowhere.

I tried to catch a glimpse before it shut, but my view was cut off by Dice.

"Trust me," he said, giving me a once-over, "you're not ready for that place yet."

"Now what? How long will this transition take? What am I supposed to do? What are you people?"

He let out a sigh and started down the hallway. "This is going to be fun, fun, fun," he said, like someone heading to get a root canal.

He hadn't answered a single question, and I followed him anyway.

CHAPTER SIX

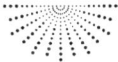

Dice stood beside a door, motioning me into a room that was mostly empty. There was a chair on a platform and a weird-looking scale off to the side, a table and a cabinet along the wall. Other than that, the room was pretty bare.

He pointed to the chair. "Sit there."

The chair was constructed of chunky wood and appeared to be made by a teenager who'd failed his workshop class, but it didn't have any restraining straps.

"What is this for?" I asked, not budging.

"Sit in the chair. I don't have all day." He stabbed his finger in its direction again.

"What do you plan on doing?" I asked, not moving an inch. I was still soaked, no one had bothered to so much as hand me a towel, and I didn't care any longer. I'd stand there all night unless I got some answers.

He took a good look at me, at my crossed arms, the puddle underneath me, and must've seen something that told him I wasn't going to move a hair.

"I do nothing. The chair does it all. It weighs your abilities and aptitudes, and if you'd go sit on it, we could be working our way through this already. You're not the only one who isn't in the mood for this right now."

Misery really did like company, because hearing he got no satisfaction out of doing this, probably didn't care if I sat in the chair or not, somehow made me feel a little more agreeable. I settled into the wooden monstrosity, waiting for a megavolt of electricity to hit and ready to grin and bear it, because it would still be better than leaving here and going back to that constant pain.

When there wasn't a jolt after a few seconds, I settled in a little more comfortably, or as comfortable as I could get in this thing.

"How long will this take?" I asked, my stomach growling. I wondered if there was somewhere in this place to get food. Now that the pain was gone, my appetite was roaring back like a lion with its teeth out. These people offering a meal was unlikely, considering I was leaving a trail of water through their building and still had no towel. Still, there might be food somewhere, and I was beyond caring.

"A couple minutes or a couple of days. You never know."

I was sure I'd be sitting here for however long that took. Everything about Dice looked unmovable and stubborn, from his short, blunt haircut to his thick, stubby fingers that were beating up the tablet in his hand.

I propped my heel on the edge of the seat, shifting again but knowing there was no comfort to be had. It didn't help that my jeans were wet, making them harder to move in, or that they had an AC vent directed right at me that felt like it was set to "arctic chill."

He was intent on the tablet. From the noises he was making, it wasn't going well. He'd tap, make a noise, then tap a few more times, each tap more aggressive than the last.

"I still don't know what this place is. What kind of aptitude test is this, exactly?" I asked, not that it should matter. The whole situation was beyond absurd. I'd sit here, regroup, figure out what was going on and, most importantly, how to stop the pain that came when I left, and then get the hell out of here again.

"We're tinkers. Now stop talking. It messes up the test." He didn't bother looking up as he spoke.

Bullshit it messed up the test. This guy just hated the sound of my voice.

"Tinkers?" I asked, pulling my other leg up until I had my knees to my chest.

"Yes, we fix things for a price. Now stop talking." He tapped on his tablet and then tapped again.

I would've pressed further, but he seemed to be having some technical difficulty. If I had to bet, I'd put my money on *user error*. The last thing I wanted was to get stuck here longer, so he needed to figure this out.

He was tapping on the tablet so hard it was echoing through the room.

The sound of a door opening and closing, along with footsteps, drifted down the hall.

Dice yelled, "Cookie, Connor, I need your asses in here."

Cookie was there first, took in the situation, and said, "I didn't come to work. I heard she was back, and I'm here to collect my winnings."

Connor, who was right behind her, sagged. "Shit. She's really here."

Obviously he was on the losing end of the bet.

"If you want me to pay up, I need you to look at this. The chair is acting up." Dice held up the tablet.

Cookie rolled her eyes, sighing almost as loud as a yell, but walked over. Connor followed.

She tilted her head, staring for a few seconds as if she wasn't familiar with what she saw. "That doesn't look right. You're doing something wrong." She reached to take the tablet from Dice. "Give it to me."

"I don't need you to do it. I just wanted your opinion," Dice said, moving it out of her reach.

"If you give it to me, I might be able to fix it. Why have me look and not let me touch it?" She reached for it again.

"Because I'm still working on it," Dice said, jerking it away from her.

Connor left them and came over to examine the chair, giving it a little shake, rattling me along with it. I grabbed the arms before I ended up on the floor. These people were a mess. No wonder I couldn't get a simple question answered.

Connor walked back to them, and they huddled, arguing over the tablet but sharing it to some degree, even though Dice was gripping it so hard his knuckles were white. Their voices had dropped, hiding whatever they were saying, but I caught Kaden's name.

"Are you calling Kaden? You don't need to call Kaden," I said. "I'm sure you can fix this on your own."

I barely knew the guy, but he had a way of rattling me worse than any of these three. I felt like I could handle them. Kaden? That seemed like slippery ground.

They quieted for two seconds, looking at me, and then continued whispering. Connor broke off from the huddle, heading toward the door.

"Where are you going?" I asked. He didn't answer, so I turned to the other two. "Is he going to get Kaden?"

They didn't answer either. They were too busy tapping, shaking, and banging the tablet.

"You don't need Kaden. If you didn't beat your electronics, they'd probably work better."

They ignored me, and I had this urge to go over and grab the tablet from them.

A few minutes later, Kaden walked in. "What's the issue now?" he asked, his gaze shifting to me. I pulled my legs up closer and then pretended to be interested in my nails.

He walked into the room and looked down at the tablet then up at me. The cords in his neck were pronounced and his shoulders rose as he took several deep breaths.

He crossed the room until he was right in front of the chair.

"Your reservation, it doesn't make any sense." The edge his voice had earlier was now sharpened into a razor. His glare darkened.

"I told you, I—"

"I know, you have no answers. Your gram did it. Apparently you have no aptitude either, at least according to the testing." His attention was focused on me, as if he were digging around my very soul.

Dice walked over. "I've never seen such bad results. What do you want me to do with her? According to this, she can't do anything."

I focused my attention on Dice, who, for all his gruff ways, didn't seem nearly as frightening as Kaden's silent perusal.

"Excuse me, but I have an accounting degree. I'm not an idiot, and I'm quite capable of doing many things." I would've stood, but Kaden was way too close to the chair.

"That's great, but you're here, and I *have* accountants," Kaden said.

He did? Was it part of his shifty business? Maybe he had a few that laundered his money. Good for him, because I wasn't going to be *that* kind of accountant.

"Look, I just want to get fixed and then be out of your hair. I'm feeling much better now. There has to be some way to reverse whatever happened so I can get back to my life and not bother you people again."

He put a hand on the arm of the chair, leaning over me. "You have a reservation. The second you stepped into this world, changes that are irreversible began shifting into place. There is *no* going back to normal."

His words were still running around in my head as he gathered with his people. No going back to normal? I was fairly certain he meant ever. My life had shifted completely, and I didn't even know what it had shifted into.

I needed normal. I'd spent my whole life trying to be normal. Working toward normal. This was not what I'd signed up for. The last week of my life was starting to bear down on me, and the sanity I'd tried to cling to had fissures running through it as I got out of the chair and marched over to the little group. From the way they looked at me, I must've appeared slightly insane, like someone on the verge of cracking.

"You say I'm stuck here, but I don't even know where here is. What you people are. I want answers or I'm going to..." To what? What would I do? The pain that waited for me beyond this place led to death. I didn't have anything to threaten them with. I'd thought I had nothing before. Somehow, as I stood here, still soaked, beginning to shiver, I had even less.

Everyone was silent for a moment. I didn't know if they were pitying me or annoyed, ready to chuck me out the door themselves, because I'd stopped looking at them, stopped focusing on anything but the new puddle forming at my feet.

"There's got to be something. Get her a room and we'll retest in a few days," Kaden said, and then left.

"Yeah, I'll see you later. I got a thing," Cookie said, clearly running for the hills so as not to get sucked into my situation. Connor didn't say anything. He just left.

The silence continued, and I saw Dice shifting on his feet, looking almost as uncomfortable as I was.

"We're tinkers," he said after another moment of awkwardness.

Apparently I was so pathetic that I'd broken Dice, a man who'd been ready to murder me, down into a state of pity. I wasn't sure if this was something to be proud of or humiliated by. My curiosity was stronger than any other emotion running wild.

"What's a tinker?"

"We get paid to fix things that people want fixed."

Oh yeah, this sounded shady for sure. "Like what?" I asked, wondering how much I really wanted to know. No matter what they said, I was finding a way out of this situation.

"More than you can imagine," he said with a laugh.

"Am I supposed to be a tinker?" Was that what they were testing me for? Would I have to murder people too? Wasn't going to happen. It wasn't how I was made.

"With your aptitude readings? I'd say not," he said, laughing again.

He might've thought he was insulting me, but it was the

first good news in a week. I sucked too much to do their dirty work.

"Well, I guess we'll find you a room." He walked out of the space, and again, I followed him because that was all I could do.

He walked farther down the hallway than I'd been as of yet.

"We don't have that many options here, since we don't usually get people staying at the outpost. The suite is reserved for VIPs." He waved toward a door and continued walking.

"Where does everyone else live?" The place was fairly quiet, and it seemed we were alone in the building.

"Most of us live in Nowhere. Some people like to keep places in Nowhere *and* Topside. Once you transition, you'll be able to last there longer, if that's what you're into." His tone implied that he found it odd.

"So I won't get that pain after I transition?" Did I just have to wait it out here for a little while and then I could get my life back? I could handle a few days, a few weeks, even a month if it meant I wouldn't have to be here forever.

"Not exactly. After you transition...there's other issues to deal with, but that can be explained later." He stopped in front of another door. "You can stay here. It's not great, but it's at least a bit more private, since you're going to be part of the crew."

Here was a broom closet with a cot tucked into the corner. The wall that didn't have the cot was lined with mops, buckets, and shelves filled with cleaning supplies.

"It's convenient enough. Looking at your aptitude results, if they're accurate, this is probably what you'll end up doing anyway."

"But once I transition, it'll get better. The pain will stop? You know, in case I want to go to Nowhere?"

No way was I going to Nowhere. I was getting back home if it killed me.

"Yes, but you don't want to go to Nowhere until you've definitely transitioned. You think Topside was bad? I've heard horror stories of people going to Nowhere before they were ready." He shrugged. "I haven't actually seen it, but I've heard the few times it happened, it was horrible."

I could make it a month if I could get back home. There were a lot of things I could handle if it meant getting out of here.

"Do I get paid for doing this?" As lousy as it seemed, anything was better than nothing. I'd still have bills piling up by the minute, interest accruing, and— Shit. I still hadn't called the landlord.

"I'm sure the cleaning crew gets paid something, but I don't know what. You'll have to ask Kaden when he comes back." He glanced around the little room, sniffing as he backed out. "You good? Because I've got some things to handle."

I nodded, and he shut the door without a glance back. I dropped my bag near the cot, looking around my new surroundings. The smell of bleach and cleaning supplies were so strong that my lungs burned and my stomach turned. At least it fixed the hunger issue.

Couple of days, maybe weeks, and I'd get out of here. Whatever Gram had done, she couldn't have meant for this. If everything she'd said was true, as it was appearing to be, I'd talk to her again. I'd hear her voice. She wasn't gone for good, and then I'd find out what this was all about.

CHAPTER SEVEN

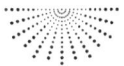

Two children were staring down at me as I opened my eyes where I was still on the cot. They didn't look older than seven or eight. The girl had her blond hair up in a messy bun. The boy was wearing a baseball cap.

"You new here?" The girl sounded like an eighty-year-old who'd lived a hard life. It was how I'd imagined my mother would sound as she got older, *if* she made it to eighty.

"Yes," I said, sitting up as the two of them looked me over, seeming a little jaded for kids their age.

"Are you part of the crew?" The boy had the same weird thing going on with his voice. Maybe they were sick?

"Yes." Dice had said as much when he gave me this room.

"We've never had a human on the crew before, but I guess you'll do. Start with the bathrooms," the girl said.

"*You're* the cleaning crew?" I asked as they walked farther into the utility room.

They both nodded as they gathered up bottles, brooms, and mops.

"You should be in school. You're *kids*."

"Hey, watch who you boss around. We're probably older than you," the blonde said.

"What are you talking about? You can't be older than eight."

"Try eighty," the girl said, and then turned to her companion. "These newbies are so annoying. Takes at least a decade before I can stand to speak to them."

The boy huffed and rolled his eyes, and then squirmed past me. They dragged over a bucket of supplies and left it in front of me.

"Start with the bathroom down the hall," the girl said.

It was now confirmed: there was no one likable in this place. *No one.* Not even these strange little people.

The girl put her hands on her hips, waiting for me to get moving, as if I couldn't be trusted to work without her supervision.

"I'm going to need a minute," I said.

"Fine. We'll wait." She crossed tiny arms in front of her chest.

"*Alone.*" I took a step toward them, not above chasing them out if needed. After all, they weren't actually children, but they were still small enough to toss out the door.

She lifted her lip, nearly snarling at me. "Fine, but we'll be checking in on you shortly." She walked out. The boy gave me his best evil eye before following her.

Shit. Literally, I'd be cleaning *shit.* It didn't matter. A paycheck was a paycheck, and if cleaning the toilets paid the bills, I'd clean every toilet in here.

Rifling through the bag of meager supplies I'd grabbed before coming here, I found a clean t-shirt and sweatpants. It was better than my dirty clothes from yesterday.

The place was quiet as I made my way out, dragging my bucket of cleaning supplies with me, trying to not make too much noise. I didn't see the two little jerks anywhere as I snooped around, but I found a kitchen. There was a platter of muffins and pastries, and a bowl of fruit beside it. I grabbed a banana, swallowing down half of it in two bites.

I looked up to see the little blond tyrant was standing in the doorway, looking at me.

"Don't worry. I'll get my work done," I said, giving her an evil look back. I wasn't above chasing her out of the kitchen.

Her tiny little mouth was in a flat line as she walked away.

I dry-heaved for the third time in an hour, wondering if anyone had cleaned this bathroom in the last year.

"I see you've decided to make yourself busy," Kaden said from behind me. The sounds of my retching must have hidden his approaching footsteps.

I dropped my stuff into the pail, preparing to see the amusement that had been clear in his voice. My hair was sticking out all over the place, and my knees were wet from kneeling.

I got to my feet. "I'm going to need to be paid while I'm here," I said, figuring a number in my head.

He leaned against the sink. "How much do you think you're worth?"

"Obviously more than you think, or I wouldn't be scrubbing toilets." That didn't mean I wouldn't charge him accountant rates. If he wanted to waste my training, that was his problem. Not mine.

"I don't recall telling you to join the cleaning crew." He shrugged, grinning at me.

If he thought he was going to get away with not paying me, he didn't know what kind of warfare he was in for.

"I need a paycheck until I…" Forget trying to explain how I wasn't staying. That was a waste of time with him. I was going to demand to be paid. "I have bills. I worked, and I need to receive compensation."

"Whatever bills you had are gone. They no longer matter." He looked me over, taking in the sweatpants that had a rip in them and a t-shirt that had been purchased on a clearance rack in a discount store.

"I can assure you, they do." I forced myself not to hunch or partially hide, even as his shirt and pants were perfectly starched. Of course he didn't think my bills were an issue. He looked like he bought whatever he wanted, whenever he wanted.

He took in a long, deep breath, forcing a smile as he exhaled. "It's a good thing we don't typically get reservations. I'm finding that explaining how things are here, and being continuously told I'm wrong, is not very enjoyable." He straightened and walked to the door. "Follow me. I need to show you some things."

I wasn't going to balk over a break. The brush hit the bucket with a splash, and I tossed my gloves off.

He walked past the door that led to his office and then opened the next door down.

This room was small and filled with filing cabinets and bookshelves from floor to ceiling. A desk was in the center with a computer that looked like it predated modern history, like maybe it was a first generation, pulled out of a garage in California. He leaned down and typed on a keyboard that looked as ancient as the machinery it was attached to. He pulled the seat out for me and waved.

"We don't have Wi-Fi here, but this computer is linked to Topside. Go ahead. Try to access your accounts."

Did he really think I'd hand over more of my information so he and his weird crew could use it against me? I didn't budge.

"How do I know your computer isn't going to save my passwords and steal my accounts?" Was I really accusing him of being a petty thief? Yeah. Pretty much. It wasn't my normal way of handling things at all. I was a peacemaker. I got along and didn't make waves, but nothing about what I'd experienced so far seemed like it was on the up-and-up. It was weird and strange, and I wanted out and didn't care who got insulted.

"Okay, let's try this another way. How much money do you have saved, including what you have access to in credit?" He waited, as if I'd give him a tally of my net worth, just because he asked.

I crossed my arms. "That is none of your business." I wasn't telling him my finances were in negative digits, that I'd need a gallon of red paint in order to sum up my accounts. Scrubbing his toilets was degrading enough for one day.

"Suppose I'm the thief you suspect—would a couple of hundred thousand cover your situation, with a little padding to boot?"

I was on the quiet side, but I wasn't typically rendered speechless. *A couple hundred thousand?* I was lucky to have fifty dollars in my wallet. That kind of money would pay off my student debt and cover rent without fighting the raise.

"I guess that would work. Why?" I asked, leaning an

elbow on the nearby shelf, as if I were completely cool in the face of that kind of money. In reality, I needed help holding me up in case he actually produced it.

"Stay here." He walked out, leaving the door open.

I scanned the room, looking at all the filing cabinets, wondering what was in them. How long would he be gone? Most likely not long enough, even though my fingers itched to dig in.

He walked back in and held out one of those reusable shopping bags. It was filled with cash. Wads of twenty-dollar bills.

"Take it."

I forced myself to grab it, almost expecting a trap if I dared touch it.

"You can hold on to that until you're sure you haven't been ripped off." He waved a hand to the empty chair in front of the computer.

I took a seat, resting the bag of cash against my leg. He was standing behind me and I glanced up. He shook his head, as if my untrusting nature was merely amusing to him. He could laugh all he wanted, but I wasn't typing anything until he moved. He walked over to the shelves and leaned there.

I typed the login to one of my credit cards. If he was a scammer, and he was trying to steal my information some-how, the credit card company would fight the charges for me. I only had a total of fifty dollars left of credit anyway.

No known user.

.   .   .

What? I retyped it more carefully, making sure I didn't screw it up, and hit enter again.

No known user.

My hand shook slightly. This time I tried my bank account.

User not found.

No. This wasn't possible. I tried the utility company, then the cable. Again and again, user didn't exist. *I* didn't exist. I switched to my social media accounts. Even they were gone.

"Before you try to come up with some grand plan on how I hacked all your accounts, it wasn't me. Your existence began disappearing as soon as you walked into the outpost."

I didn't say anything, didn't look at him, but typed a few more things into the computer, random accounts on stupid sites that most people wouldn't think of, especially if they were trying to scam me. I existed on none of them. Even my obscure reading group account was gone. How was this possible?

I leaned back, staring at the computer and then finally dragging my eyes to him. "I don't want to be here. I don't want to be a tinker and do whatever it is you people do. I want my life back, and I'm not going to stay here." It wasn't a plea. It was the way things were going to be.

"Maybe you should've taken that up with Gram before

she made that reservation. There are certain things that, once they are put in motion, can't be undone." He shrugged, as if none of my words mattered. "Take as much time as you need," he said before he walked out, as if he'd sensed I wouldn't let it go that easy.

He left.

I thought up some more sites to check.

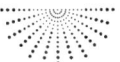

CHAPTER EIGHT

I pulled my phone out again, trying to get a signal. It was my fiftieth attempt today. Walking the hall, I held it out like an old guy combing the beach with a metal detector.

"That's not going to work here," Cookie said from the couch, where she was watching *Friends*. Dice was on the other couch watching too. Connor was in the chair, nose-deep in a car magazine.

"Is there anywhere I can get service in this place?" I didn't give up, going up on my tiptoes every few feet. I'd been gone all day. My mother might not notice my disappearance, but Johnny would, especially when he couldn't get a call through.

"Getting things from Topside to work here is a real mess. Why do you think we're watching DVDs? We're too cheap for cable or something?" Cookie asked, making the guys laugh.

"How do you make calls? That thing?" I asked, pointing to the mustard-yellow phone on the wall.

"Hell no. That's only for certain situations. We all have

special phones that forward our calls while we're here," Dice said. Connor nodded.

I walked closer, fidgeting with the back of the couch as I spied one of their phones on the table in between the couches.

It was a small favor, but things were already weird in this place. If it got any odder, I might not be able to stand it. Normal people would've offered to lend me a phone to make my calls. These people were definitely not normal.

I rubbed my hand along the tweed fabric of the couch, trying to size up who would be the best to ask. Cookie and Dice were... Yeah, they were something, all right. Connor didn't speak enough to figure out.

Cookie turned toward me. "Dude, you're lurking. You gotta either sit or move. Whatever this energy is you're putting out right now is weird."

I was weird? I'd let that one go—at least until I got my hands on a phone.

I moved and took a seat on the couch, eyeing up the phone on the table. It looked like one of those old flip styles, and my fingers itched to pick it up.

"Is it possible to borrow someone's phone?" I scanned their faces, pleading my case to everyone. "I'd only need it for a minute. If I go out to the bridge, who knows how long it'll take to get another opening and get back." If the bridge guy would let me back in. He'd hated me instantly, like I'd stolen his lunch money in a past life.

Dice cracked up laughing, wiping a tear from his eye. "Yeah, those bridge openings can take a long time until you get to know the schedule."

They all laughed for a good long time, and I waited, hoping someone would remember the favor about the phone. Unless they were forgetting about it on purpose.

"Oh, you wanted a phone, right?" Dice asked.

"Yeah, if one of you wouldn't mind."

He'd already gotten up and walked over to a drawer, where he pulled out another ancient flip phone and a charger. He dropped them on the couch beside me. "Here. That'll work."

"Thank you! I'll bring it right back after I make a call." I grabbed it, ready to hightail it back to the utility closet that served as my bedroom.

Dice was already back to watching his show. "You don't have to bring it back. That's yours. It should forward your calls from your other phone when you're here. Programmed it yesterday. I forgot to give it to you."

I'd sat here going out of my mind, pacing the halls with a phone that they knew didn't work, and nothing had jogged his memory to give this to me?

I swallowed back what I *wanted* to say. "Oh, that's great. Thanks."

My calls would get forwarded here? How was that possible?

"How…" *Don't ask.* The less I knew about this place, the better, because I wasn't staying. If it was some kind of mob organization, I didn't want to hear anything that could lock me into this.

"Now she's catching on," Cookie said, glancing at me and giving me an approving nod.

I faked another smile and headed toward my utility room.

"She hates it here. I'm pretty sure she hates us too," Connor said in a flat tone as I walked away.

For some reason, they all couldn't stop laughing at that. Their laughter rang down the hall, haunting my steps as I tried to get away from them.

He was absolutely right. I did hate them and this place. I would rather do a year in a state prison or a forced labor camp than stay here any longer than needed.

I closed the door to my utility closet, in spite of the overwhelming smell of bleach. Those two little cleaning psychos had probably spilled some just to torment me.

I dialed Johnny first. "Hey, it's me."

There was silence.

"Johnny? It's Billie. Are you there?"

"Oh, Billie," he said finally, as if he'd actually forgotten my name for a second. He couldn't have been *too* worried about me missing.

"Is this a bad time?" I asked.

"I'm sorry. I was distracted. Still finishing up work."

There were clicking sounds, as if he were sitting in front of his computer, and then papers rustling.

"Oh, well, I won't keep you long. I just wanted to say I was going to stay at Jeannie's tonight. I didn't want you to worry about me if I missed your call."

There was more clicking and rustling, but no response.

"Johnny?"

"Oh, yeah, sorry. Not a problem. I have a lot still on my plate right now. I'll talk to you tomorrow," he said.

"Sure. Love—"

The phone beeped, signaling he'd ended the call. He'd gotten a promotion a couple of weeks prior. He was going to be distracted. If my life wasn't falling apart, I wouldn't have thought anything of this. It was just because *I* was in a crazy way. As soon as I got this situation fixed, everything would be normal.

I dialed my mother next, but she didn't answer. *That* was completely expected, as she was probably passed out on the couch.

I dropped onto the cot, staring at the brooms lining the walls, the smell of bleach making me nauseated. The room was going to have to get aired out before I fell asleep.

Maybe I should go try to find a muffin, or even a cracker. It was better than lying here, staring at the walls.

The others were all lounging around still as I walked past again, heading to the kitchen area that was right next door.

"These reservation people never work out," Dice said, not even attempting to keep his voice down.

"How would you know? We've never had a reservation person," Connor said.

"Okay, you're telling me this is working out?" he asked.

This. I wasn't even a *she.*

I grabbed a muffin from a platter and walked to where I could watch them while they discussed me, instead of only hearing every word.

"It's a little rocky, but I might be willing to take that bet," Connor said, and then gave me a wink, like he was on Team Billie. If he was with me, he'd help me get the hell out of this situation.

All three of them perked up, as if a magic word had been uttered.

"Get the book," Dice said.

"You think I won't?" Connor got to his feet. "You thought wrong."

"I'll take some of that action," Cookie said.

"You're going to bet on me?" I stopped, staring at them, muffin crumbs dropping onto my shirt. "Do you realize I'm a person who is basically stuck here against her will? That all I want to do is go home but am too terrified of being in agony and dying?"

All eyes were on me for a few seconds, as if they were

shocked the subject of their bet was speaking, as if the insane person was about to start spitting or throwing feces.

The silence didn't last long.

"Somebody's a real killjoy," Connor mumbled, clearly jumping off Team Billie at the first rough wave.

"Are you getting the book or not?" Dice asked. "Or are you chickening out because she looks like she's cracking?"

"I'm not chickening out on anything," Connor said.

I turned, planning on heading back to the kitchen. Talking to these people merely encouraged them.

I spun, finding Kaden had appeared at the other end of the hall.

"Cookie, Billie." With a tilt of his head, he disappeared into his office.

Cookie was up and following him. She walked around me on her way. "You coming? He called you for a meeting."

That's what that was?

I could go back and listen to them betting over how much of a disaster I was, or sit on my cot and smell bleach. I shrugged, and then followed. It wasn't as if there were anything else pressing on my schedule.

Cookie was sitting on the arm of a chair, a boot planted on the seat. I didn't bother sitting at all.

Kaden was leaning back on the ledge of the window with the strange landscape. "Cookie, you need to take Billie with you tonight."

She glanced about the room, as if there must be a whole other Billie that had walked in behind us or her world no longer made any sense. When she couldn't locate this new and improved Billie, she glanced at me and squinted. Our eyes met and she broke the connection quickly, as if she might have caught something.

"You mean…" She jerked a thumb at me. "Are you saying this Billie?" she whispered, as if I wasn't still going to hear her from three feet away.

Kaden looked at her the way I wanted to but couldn't because I was still attempting to get along. "There isn't *another* Billie, so yes, *that* Billie."

"But I thought that… *You know*." She shrugged.

"That I have no aptitude?" I asked, my voice devoid of sarcasm. Cookie was completely right. Bringing me anywhere was an utter waste of time. Plus, I didn't want to go.

"I'm aware of how she tested, but I want you to take her anyway." He was opening up his desk drawers, shuffling through them.

"On assignment?" she asked.

"No. To get ice cream. *Of course* on assignment," he said, not bothering to look up as he kept searching for something that seemed to be more important than us.

"I can't go anywhere. I'll be in agony," I said.

"You'll be back before it kicks in," he answered.

I looked at Cookie and then back to Kaden. "I don't want to go on a job."

"Then you'll really have a problem, because this is my outpost and I'm saying I want you to go," he said.

Cookie looked at me. "I guess you should probably follow me." She took a few steps toward the door, very slow steps, as if to give me every opportunity to argue against this again.

It wasn't happening. The way I saw it, the sooner I failed abysmally, the quicker he'd figure out how to send me back home. I wasn't buying Kaden's story about not being able to fix this situation for a second.

We made our way out of the outpost, and a bright

orange Mustang was waiting for us on the bridge, the traffic flowing around it as if it had its own lane.

She glanced down at my outfit. "We should've done something about that before we left. You look...not good. Like someone who *wants* to be an accountant. Even your beat-up stuff is boring."

"That's probably because I did want to be an accountant. I might've already had a job as one if..." I threw my hands up, having no words for what life was now.

"Oh," she said. "Thankfully, you were saved from that fate. I can't imagine how hideous that would be. Probably as bad as being a lawyer. How does that even happen to a person?" She wore the expression of someone watching a horror movie that had chainsaws and lots of guts flying around.

"I don't know. I guess I was confused on the day I decided to take that path in college? And then wandered around confused for another four years?"

She shook her head, clearly not picking up on the sarcasm as she got in the car.

We took off, wheels screaming and the engine roaring like a dinosaur trying to traumatize its prey, which was working. I gripped the car door as if that could save me. After some close calls with a few pedestrians, I closed my eyes.

A few minutes later, the car jerked to the side so fast I slammed into the door.

"Come on. You can open your eyes now. We're here," she said, then got out and walked into a boutique shop.

I sat there for another few minutes, trying to get my bearings and taking in the store. It looked like an eighties rocker's closet. It looked like everything *she'd* wear, and there was no doubt she was picking me out an outfit while I sat here.

I hightailed it into the shop, finding her with a heap of clothing already in her arms.

"I thought we were going to a job of some sort?" This didn't look like the type of clothing I'd wear for something even remotely professional. Then again, their work might be anything but that.

"We are, but it's at a concert at a small venue, and I can't take you in like that. You'll stick out like a sore thumb."

Cookie grabbed another pair of jeans and a halter top. She was carrying a rainbow of shredded denim, leather, and latex. She dropped them into my arms, spun me around, and steered me into one of the dressing rooms that lined the boutique's wall.

I pulled on a pair of pants, then another, skipping the latex altogether. She shoved some boots under the door while I was changing.

"Well?" she yelled through the door not four minutes later. "We're running late, so just find *something* and go with it."

I settled on a ripped pair of jeans and a bustier that didn't look too horrific under a jacket.

"Hope you didn't take that personally back there," she yelled over the door. "It's not that I don't like you. It's only that I can't understand the point of bringing you along,"

"Don't feel bad. I don't know why I'm here either." I slipped my feet into the shoes that were somewhere between a heel and a combat boot, but couldn't quite commit to either.

Everything I was wearing looked like something my father's wife would wear, or his daughter. I wanted to rip it off immediately, but that wouldn't get today over with.

I turned sideways, realizing I didn't look half bad in this getup. So I'd have a night out, play dress-up, and then go back to my life. It wouldn't be that bad as long as it didn't last.

I opened the door, and Cookie gave me a once-over. "Much better."

I nodded.

"I'm relieved you realize this probably won't work out," Cookie said. "I just don't see what you're going to do, with no aptitude and all. Maybe you can keep cleaning until something else is arranged?"

Normally I'd find that a little insulting, except that I wanted out of this more than I cared about being wanted. What needed to be arranged was going back to my old life. And if everyone else agreed, maybe I could make that work for me.

Kaden didn't seem to be the type to be swayed by popular opinion, but what if I could stir up a revolt? A strike? That would surely put a crimp in his bigger picture, whatever *that* was.

"It must be hard to work with someone who has no clue. You must be a really good employee to be willing." Too good an employee, if Cookie gave it some thought.

"Well, we don't usually get many new people."

"Still, it's got to be a real hardship on you. Not only do you have to do your job but you're expected to have to deal with me too? That seems like a lot to ask."

"Well, maybe after today he'll realize this isn't working and put more of an effort into helping you get out of here. When Kaden sets his mind to something, he gets it done, no matter how impossible."

She looked about the boutique and screamed toward a

woman in the back, "Hey! We're done here! We'll be leaving now."

CHAPTER NINE

The bar was one of those places that had scribbles on the wall, worn wooden furniture, and surfaces I didn't particularly want to touch.

"I'm just watching, right?" There was no way I was doing something illegal, or *fixing things*, as they called it. Maybe I could stand by the bar and not even get close to whatever it was Cookie was going to do.

The bar might not be safe either. What if she drugged someone's drink? I'd have to find a corner to hide out in. Maybe have some mysterious stomach issue?

"I don't know what you're doing here, but I've got my hands full. This guy we're here to tinker has been a real problem. The issue is, he's about to kick it in a week, and—"

I backed away, hands up. "I don't need to hear this. I really don't want to know."

She grabbed my arm and dragged me toward the bar with her as she said, "We're not killing him. We're cleaning up one of his messes before he kicks the bucket."

She was swerving us in and out of people, yelling over

the background music, and no one so much as blinked an eye in our direction.

"He's been a real bastard, trying to screw his ex out of support with the kids. The only reason he's getting away with it is he's got some dirt on her family she doesn't want to get out. Apparently her father likes to cook books." She didn't stop tugging me until we were at the bar. "What do you want to drink?"

"I don't care. Should you be talking about this so loudly?" The place was getting busier by the second.

"Nobody will hear what I say to you."

My mouth was gaping open while I tried to determine exactly how crazy she was or if there was something odd surrounding these people too.

"This guy is going to drop dead in a week! Anybody here give a shit?" she yelled at the room, and no one turned to look at her. "See?" she said, and then yelled down to the bartender, "Two Jack and Cokes."

The bartender, a cute guy in his twenties, stopped what he was doing and smiled in our direction as he made our drinks. He placed them in front of us, not asking for money or anything. It was almost like the boutique, but I'd assumed Cookie had some sort of tab. Did she have a tab here too?

"How do you know he's going to die?" I asked. This knowledge might come back to haunt me, but if they were going to do something...

"Because it's part of the business. Some things we get to *know*. I don't know how, but he's a goner for sure, and this has to be fixed before he goes." She was on her tiptoes, looking around the crowded bar. "Found him." She picked up her drink, downing it in a few gulps. "Watch what I do. If it doesn't work, give it a go afterward. Kaden wants to feel you out, so we're going to put you on a real test drive."

"You want me to try?" I backed up. "I think I should wait over there so I don't get in your way." I pointed to a corner by the front door and took a step in that direction.

She grabbed my arm, pulling me along with her again. For a small girl, she had a good grip on her.

"Stop looking so panicked. You're not going to actually do anything. There were twenty tinkers who tried before me. Odds are, I'm going to fail, so you *definitely* will."

"You're sure I won't do anything?" If she was positive this would be a colossal failure, it only worked to my benefit. It was sort of a win-win. Do this, look like you were willing, and then look useless.

"I'm going to talk to him. That's it. I'll try to convince him to do the right thing. It'll work or it won't. Most likely it won't. Okay?"

"That's it? We're just going to ask him to do the right thing?" None of this sounded that bad, or that mysterious. They were trying to get a guy to do right by his kids. How could that be nefarious?

"I guess you could say that. We have a way of talking to people that helps them. You'll see."

"Okay," I said. She'd let go of my arm, and I yanked it away before she grabbed me again. "I can make it over there on my own."

She tilted her head, taking a few steps and then making sure I was indeed capable of following.

"Danny? Is that you?" Cookie asked as we got close to the man.

Danny was wearing a suit and looked a bit out of place here. The way he was talking to the band that was about to play, my guess was he was either a manager or promoter.

Danny turned, squinting. "Do I know you?"

"We went to high school together. Don't you remember?"

The guy was looking at her as if he had no clue. They definitely had *not* gone to school together. Cookie looked twenty-five, tops. This Danny guy looked like he was getting ready for his midlife crisis.

She laid her hand on his. "Me, you, and your wife Sabrina?"

He pulled back, glaring at where she'd touched him. If this was tinkering, I was glad I hadn't shown an aptitude. I wished I was on the other side of the club right now, because Cookie was looking like a whack job or stalker. Probably both.

Maybe I could slip out of here real fast. I took a step back and then glanced at them, to see if my escape was possible. Were they even looking at me?

For some reason, the guy was staring at me, nearly transfixed. Cookie was looking back and forth between us. Yeah, there would be no escape.

Cookie stepped forward and grabbed my hand and his, forcing us to shake.

I went to take mine back, afraid I'd get the same disgusted glare, but he gripped me. He kept staring, fixating on me.

"Did I go to school with you? You look so...familiar." He sounded almost dreamy.

Cookie smiled wide. She angled so he couldn't see her as she mouthed, *Say yes!*

I wasn't killing anyone. Was there really any harm in encouraging him to take care of his kids? Years of ripped clothes and ill-fitting shoes dogged my memories, and some other part of me kicked in.

"Yes." The lie flowed off my tongue, as if I were a polished con artist. It used to be that I'd trip over an untruth, my cheeks flaming with every attempt. Not this time.

"I *knew* you looked familiar." He was grinning, big almond eyes opening as he stepped closer. He took me into a hug. Cookie nodded, looking like she wanted to jump up and down after her favorite team had scored a goal.

"I'm so sorry about your separation from Sabrina. I know you really cared about her," I said, every word flowing out naturally. I had no idea who Sabrina was, and yet I sounded believable even to my ears.

He stepped back a little, a hand still resting on my arm. "Thank you. It was a tough breakup. I never thought I'd ever divorce her."

"It happens, but I'm sure you two will work out what's best for the children."

Instead of looking at me like I was prying, or worse, telling me to mind my own business, he nodded. He stared at me like I were his best friend.

"It's been pretty ugly, but I do want what's best for the kids," he said, as if I'd fed him the line. I guess I had.

"I know you're a generous soul and you want to help them as much as you can. I'd expect nothing less from you." Even as I said it, I could almost picture Sabrina and his children. Of course, I'd always had a vivid imagination, so it wasn't surprising I'd conjure up a mental image.

He smiled softly, his eyes warming as he held my hand with both of his. "You know, I really do want to help them, including her."

"She is the mother of your children. Of course you do," I said. Was that it? Was this done? Had I tinkered someone?

Cookie held her hand up to her ear, like she was talking on the phone. She mouthed, *Call his lawyer.*

"You know, I bet you'd feel so much better if you called your lawyer tonight—now, even—and tell him that." Some instinct in me infused urgency into my voice. "I think you should go outside, where it's quieter, and call this second."

He was looking at me like he was a child. "I'm going to do it."

He didn't even say goodbye as he walked away and beelined it right out the back door.

Cookie inched closer. She looked me up and down in a sort of analytical manner, before squinting as she examined my face. "How did you do that? I thought you sucked. You came up with zero aptitude," she said.

I'd been insulted enough to know when someone was intentionally trying to hurt my feelings. She was honest-to-goodness stunned. Cookie's way of communicating wasn't really smooth. It was closer to getting hit with a boulder.

"I don't know. What exactly just happened?"

"You tinkered. That's what. And not only that, you were brilliant." She grabbed me and pulled me after her toward the exit.

"Cookie, we really have to work on this dragging thing," I said.

She stopped and looked down at where she'd latched on to my arm. "Oh, yeah, sorry about that. I don't know why I do it."

Maybe Cookie wasn't that bad. I could grow to like her. I didn't plan on being around long enough to, but I could.

"I gotta get you back, and now," she said. "Kaden is going to want to know about this."

"Wait, I don't think we should share this. It was a fluke at best."

"Are you kidding? I have to tell him." She latched back on to me. Yeah, she was definitely not likable, and she was going to blow up my life even worse. I was supposed to be bad, *horrible*, in fact. Who was going to help me leave if I was an asset to them?

If Cookie's driving had been bad on our way to the job, it was even worse on the return. By the time we'd pulled up to the bridge, my stomach felt like it had gone through a cement mixer. It felt so wonderful to be on solid ground again and out of that deathtrap.

Cookie left the car on the side of the bridge and yelled to the toll guy, "Hey, Hank, I need an opening."

He smiled and yelled back, "Of course. Right away."

I didn't even care that the guy obviously had been giving me a hard time. Solid ground was making me too happy to be mad.

"How bad you bomb?" Dice asked as we walked into the outpost.

"We didn't. Or I should say, *she* didn't." Cookie pointed at me.

Dice looked up from his magazine, lips parted but nothing coming out.

Connor looked up too. "Huh?"

Their stunned looks were ripping away any hope I'd have of this being played down.

"I'm pretty sure the guy had come to the decision earlier. I don't think it was me," I said, shaking my head.

I might've been able to sway them if Cookie didn't jump back in. She stepped closer to them, angling herself slightly in front of me as if I were talking gibberish and shouldn't be paid attention to.

"Not only did she not fail," Cookie said, playing to her audience, "she *killed* it. No idea what she was doing, but she led the guy like a puppy dog with a bone. It was crazy."

"No one's been able to get that guy. He had to have been primed from all the previous tries. It's the only thing that makes sense." Dice glanced in Connor's direction. He nodded in agreement.

"Makes sense to me," I said loudly. "I've got zero aptitude. I'm certainly not some sort of tinkering savant." Nor did I want to be. I hadn't even wanted to do that job. Why I'd stepped up to the occasion still wasn't clear, other than bad judgment on my part.

Dice and Connor were looking as if they weren't buying it either. Kaden would never buy into it. It would be okay. I hadn't utterly screwed myself.

"No. Fucking. Way. I approached the guy first, and let me tell you, he was one stubborn son of a bitch. He was not ready to go down in any way," Cookie said, looking like she was ready to go to the mat to defend her position.

Dice and Connor looked at each other and then back at Cookie. They shook their heads in unison.

"You're being idiotic," Dice said.

Cookie's arm sprang out, making me jump back a few inches to stay out of her way.

With her arm outstretched and her finger pointed at the yellow phone, she said, "Call it in. See if payment was made if you're so sure."

"Payment from who? Who pays you people to do this? Who are you calling?" I asked.

Connor raised his brow. "Technically, who paid *you* to do this. Depends on who wants things tweaked.

Could be anyone, but we call the IBA, also known as the Independent Board of Adjusting. They're a third party who holds the funds during transactions. Think of them like a title company when you sell or buy a house."

While Connor was explaining this, Dice got to his feet and began a fierce stare-off with Cookie. They looked like they could've been two combatants in a dark alley, about to pull knives on each other. Connor didn't seem overly concerned, but that might've been because he was as crazy as they were.

If it came to blows, did I step in or let them kill each other?

Before I had to make a choice, Dice said, "Fine." He walked over to the yellow phone. His back was blocking the numbers, but then he said, "Yeah, calling to see if we received a payment for tonight."

He turned a little, his eyes shooting to me and his mouth dropping open. "Uh huh. Yeah." He hung up. His eyes still on me, he said, "They paid and gave us a bonus."

Cookie yelled, "Yes. Told you so, suckers."

I barely heard whatever else was said over the loud buzzing in my ears from my blood pressure shooting up. I couldn't be stuck here. I wouldn't be. No. No. *No.*

"Where's the boss? He's going to want to hear about this," Cookie said.

Connor hooked a thumb down the hallway, toward Kaden's office.

That was all Cookie needed. She grabbed my hand and dragged me after her with such gusto that my head snapped back.

"You know, I'm not sure..."

Too late. We were in his office. Kaden looked up from

his desk as we walked in. His eyes met mine, and seemed to darken. I was grateful when Cookie started talking.

"You aren't going to believe this, but she's a natural," Cookie said.

"Really," he said. "What exactly happened?"

"Nothing. I think it was a fluke," I said.

"Cookie?" Kaden asked. He moved his attention off me, and I could breathe again.

He leaned back, listening to her outline every last detail and then adding some flourishes like she was performing a play. His expression remained calm and controlled, his attention shifting my way ever so often.

He wasn't anywhere near as surprised or dismissive as I'd hoped. He was supposed to laugh this off, or dismiss it out of hand.

I crossed my arms and then immediately dropped them, refusing to look defensive. I stared at the floor, the wall above his head, my nails...

She finally finished her act, and Kaden's attention was solely on me. His fingers were running along his chin, and I could see him calculating something.

"I think you might be overstating it slightly," I said to Cookie. "The guy wasn't *that* persuaded by me." I turned, glaring at her, not that she seemed to be aware.

She continued carrying on to Kaden. "She had him eating out of the palm of her hand. I've never seen a newbie pull off something like that. It was insane."

With every word she said, I could almost feel the door shutting on me ever getting back to a normal life.

"Interesting," Kaden said, again, not sounding surprised.

Had he expected this? Why would he? Their test had labeled me a waste of space. And yet, even as shuttered his emotions, as glib and smoothed over as Kaden was, there wasn't even the tiniest flicker of surprise. Had he considered this a possibility? Was that why he'd sent me with her?

Cookie's phone buzzed, and she looked down. "Shit. Forgot I double-booked today. You got this all? I gotta run."

"We're good. Go handle your business," Kaden said, as his attention shifted fully to me

Cookie was out the door. I turned to follow her but didn't make it out before my name was out of his lips and he was uttering the words I knew would bring my doom.

"Billie, we need to have a conversation."

CHAPTER TEN

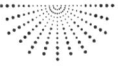

I was still staring at the open door, trying to force myself to turn back around. There would be no avoiding this conversation with Kaden, and there was nothing good that would come out of it.

"Shut the door," Kaden said.

No one tells you good news with the door shut. I did as he asked, the sound of it closing echoing through the room. I turned, still standing in the same spot.

"Why don't you take a seat?" He motioned toward the abandoned chair with a tilt of his head.

The more cordial he was, the more dismal things were probably going to be. I walked, slowly, until I dropped into the seat across from him.

"What did you want to talk about?" He hadn't said it yet, but my body and brain were already reacting as if I were screwed. That it was a done deal. I was stuck here, and this conversation would merely confirm it. Had I been screwed before Cookie gave him this information? That question would probably haunt me in the coming days.

"I know you've been hoping to reverse your reservation. The possibility has always been unlikely. Now that you've tinkered, I think you should be prepared that the changes are likely irreversible." He rested his chin on his fist, his legs stretched out before him.

One would think he'd at least pretend to be disappointed for me instead of this casual *oh well* attitude.

"If I'm screwed, just say it and let's be done with it," I said.

"Fine. You're screwed," he replied with a shrug.

There hadn't been a second's hesitation. No remorse. No *I'm sorry. Definitely* no sorry. He didn't seem to be bothered at all that I was stuck here. Why would he? He'd just picked up another asset for his business.

He could think whatever he wanted. I wasn't accepting it.

I got out of the seat, no desire to stay in this room with him. I headed toward the door and then swung back around, probably looking as erratic as I felt.

"What exactly is the issue? Why are you acting as if this is final? Because of some fluke? What does it matter if I was responsible for that man's actions?" My voice was only a touch shy of a shriek, and I didn't care. I was beyond worrying about decorum. The only thing that mattered was going home.

His head shifted the slightest amount to the left as he stared at me. When he watched me like this, it was as if he were seeing so much more than I could fathom. His expression was so unyielding that I knew he wasn't going to try to help me. In truth, I'd known from the second I'd met him.

"You implied you only wanted to know your status and we'd move on from the subject?" he asked, as if he'd believed that for a second.

I gripped the back of the chair, forcing myself to calm down. I wasn't used to being the lunatic in the room. It never helped the situation. What was needed was information.

I took a long, deep breath as he watched me with slightly removed interest, like I was a science fair project.

I calmly said, "I'm going to need an explanation as to your logic. Why do you believe that I'm past the point of no return?"

He looked as if he were suppressing a smile. Why he found any of this amusing simply showed what a crazy person he was.

He shifted slightly, making himself even more comfortable. "The fact that you're tinkering means you've already transitioned too much to possibly reverse this, if it could've happened in the first place. The fact that you're proving to be so adept this early on means that whatever *Gram* did, whoever she is, she did it well. There was no way to unwind the reservation she put in place." He rubbed his jaw as he watched it all sink in. "You do realize reservations are extremely coveted? The opportunity you're being afforded is one that's sought by many."

I wasn't used to people looking at me as if I were an ingrate. I'd spent the majority of my life being grateful for whatever I got. But I wanted nothing to do with whatever they had going on.

"Look, I'm sure you've got a great gig here, but it's not where I belong." I didn't understand what this place was, what exactly they did, and I didn't want to.

"What exactly is your objection to being here? Does the lure of being an accountant hold that strong a pull on you? Hard to break away from the draw of tax season, long, wild nights punching numbers into a calculator?" His arm was bent, his fingers waving as he spoke.

"Mock me all you want. I'm not accepting this situation. How can I work here? Live here? What do I tell my family and friends? I have a *life*. You can say whatever you want, show me all my accounts disappearing, hand me a pile of cash, I don't care." I spun away from him but didn't stop talking. "I can't stay here."

"You don't have a choice any longer. You're changing, and it's not something that's going to stop. You've already stopped aging, even at this point."

Stopped aging?

"You mean..."

"I mean you won't age," he said.

Immortal? That nearly made it worse. Immortal and living in a broom closet. I'd be spending the rest of eternity smelling bleach and sleeping next to dirty mops. Why would anyone think that this, day after day, was something good? The only thing he'd accomplished was making me a hair short of hysteria.

"I don't believe that. There's always a choice." I shook my head, pacing in front of his desk. "I can't be here. I can't live here. People will eventually want to come see where I moved. I have people who care about me."

"That won't be a problem for long."

I stopped walking, dread filling me. I walked up to his desk, staring him down. "Why? Are you going to tell them I died? Don't you dare."

My mother. She wasn't going to win any awards, but to lose her own mother and then her daughter in such a short gap... I groaned, imagining how badly she'd spiral after that.

"I won't have to. They're going to forget about you," he

said, and finally a flicker of remorse was in his cool eyes, only a flash that happened so fast I might've been imagining it.

"My mother is going to forget about me? I know the woman has her flaws, but I don't think she'll forget that she birthed a human." There was a limit to even their tricks. This couldn't be true.

He stood, turning and resting his shoulder on the window frame while staring out at that strange landscape. "Except she will. At first she'll start forgetting to call you. Then it'll progress to not knowing you at all, even when you're in front of her, but that takes longer." He spoke so coldly, as if none of this mattered. Why would it? Someone else's life falling apart probably meant nothing to him.

"What about my boyfriend? We were talking about…" I shook my head. I couldn't say it, or didn't want to. But the words were blaring through my head. Marriage. Kids. We'd talked about children. What if I'd already had them? Would they have forgotten me?

"Yes," he said, looking back at me. "Yes to every one of them." His thoughts were firmly shuttered away now behind cool, dispassionate eyes. They fit him perfectly.

His voice was calm as he explained to me the rest of the dreary details that would unfold. If I knew what he was going to say, I might've asked him to stop right then, but I didn't.

"They will all get more distant. Eventually they'll stop calling you as much, forgetting you exist," he said.

The last phone call I'd had with Johnny played out in my mind. How my mother had been startled last time I walked into the house, looking as if she didn't recognize me at first. No. Those were just flukes. What he was saying couldn't be true. It was too absurd.

"They aren't going to forget me," I said, my voice growing weaker in the face of the truth. That day in the park, Johnny had walked right past me. Had he really been distracted by work?

"But they will. That is how this thing of ours works. Once you no longer belong in that world, your ties to the people in it lessen. It'll happen gradually with some and faster with others. They'll lose the urge to call you, stop wondering what you're up to or checking in. You'll become that distant relative that shows up at an occasional holiday, until you aren't even that anymore and they forget you existed at all. At that point, your birth certificate will have been long gone, along with any other evidence you existed." He was facing me now, his arms folded as he watched to see if I'd crumble.

I wouldn't cry. I wouldn't do it. I'd rip my eyeballs out of their sockets before a single tear dropped in front of this man. I spun and walked out of his office, intent on going somewhere other than *here*.

I didn't think he'd follow, but his footsteps sounded behind me.

"Being upset is a waste of energy," he said.

I stormed back in his direction, staring at him as if he'd lost his senses. Or was he so inhuman he couldn't fathom what a human life meant? It took every last shred of restraint I had not to grab his freshly pressed shirt and shake him.

"I'm going to live in a mop closet for the rest of my life and you think I should just accept that?" I asked, not caring that I was a foot away from him and on the brink of screaming. The reality staring down at me deserved at least that amount of rage.

He stood as calmly as ever as I started gasping for air.

"There's no air in this place," I said, breathing heavily. "Did you do something?" I reached out a hand, bracing it on the wall.

"You're having a panic attack."

He might be right, but nothing about hearing the words aloud did anything to halt it. Instead, I was gasping more.

This wasn't me. I didn't lose control and gasp and freak out.

But he'd just informed me my entire life was slowly disappearing. Screw holding it together. If there was ever a time to freak out, this was it. He was lucky I wasn't sobbing, although considering my current lack of control, that might be coming next.

He leaned on the opposite wall, watching me gasp for air while his breathing was perfectly fine.

Nothing mattered at the moment but the fact that I had no job, would have no family or friends soon, and I would go to sleep at night with the fragrant smell of bleach and urine-soaked mops.

"You'll eventually be able to live in Nowhere, or keep a place in Topside. It's not as if this outpost is it," he said, as if he'd sensed my thoughts.

Topside, a place where no one would remember me. Or Nowhere? That place? Where there were no laws, and it sounded like utter chaos that I dared not even go into yet? That was supposed to make me feel better?

I had to stop talking to him or the hysterics would only get worse, and I was a hair away from a full-blown melt-down. I'd never had one in my life, but that didn't mean I didn't recognize it running down the tracks toward me.

I didn't respond as I focused on slowing my breathing, getting back under control.

I barely noticed the sound of other footsteps headed

our way until Connor said, "Oh shit. She's cracking. It's the mop closet, right? I told Dice to put her in the suite, but you know he likes to save those rooms for his extracurricular."

I didn't *have* to stay in a mop closet? Seriously? There were other options and no one had bothered to mention them?

By the time I straightened off the wall, Kaden was already in between us, blocking Connor's view as I pulled myself together.

"We need a few," Kaden said.

Connor's footsteps retreated down the hall, away from us as he grumbled, "Not my fault Dice is a pig."

Kaden waited another few moments, until Connor was completely gone, before he took a few steps in the opposite direction.

"Follow me," he said. When I didn't move, he added, "At the very least, this will make your stay, however long, more comfortable." He waited to see if I'd follow then.

The idea of staying one more night with the bleach made my feet move.

He made a few turns, down a hall I'd yet to explore, and opened a door. The inside was about as comfortable and inviting as I could've ever imagined. Cozy, almost, and utterly unexpected. I felt like I'd just walked into an English cottage with a stone fireplace and a door that led to what looked like a separate bedroom.

"This will be yours until you're ready to move somewhere else. Dice should've given you these rooms, but as Connor mentioned, Dice likes keeping this available if he has company and he doesn't want to bring them to his place."

I nodded, and then he was gone, as if he sensed my

desperate need to be alone, or feared what he'd have to deal with if he stayed.

I walked into the bedroom, shut that door, and flopped down onto my belly. I buried my face in a pillow so no one would hear me crying, mourning a life I no longer had and the people who would forget me soon.

CHAPTER ELEVEN

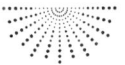

My head was down as I read through one of Connor's magazines in a chair off to the side, trying to pretend I was okay. That I wasn't on the brink of another breakdown. That the smell of bleach didn't make me want to bawl my eyes out. Connor, Dice, and Cookie were spread out among the couches, being quieter than normal, as if no one wanted to be the reason the pin on the grenade got pulled.

The sound of the door to Nowhere opening and closing barely registered until I sensed someone else in the room. A woman with purple and pink striped hair was standing just inside the lounge, trays in her hand.

She looked at me. I looked at her.

Cookie's gaze flitted between the two of us. "Wanda, that's Billie. Billie's new on the crew. Wanda is our caterer."

Wanda nodded toward me, and I returned it. She walked out of the room, and there were sounds of her dropping things off in the kitchen before she returned.

"I'm heading out," Wanda said to the gang before turning to me. "Billie, if you'd like anything in particular to eat, leave a note on the table and I'll add it to the order. See you tomorrow."

"Thanks," I said.

She nodded and headed toward the door to Nowhere.

Nowhere. I wasn't going to get answers on how to get out of this place in Topside. These people didn't have any inclination to help me, either. But Nowhere was filled with people who would know all sorts of things. That was where I had to go. Maybe they were trying to keep me out of there on purpose, because that was where all my answers lay?

I got up, trying to maneuver to a spot close enough to see what was beyond the door. What was this Nowhere place all about? That weird yellow phone probably called someone there.

The door opened and closed so quickly that it was hard to see more than a glimpse of a city.

"So what's Nowhere like, exactly?" I asked, looking around.

Cookie was the only one who glanced up from what she was doing. "Nowhere is the place you go when you've seen behind the curtain and don't like the game, or playing by the rules. It's where you make your own rules and everyone is free in the purest sense. In some ways, that's good." She made a point of looking me up and down. "But if you aren't prepared, you won't make it a day."

Dice decided this was his moment to chime in. "Until you transition, I wouldn't get anywhere near that door. You think Topside is uncomfortable? What you felt there will be a minor tickle in comparison to what setting foot into Nowhere will be if you go before you're ready. I wouldn't even get close enough to that door to accidentally trip."

Scary words to keep me from going in? Stall tactics? Possibly. It would be idiotic to trust anything that came out of the mouths of people who had been willing to kill me not even a week ago. They'd been ready to toss my body in the river, the way others brought out the weekly trash to the curb.

There certainly wasn't any urgency on anyone's part for this mysterious transition to happen.

"If I've already tinkered, wouldn't I have transitioned?"

Dice glanced at the other two like he was hoping they'd field this one. When neither were forthcoming, he said, "No. Remember the whole boiling conversation? Just because you can stir the water, doesn't mean you won't still boil if you go in there."

"How much longer do you think this is going to take?" I stared at that door, wondering how much of what they said was true.

"Not sure. We can test your progress if you want," Dice said.

"You can?" I swung to face him, wondering why no one had mentioned this before. It was the phone all over again. Or was it?

He got up, looking at the door and then me, as if he were ready to pull me away from it. "Yeah, come on. I'll hook you up to the machine and see how you're doing. You've been hanging around for a few days now. We can see if there's any progress."

He walked toward the hall, waiting to see if I'd come. I did.

He led me into the aptitude testing room and this time went to a latch high on the wall. A panel dropped down like a Murphy bed, except it wasn't a bed but a small platform. A couple of wires hung with finger sensors, like the kind they used to test your heart rate or oxygen at the doctors. There was also a row of lights, like that punching game where you could see how strong you were.

"Step right up and try your hand," he said, as if he were a carnival barker.

I did, and he attached wires to my pointer fingers. "This might tingle, but it won't hurt," he said, then flipped the switch on the wall.

There were twenty lights in the row, and only the bottom two lit up.

That might be good, or bad.

He hummed, rubbing his knuckles over his jaw. "Maybe it's acting up. I'm going to power it down and try again."

Okay, that was bad.

He flipped off the wall switch and then waited. "It's usually good to give these things ten seconds or so before powering up again."

Was this like a cable box kind of deal? It better be more reliable. For some shady land of magic and mystery, they seemed to have quite a few technical difficulties.

We stood there, both counting softly. He looked at me, as if to ask if I thought that was long enough. I shrugged, having no idea. This was their weird stuff, not mine.

He flipped the switch again. This time only one bulb lit. The measurement was worse, if that were possible.

He hummed again. I was beginning to find his hum slightly irksome.

"Switch places with me." He waved me off the platform and motioned to the spot he'd been standing. He stepped onto the platform and pointed to the wall. "Okay, flip it on."

All the bulbs lit up instantly. He hummed again.

"Hang on." He walked to the door and screamed like he was dying, "Cookie! Connor! I need you."

Cookie came running. "What the hell? I thought someone was getting electrocuted."

He pointed to the scale. "Get on. I need to measure you."

"Why?" She looked at him as if he were too stupid to know how to breathe.

"I'm testing the machine."

She shook her head, mumbling, "You're such an annoying idiot it's almost unreal. Like if the people I bitched to hadn't met you, they might not even believe me when I'm talking shit about you."

"You getting on or what?" Dice said.

She got on the scale. Dice flipped the switch. All the lights lit.

"Looks like it's working fine. Like I said before…" The insults hung in the air.

Dice hummed again, ignoring Cookie.

"What's the issue?" Cookie asked.

"She only got one light," Dice said. He glanced back at me. "Everyone gets one light. It's to let you know the machine is on."

I didn't get a single light? Not even that one counted?

Cookie went to the door. "Connor, get your ass in here or I'm going to beat you." She screamed so loud I covered my ears.

Connor walked in a minute later with a scowl and shook his head. "Why do you people keep screaming?"

"Get on the scale," Dice said.

Cookie pointed to the platform.

"Why?" Connor asked.

"We're testing it," we all said.

Even my voice was rising.

Connor squinted at us but got on the scale. Dice flipped the switch. Everything lit up.

Cookie and Dice hummed in unison. I officially hated the sound of humming.

"Is there an issue?" Connor asked.

"It's not lighting for Billie," Dice said.

Connor hummed. I took a long, deep breath.

"Get on again," Cookie said.

I would've declined if I didn't think they'd all drag me on anyway. The switch was flipped. Even the test light appeared a little duller, like I was sucking the life out of the machine.

Three hums sounded around me. If I heard another hum, I might have to start slashing vocal cords.

Tuning them out, I fixated on the one dull bulb. Was this a setup so I wouldn't attempt to go into Nowhere? I glanced at the three hummers. This did not appear to be some master plan, as convenient as that would be.

I *had* to get back Topside, and in order to do that, I might need to go to Nowhere. Now my chances of getting out of here seemed even worse. Instead of transitioning, I was stagnating. This was the only place that didn't make me feel like I was going to die after a day, but it dulled my brain and sapped all the joy out of my life.

I hadn't been paying any attention to anyone else in the room until someone said, "Kaden."

"Did you just call Kaden?" I asked, catching Connor with his phone halfway to his pocket.

"Yeah. Figured he needed to see this. Something is definitely wrong." He wasn't looking at the machine anymore but at me. So were the other two. We'd transitioned from restarting the machine to trying to determine if there was a way to reset me.

Yeah, this wasn't a staged plan. You couldn't fake this level of confusion.

"I really don't think Kaden needs to come. You should call him back and tell him to forget about it. I'm sure something will kick in soon," I said, not believing that for a second.

They all looked at me as if I were stupid.

"Too late. He said he was on his way over," Connor said.

"Call him back and tell him not to. I don't want to bother him. I'm sure this can wait," I said.

The last time Kaden saw me, I'd nearly had a panic attack. Something about being so raw in front of him yesterday... I didn't do that. I didn't have those, or not in front of people. That wasn't who I was.

The sound of a door closing in the distance signaled that it was indeed too late. Kaden walked into the room a moment later.

"What's the issue?" he asked, glancing in my direction, because of course he'd assume the problem had to do with me. It very much *was* my issue, but it was hard not to resent the assumption.

"I don't think she's transitioning," Dice said. "At all."

"Not even a little," Cookie added, because she really enjoyed having her opinion out there for the world to hear.

"It could be the machine. It's not necessarily me," I said, trying to sound strong, the exact opposite of the woman who'd nearly had a meltdown in front of Kaden.

He gazed down at my sweatpants. "What are you wearing?" he asked, as if I were in some alien gear he'd never seen.

"Sweatpants?" The drawers in the suite had been filled

with brand-new clothes with tags. I'd thought they'd been put there for me, and as I had limited items...

"What's on them?" he asked, as if he'd never seen them before.

"Strawberry Shortcake." As soon as I put them on, they'd made me feel a little bit better. They reminded me of the dolls my grandmother had gotten me as a child, not that he deserved to know anything about that. His gaze moved to the slippers that looked like little Shih Tzus stuck to my feet.

He shook his head but turned his attention back to his people had huddled up to discuss me. "How many lights is she getting?" Kaden asked.

"Only the test light," Cookie said, and it was clear she was putting up a valiant effort not to laugh.

"That's it?" Kaden asked.

Cookie cleared her throat, trying to disguise her laughter. There was some more coughing, as the urge to break into hysterics seemed to be spreading.

"Go," Kaden said, waving to the door. "I'll handle this."

The trio ran from the room as if they were having trouble holding back. I'd almost rather they stay and laugh. Whenever Kaden was in the room, my movements always felt more awkward, my thoughts stilted. When it was just him in the room, it seemed to grow even worse. And he didn't seem to be affected at all. Nothing I did rattled him.

"Get back on the scale."

I took a step back. "Why? What are you planning?"

He looked at me, raising a brow, as if to say, *Do we need to have this fight over everything?*

I shrugged and took a step on, choosing my battles. For some reason, when it came to Kaden, my instinct was the more battles the better, even if logic disagreed.

He reached out, taking my hand before I could pull it away, and a tingling feeling grew, spreading up my arm.

"What are you doing?" I asked, trying to yank it back, but he wouldn't let go.

"Trying to recalibrate you," he said.

He dropped my hand and then flipped the switch. Four bulbs lit. It was definitely progress.

"Can you speed the transition?" I asked.

Instead of mirroring my happiness, he looked disappointed. Had he not seen the lights?

"I lit up the bulbs. Wasn't that a good thing?" I asked.

"No," he said. "They lit because of what I did, and it won't last. I was hoping you weren't reading accurately. Obviously you are."

I watched the light slowly dimming from one of the bulbs until it went out. The next one began to dim. It was too disappointing to watch. Kaden must've thought the same, because he flipped off the machine before another went dark.

Could I be stuck in the outpost, limbo land, forever?

All the bulbs were dark and I still couldn't stop staring at them as I tried to process what this new turn of events meant. I felt like a grade schooler trying to pass the bar exam, not even understanding the language.

"Now what?" I asked.

"You showed up with a reservation that you said came from your gram, but act as if you don't know anything. You don't read as having any real aptitude for anything, and yet you go out and sway someone you never should've been able to. Now you look at me as if I should be able to tell you what the problem is?" He looked at me with as much trust as I had for him.

I'd been floundering so badly, so thrown off my game

and out of my league, that the extent of his distrust hadn't been fully obvious until right now. Who did he think I was?

"If you're uneasy with my situation, maybe you should figure out a way to get rid of me," I said, knowing that I might be treading into dangerous territory. There was more than one way to handle a person you didn't want.

"Why would I bother doing that when I think you'll end up being an asset?" he asked.

So even if he didn't trust me, didn't totally believe my story, he would still exploit me if at all possible.

"Are we done?" I asked, stepping off the scale before he answered.

"Yes. I'll see you tomorrow afternoon. I want to feel out your skills for myself," he said.

"Why?"

"Because I do. Maybe you'll get lucky and I'll realize you shouldn't be here." He smirked.

I scowled and left.

CHAPTER TWELVE

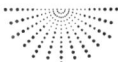

Cookie inched closer on the couch. It was the third time today. It was getting so that sitting on the same couch was becoming awkward. I tried to shift over, again, hoping she'd take the hint that some people preferred a little more space.

Dice let out a deep laugh from the other couch, where he was leaning forward, oiling the pieces of his guns that were spread out on the table. "You know why she's doing that, right?" he asked.

"I'm not doing anything," Cookie said. In spite of her denial, she subtly leaned in the other direction. It was like wiping the crumbs off your face after everyone watched you eat half the cake.

"Oh yeah, sure you're not," Dice said. "You've been hanging on Billie like a sleazy date trying to get a cheap feel all day. Is it the hair, eyes? Nose?"

Nose? Was she sizing up my body parts for something?

Dice stared at her, waiting for an answer. I watched to make sure she didn't reach for one of her knives as I inched a little farther away from her.

"What are you talking about?" I looked at Dice and Cookie.

Cookie shot Dice a look that made it clear he was the one she was looking to cut up.

He laughed as he said to me, "There's an old wives' tale that says you turn into the people you're closest to."

"Huh?" Was this a Body Snatchers-type situation? I was about to throw myself through the door to Nowhere and take my chances.

"Shit, you really know nothing," Connor said, not bothering to look up from his magazine. It might be a good thing he didn't speak often. Maybe his silence was a survival mechanism.

"Can you please explain this to me?" I asked Dice, the only one who seemed to be forthcoming.

"We don't age like normal people. You'll never look older than you do today. What happens is we morph. It's slow going but unavoidable." He dug out his phone and held up a picture of some guy with platinum hair, brown eyes, and a hawkish nose. "See this? This was me about twenty years ago."

"That was you? You're kidding me, right?" There was no resemblance to the man in front of me. Wait, maybe the ears? I looked again. No. Not even them.

"Nothing." He swiped at his phone again and held up a screen with two more people, a man and a woman standing together. "That was Cookie and Connor."

They were unrecognizable from the people in this room.

"What about Kaden?"

He froze for a second and then pocketed his phone, as if there hadn't been a glitch, as if Connor and Cookie didn't drop their heads down another smidge, as if they hadn't heard the question.

"Yeah, I don't think I have any pictures of him on this phone."

He pulled off a lie about as well as a toddler pulled a two-ton boulder. I hummed, nodding, as if it were believable he'd have pictures of Cookie and Connor but no Kaden.

"So that's why she's…" I tilted my head toward Cookie.

"I think it's your eyes. She's been pretty unhappy with her current shade," Connor said.

"It's not her eyes, know-it-all." She shifted toward me, right back to brushing shoulders. "It's her hair. I've never had red." She lifted a lock of my hair. "I think I'll wear it well." She glanced at my t-shirt and jeans before going back to her magazine, giving the sense that she didn't think I was wearing it well at all.

At least she'd stopped verbalizing the insults.

"How long does this take?" How long could I expect a Cookie glued to my side?

"The hair? I'm not sure that it works, but she's stubborn. Or the total morph? You'll look like a completely different person in about fifteen years."

"In twenty years, I'll be unrecognizable to anyone I know?" I touched my face. I'd never been enamored of my appearance. But to look completely different? It would be another tie to my life severed. No one would remember me. No one would recognize me. I'd think back to my family, friends, still have all these memories, but no one to share them with. For all intents and purposes, I'd cease to exist.

"Yeah, thankfully," Cookie said. "Otherwise, how would you explain that you didn't age? We think that's why it happens, keep the idiots in the dark and all, but we're not sure."

Cookie grabbed the remote and turned on season five of *Friends*, signaling she was bored of this conversation. Dice and Connor had already checked out.

I absently touched my face.

"You'll adjust. It'll get easier," Cookie said, showing she was a little more aware than she was acting.

Kaden walked into the lounge, glanced in my direction, and said, "My office," before continuing on his way.

"Does he always assume everyone will follow him?" I asked. I continued to sit there, watching his back until it disappeared.

"Yeah," Cookie said.

"Why?" I asked.

"What do you mean?" Dice asked, looking up from his oiling.

Connor was watching me over the top of his magazine, as if his life might be upended if I didn't follow Kaden.

Cookie looked at me a moment later, when I hadn't gotten up. "I don't know why you're fighting it. He *always* gets his way."

"Al-ways," Connor said.

"Maybe he shouldn't always get his way?" I asked. Did that never occur to any of them? Did they not care?

The three of them laughed. The most grating part of it all was that I *wanted* to hear what he had to say. If I was going to get out of here, I couldn't walk away from any information. I could make a point or I could get answers. What was more important? My pride or figuring out what was going on?

I got up. Their laughter popped new holes in my battered ego.

They could laugh, but I wasn't knocking. Nope. I'd stroll right in, no matter how rude it might be. Of course Kaden ruined that as well, leaving the door open.

He wasn't sitting behind the desk but in a chair facing another only a few feet away.

"Sit," he said, pointing to the empty seat.

"I'm fine." I remained on my feet. This was going to be short and sweet. We'd do this on my terms. "And just so you know, what happened with that guy? I've been thinking about it. It wasn't me. It was a fluke."

He leaned back, resting an arm on a table, stretching out his legs and taking up too much space.

"Sure," he said.

"I'm glad you agree," I said, as if that had been a legitimate agreement of some sort. Some weird shit had happened, and I wasn't taking credit for it, no matter what he wanted to think.

"Something upsetting you?" he asked, looking pointedly at my arms. I had them crossed in front of my chest, my hands fisted.

"Nothing at all," I said, dropping my arms and leaning a hip on his desk. He wasn't the only one who could *lean*.

"Then are you ready?"

"For you to test me? No. I'm not. There's no need." Because if there was something funny going on inside me, he was the absolute last person I'd let know.

Not that there was.

His eyes hardened. "Let's make something clear. You came here, to me. You say you don't know how, that you didn't want to, but you are here. If you can be of use to me, you're going to be of use to me."

His tone was soft but lethal. This was the predator I sensed every time I walked into the room. This man, the one showing his true colors right now, was one of the main reasons I needed to get out of this place.

"You're not using me," I said, every bit as serious as him. I might act calm, but I'd be every bit as savage as him if needed.

"*You* came here. You weren't invited. You showed up and then called reservation status. Now you need to carry your weight. So we're going to do a little testing, and then you're going to start taking assignments and tinkering." His eyes, tone, everything about him was unyielding.

I'd taken care of myself, and my mother, the majority of my life. If he thought at twenty-four years old, after living the life I had, I'd roll over and take orders from him for no other reason than I'd happened upon this place, he was more lost than I was.

"I'm done."

I turned and had made it halfway across the room when he said, "I think you should sit down and smile, Wilhelmina."

His tone was pleasant, calm, cultured, and I wanted to tell him to go screw himself, but I couldn't. I couldn't take a step toward the door. I couldn't speak. Most importantly, I couldn't resist the urge to do exactly what he said. I fought it for a few seconds more, but the compulsion continued to grow until I was walking back and taking a seat.

The icing on the cake, the thing that made me want to punch him the most? I was smiling. He'd used my name, the one I hated, and made me smile while he did.

The compulsion slowly drained away, the feeling of being a puppet softened, and my body became my own again.

"Don't ever do that to me again," I said the second I could.

"You don't like it? Learn to stop me."

All I wanted to do was get up and go to the door. I'd never felt so helpless in my life, but there was nowhere to go, no one to help. This was it. The only thing that had saved me from dying was some strange reservation that I didn't understand and no one explained. As far as my life went, he was king. I had no recourse, and even though I had full control of my body, the weight of what held me in this place felt heavier than ever.

"Are you ready to try to focus now?" he asked.

I opened my mouth, the words *go screw* primed for release. I could nearly taste the joy of seeing his face as someone finally said that to him. I suspected he heard it much less than was deserved. Yet the words didn't come, and it wasn't from lack of balls. I'd been accused of having too much passion in my past, but I wasn't an idiot. I was playing in a world, a game, where I didn't know the rules. If I wanted out, I had to learn how to survive in it first. I'd figure out this place and then turn it inside out and get my life back.

"I'm ready," I said, my tone calm because it had to be. I was a numbers girl, and the deck was stacked against me, but damned if I wouldn't try to turn this hand around.

I was going to have to learn how to maneuver in this world, one where he had control, for the time being. I'd learn it so well I'd find a way to rewrite the rules.

When his gaze met mine this time, it seemed to get stuck as we both reassessed the parts we played.

He nodded slowly and cleared his throat. "Let's begin. You're going to tell me what to do in a benign way, as if you were asking me to hand you something. Most tinkers need to form a physical connection. Skin to skin is best, but as you get better, you might be able to do it with a layer of clothes in between." He rolled up his sleeve and held out his arm.

"What about how you just did it?" I asked. That was a neat parlor trick I'd like to have in my back pocket.

"We'll see," he said, not seeming evasive but honest.

I wrapped both hands around his wrist, ignoring how physical contact with him made me even more unsettled.

"You're not concerned that I might make you do something you don't want?" I smiled.

"No." He smiled back.

There was no hesitation in his belief that I couldn't possibly do anything to him. I gripped him tighter.

"You're going to find a way to get me out of this godforsaken place," I said, focusing every thought, every ounce of energy I had, on him.

His face went slack, his eyes dazed.

Then he said, "Not as horrible as I feared, but you'll have to practice your focus. It feels scattered and all over the place."

I dropped my hand and could see his amusement as the corner of his mouth lifted.

"I'm a very focused person. I've never been called scattered in my life, not even as a kindergartener."

"According to what I feel?" He raised a brow. "Scattered."

"You're mistaken," I said, trying to keep the calm façade even as I wanted to punch him in the face and storm out. Unfortunately, the latter had already been attempted and failed.

"I think I'm capable of judging."

"And you're never wrong? Why does that not shock me?" I asked, poking at him the only way I had left.

"Continue," he said, looking down at his arm. "But put a little more effort in this time." He grinned.

You can't win a game when you don't know how it's played. I'd let him bully me and talk down to me as long as it took to learn, because I was going to become a master of this, if for no other reason than to beat him.

CHAPTER THIRTEEN

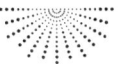

ookie, Connor, and Dice were sitting around the lounge area, another marathon on the television as they continued their endless mundane chatter, which usually included something about lollipops, bets, what some human did, or another idiotic topic that made me want to be knocked unconscious.

This was it? This was my life? I couldn't stay in the normal world. I couldn't go into Nowhere. The only place that was bearable was here, the outpost, *his* outpost. It was unacceptable. What if I never transitioned enough to get beyond this? What if things went on this way for years?

No one called me. When I called them, they didn't answer. I'd even left a message with my mother's landlord, telling him I wanted to prepay the rent, and still couldn't get a call back. I couldn't live in this limbo indefinitely.

I wandered toward the door to Nowhere, laying my hand on its surface, seeing if I could feel any kind of strange energy. What was happening behind it right now? What would I see if I opened it? Stepped through it?

"So this door would open up to Nowhere, even if I were to open it?"

"You know you can't go there." Dice's attention snapped toward me.

"Yeah, I know." I ran a hand across it, seeing if I could feel anything. "I'm just wondering, what would happen if I did? Would it lead to nothing because I opened it, or would it go to Nowhere?"

When he didn't answer right away, I looked back, and all three of them were staring at me.

"I would suggest you don't go through that door," Connor said, his hand bunching his magazine.

I shrugged. "I know. I can't do anything. I can't go back and I can't go forward. I've heard." I moved my hand down to the knob. "But if I did go, without being transitioned, what would happen?"

"Billie, I'm telling you, you don't want to go through that door. It would be very uncomfortable." Dice was on his feet, his hands in the air.

"But what would happen? Would it help me transition?" I asked.

Unless they told me it would kill me, I was going through this door. Short of death, this was happening. I tightened my hand, ready to put up a fight if they tried to stop me. Even if they did, I'd come do it when I was alone.

"It might force the transition, but it'll hurt like hell." Dice took a step toward me.

I spun the knob. "But it won't kill me?"

Dice wasn't answering, and neither was Connor.

"No, it won't," Cookie said.

"Why the fuck did you tell her that?" Dice asked.

"Because it should be her choice," Cookie said. "Let her handle shit the way she wants. She's tough. She'll be okay."

As they bickered, I swung the door open and, for the first time, got a good look at Nowhere. It was a city of sorts, but nothing akin to anything I'd ever seen.

"Come on, Billie, let's…"

Dice's voice died as I took a step into Nowhere. No one was stopping me now. If this was going to be part of my life, the way it was everyone else's, then *let* it be part of my life. I was tired of only having half the information and world available to me.

The entire scene was almost overwhelming. My breath caught in my throat. The sky above was filled with so many stars, glittering like I'd never seen. The Milky Way was there, glowing, but other solar systems as well, all over. I could spend a month just staring up and never stop marveling. It was as if this place was smack in the middle of the universe.

The air was crisp, with a hint of spice I couldn't place drifting on the air, and the sounds of life were practically bursting out of the place. I looked down the street, and it didn't seem to have an end. The road looked like solid black stone and was lined with buildings and storefronts, with signs that moved, like they were written with snakes, or twinkling like the stars above lent them their light. Warm, flickering lanterns hung everywhere. Then, every so often, there was a building that glowed like it was plucked from a Kinkade painting.

Then there were the people: some of them looked human, others not even close, with scales or horns. Some almost shimmered.

This was Nowhere? The underbelly of the universe, so to speak?

I was standing there, looking like a tourist, mouth gaping open, when I got a cramp in my side, like you'd get from running after a long time off. Well, they'd said it might be painful. I pinched my side and took another step, and that was as far as I made it before the cramp grew. Before I could pinpoint the exact location, it spread to nearly every part of my body.

My knees hit the ground, followed by my hands. The pain racked every part of me; even my fingertips throbbed. I vomited on the beautiful street I'd just admired.

Dice knelt beside me. "Are you a dumb shit or what? What did you not understand about *don't go through the door?*"

"She looks a little worse than I anticipated," Cookie said, standing on the other side. "We better get Kaden. I think this might be above our pay grade."

"Nothing to see here, folks. Just her lady time," Dice yelled.

My heaving onto the street, along with the groans, must have gathered a little attention.

"Her *lady time?*" Cookie asked. "Are you an idiot? Does this look like her *lady time?* If this was normal, we'd all be dropping like flies once a month, you weirdo."

"It worked, didn't it? They all kept walking," Dice said.

"Probably because they figured you were insane and didn't want to get anywhere near *you.*"

"What would you have said?" Dice asked.

Cookie opened her mouth to give a retort. There was nothing but silence for a few seconds. I flopped onto my back, watching the two of them argue over me as I lay half dead.

"Yeah, I don't know." She threw up her hands.

I couldn't hear what was said next, as I had to lean on my side to vomit again.

"He's on his way," Connor said.

Just what I needed. Kaden.

"What do we do with her until he gets here?" Connor said, then looked where I'd just vomited and took a step back.

"I have no idea." Cookie turned to Dice. "If anyone starts poking around, keep screaming about lady time like a weirdo."

"You're a real asshole, you know that?" Dice said.

"What are you bitching about now? I'm serious. It worked," she said.

Connor walked through the outpost door, which was still open and attached to what appeared to be a brick building on the street. He came back out with a blanket, which he threw over me.

Dice pointed at the mustard-yellow and green striped grandma blanket that covered half my body. "And you complain about me?" Dice asked Cookie.

"Oh, you're getting plenty of credit. Loads of credit," Cookie said.

Connor pulled the blanket up just shy of my chin while Dice continued fighting with Cookie.

"Just so you know, I left the last purple lollipop for you, and this is how I get treated?"

"What happened?" Kaden asked, bringing their bickering to an end. "She wasn't supposed to go through the door and yet here she is, with all of you here? No one could stop her?"

I closed my eyes, telling myself it was just to rest through the pain. That it had nothing to do with the vomit next to my head or the fact I was too weak to even get off the street.

"I told her not to go through the door," Dice said.

"She was getting impatient," Cookie added. "She's the one who has to pay the price. Figured it was her choice."

Connor didn't say anything, but I could imagine him shrugging.

"You can go now," Kaden told them.

The entire time he was talking, I wondered if I had puke in my hair.

"Do you *ever* listen?" Kaden asked, so close he must be kneeling next to me.

I opened my eyes, irritation pushing back the humiliation enough to stare right at him. "To people I don't know and can't possibly trust? I have to admit, I've never been very good at that."

I would've sounded so much cooler if I didn't have to roll onto my side and vomit right after.

He stayed kneeling next to me, waiting for the spasms to end.

"Did you have a plan for what you were going to do next?" He was perusing me as if we had all the time in the world.

"Look, this wasn't my best choice. Can you get me out of here, or are you waiting for me to beg? Can you bring me back to the outpost?"

He'd be the type that *would* make me beg for help. Didn't matter that I was being tortured and had obviously made a wrong step, literally.

I was lying on the ground, curled on my side, pain shooting through me. There wasn't one part of me that wasn't in excruciating agony, from my scalp to my little toe.

"I can, but it'll make it worse, if you can imagine that. Once you force the transition the way you did, it's best to wait it out here."

I rolled on my back, trying to breathe through the pain. When that didn't work, I turned to my other side. Switching positions wouldn't help, but lying still seemed impossible.

"How long?" I asked.

He laid his hand on my cheek and then moved it down to my neck, his eyes intent, as if he were taking my measure. "Depends on the person, but I don't think it'll be too bad. There's nothing I can do until it starts to wane a bit. Good news is you'll survive it."

I moaned, closing my eyes. Why did I have to be so stubborn? Why? Worst part was that I wouldn't learn. I'd do something stupid again in a month, a few months, a year. It was like the reckless, rotten part I'd gotten from my father had to leak out here and there.

"I'm going to have to carry you. This is going to hurt, but you don't look especially mobile."

I had no delusions of being able to walk. None at all.

He waited, giving me a moment to prepare myself. I nodded.

Every place he touched my skin hurt. I focused all my energy on trying to breathe and not vomit. When he hoisted me over his shoulder, I barely kept the vomit down.

"Try not to move too much," he said.

"Why?" I swallowed, and swallowed again, regretting talking at all.

"I'd rather people assume you are passed out or dead so they don't pay as close attention."

There wasn't anything he could've said that would've been worse. That a presumed dead or incapacitated body would draw the least attention spoke volumes of the place I'd been so anxious to enter.

He walked at a brisk pace, my weight not hindering him at all. I didn't open my eyes or stir, and it had nothing to do with what he'd said. It took every ounce of control I had left not to humiliate myself further by getting sick all down his back. I didn't look until we were climbing the stairs of a stone building.

He placed me down on the sofa, more gently than I'd imagined him capable. I sized up my new surroundings, taking in the clean lines and minimalistic style. The large open-floor plan and use of stone and wood. My appraisal ended there as another wave of pain racked my body.

There was a clinking sound as Kaden placed a glass of water on the table beside me and then picked up a remote, turning on the large TV over the fireplace.

"Harry Potter marathon to pass the time while you wait this out?" he asked, glancing back at me.

"You like Harry Potter?" Telling me he was the devil would've shocked me less.

He shrugged. "No idea. I never watched it."

That made more sense somehow. I nodded, trying to find a comfortable position that didn't exist.

The familiar sounds of the opening theme started up, and I shifted to get a better view. He settled on the other side of the sectional.

"You're going to stay and watch it?"

"I've never seen it," he said, as if that had been a strange question.

I lay there watching for a while and then closed my eyes, listening instead. I'd never admit this aloud, but there was something comforting about having another person there, even if it *was* him.

. . .

Kaden's hand grazed my head, startling me, and my eyes flew open.

"What are you—"

"It's subsiding. It's time to try to sleep."

I felt a pull toward darkness that was nearly impossible, just as he'd done in the office. He'd just tinkered me, and I couldn't do a thing about it but lie there, fighting it.

"Stop resisting it," he said, running a hand through my hair in a caress that seemed almost too gentle to come from this man.

He was pulling my shoes off, and I rolled to my side. I let my eyes close, unable to fight the urge.

"It's all right, Billie. You're safe here," he said, smoothing my hair back from my face.

I felt surrounded by warmth, as if nothing could touch me. It was the first time I'd felt so safe in more than a decade. It was the very last thing I remembered.

CHAPTER FOURTEEN

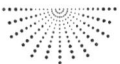

I woke alone, the pain still there, but a faded echo of what it had been. It was still dark outside, and I was in the middle of a very large bed, on sheets of silver gray. Although the room felt sumptuous, with a thick white rug and beautiful artwork, it had a certain lack of personal effects.

As I stood, the silky fabric of the pajamas I was wearing slithered over my skin. It was hard to be annoyed that Kaden had taken it upon himself to change me when I wouldn't have put someone in bed the way I'd been. The fact that he'd seen me naked... I wasn't going to think about that.

There was no clock in the room. I might've slept for a few hours or a few days.

I used the attached bathroom while searching for my jeans. The way these pajamas fell, they were sexier than some of the lingerie I've seen. I checked every corner and couldn't find my clothes.

I opened the door, prepared to search downstairs, and

heard voices. I crept slowly down the hall and then took one step at a time until I could hear them clearly.

"But why would you bring her here?" a woman asked, obviously annoyed by my presence in the house.

"Where else would I bring her?" Kaden asked, as if she already knew there wasn't another viable option. "Was I supposed to leave her on the ground?"

"Why didn't you have one of your people bring her to the outpost?" she asked, pushing even when I could tell he was losing his patience.

Whoever this woman was, she *really* didn't want me here.

"She forced the transition early. You know that wasn't a viable option unless I wanted to drag it out longer," he said, his words becoming more clipped.

"She chose it. If there was a cost, maybe it would be a good lesson for her to learn, for her own welfare. She needs to understand that this world is different."

As if this tactic wasn't transparent, she was going to use the *torture her for her own good* line. Glad she wasn't there when I was groaning on the ground.

"I wasn't in the mood to watch her suffer more than necessary, even if it was her doing," he said, sounding as if he didn't hate me. This was getting interesting.

"I don't know why you're becoming irritated with me. It's only natural for me to ask when you say she was thrust upon you but you keep showing so much interest in her."

"Nettie, she's an obligation that I'm stuck with. As for last night, I wouldn't have left a dog in the street like that. Stop making more of it than there is."

Hearing that everyone thought I was a burden didn't give me the warm fuzzies. Or that he'd taken pity on me like I was a stray dog. That wiped out any bonus points he got for being kind of nice.

"Except it seems more than that. You seem...*curious.*" Her voice softened, some vulnerability leaking into her tone.

Did she think for a second he was interested in me? He probably hadn't told her all my details.

"I'm not. Now is this going to be an issue?"

Nettie might not have realized it, because she seemed a little thick, but even I heard the warning in his tone, hiding around the corner like I was.

"I didn't say it was," she said, sounding a little desperate now. So she *wasn't* deaf.

There was a long, quiet pause, just enough time to make me wonder if I could walk in now as if I hadn't heard a thing. Right when I thought it was safe, Kaden's voice broke the silence again.

"I've never given any pretenses about who I am and what I'm capable of giving. It has nothing to do with you. It's who I am, but I'm not going to change."

Ugh. I grimaced for her. If I was this woman's friend, I'd be screaming to run as far and fast as she could. This man wasn't going to be her white knight. He never would. He was telling her point-blank that this was it.

"I didn't say I was unhappy with our situation."

I could just imagine her clinging to his arm as she spoke. I backed up, thinking better of walking in. I'd hightail it up to the bedroom and wait for someone to come and find me, whenever that might be—an hour, a week, whatever.

I turned to escape and the floor creaked—loudly. They'd been silent as it happened, too.

Fuuuuuck. There was only one thing to do: walk into

the middle of the wreckage. I strode into the kitchen as if I hadn't heard a thing.

I forced a surprised look on my face as I saw them. Saw *her*, Kaden's girlfriend. She was slender, finely boned, and the kind of beautiful you usually only saw after a lot of filters and Photoshopping. She had a presence about her that made it clear she knew *exactly* how stunning she was.

"I'm sorry. I didn't realize you had company. I'll come back," I said.

She smiled like a viper. "Not at all. I'm Antoinette, a close friend of Kaden. I'm here enough to hardly qualify as a company." She hadn't called herself his girlfriend, but she was trying to get the point across as loudly as possible, short of screaming it.

She hadn't liked me before she met me, and now she hated me even more for some reason. I could see the venom dripping as she stared my way.

She needn't bother. He was all hers, or as much as he'd allow her to have. How anyone could tolerate a relationship like that was beyond me. I didn't care how attractive he was.

Not that I found him attractive.

Kaden merely nodded in my direction and walked out of the room, leaving me here. Alone. With her.

"I'm so happy I could lend you something. Kaden said you were in rough shape." Her gaze lingered on my hair.

I reached up, smoothing down the out-of-control mass as the length of the silky pajama pants made sense. I felt like a munchkin with puffed cheeks staring at the cheekbones of a face that could make a cosmetic company a fortune.

"Would you like a pastry?" she asked, holding a plate out to me.

"Thank you," I said, taking a croissant. I'd been starving a few minutes ago, but now I was just trying to get along and be polite. Clearly this was a relationship that was going to need some work, if I ever saw her again. If she was dating Kaden, it was likely.

I nibbled at the corner of the pastry. "Tasty."

"Take the rest of them as well. I don't know why Kaden gets them. Neither of us eat that kind of food." She smiled as her eyes dipped to my hips.

Curvy hips ran in my family. It didn't matter how thin I was or how many croissants I skipped. The hips curved. The butt popped. That was my fate in this life.

Just get along.

She walked over to a chair, where I saw my jeans.

"Kaden had your clothes laundered, but I'm not sure they did a good job," she said, running her hand over a spot on my newly cleaned shirt. "See? Look what they did. It's like they scrubbed them with rocks or something. They should have to replace them, they're in such bad shape. I have plenty of old things lying around here I won't wear anymore that are better than this if you need to borrow something."

"Yeah, I'm sure they're fine." I grabbed my stuff off the chair before she could find more fault with them, me—everything. "Hopefully Kaden can point me in the direction of how to get back to the outpost and I'll be getting out of your hair."

"I'll make sure to tell him you're waiting for an escort back. Lord knows he's not good at being a host, probably from lack of trying, but we all have our weaknesses."

"Well, thanks," I said, retreating to the guest bedroom before she could verbally slice me up any more. I wasn't coming out until this woman was long gone.

. . .

Kaden stood in the door of the guest bedroom.

"You look better," he said, walking in and his eyes running the length of me.

I was already back in my own clothes, but even clean, I felt a little rattier.

"What time is it?" I moved to the window, looking down on the town below. It was unlike anything I'd ever seen in a tourist magazine.

"About nine in the morning."

"What time does the sun come up?"

"Five years, give or take a week or two."

"Five years?" I turned to look back at him, and he didn't appear to be joking.

He walked over and leaned on the dresser. "Don't mind Antionette if she was a bit abrasive. She can get territorial with new people, but she doesn't mean any harm."

Okay, so he knew she'd be a bitch and also expected me to take it on the chin. Got it. Didn't *like* it, but message received.

It wasn't a secret that I ranked low on the totem pole around here, but having to suck up abuse from his girlfriend was the icing on the cake. The sooner I learned the ropes, the quicker I got my footing, the faster I'd get out of this situation. And I would. I'd get out of here and back to my life if it was the last thing I did.

"I should be able to move around now without an issue?" I asked, trying to sound casual.

"If you mean going back Topside and living there, this doesn't change anything. You'll be a ghost to those people. Even if they see you every day, they won't remember you."

Then how did this ever end? In essence, I was stuck in this world as thoroughly as I had been before.

No, that wasn't completely true. Kaden said there was no return. That didn't mean there wasn't a way he wouldn't tell me about, or he didn't know of.

"Yes, but before you go, we need to set up some ground rules."

Ground rules? On top of taking crap from his girlfriend whenever she wanted to dish it out? Great. Just heap it on. I'd stash it away in my I-don't-give-a-shit folder and do what I wanted anyway.

"Sure," I said, smiling and leaning on the windowsill.

"Is there a problem, Wilhelmina?" he asked, crossing his arms and tilting his head slightly.

It was as if he somehow knew I hated my given name. He probably did. There was probably a folder on me around here, with a list of all my dislikes that he was planning on using against me. Maybe that was how he knew I liked Harry Potter.

"Not at all. I have some ground rules I'd like to discuss as well." I kept my smile in place, even as I feared my face would crack from the strain.

He waved a hand. "Go first, please."

I thought back to the very first time he'd tinkered me, making me sit. Last night was the second, and although sleeping through some of the pain hadn't been a bad thing, a line needed to be drawn now. No one was controlling me like that, ever. I didn't willingly relinquish control, not to anyone. You didn't grow up the way I had without knowing what harm could come from doing that.

"Don't tinker me again," I said.

"I was trying to save you a few more minutes of pain if I could. I didn't think you'd mind."

"I understand why you did it, the *second* time. Don't do it again."

"Next time, I'll run it past you before I do anything," he said.

It was a win on paper only, but he'd left himself an opening. He hadn't said he wouldn't, only that he'd tell me first.

I nodded, as if I believed I'd gotten a true win. It was easier than fighting for a win I wasn't going to get. Not yet, anyway.

"Now for my rules. You aren't to come here alone." His voice hadn't changed, but his eyes had grown hard, chilling almost.

"Why is that? No one else seems to have that restriction on them. Am I special for some reason?" What was here that I wasn't allowed to have access to? Whatever it was, I hoped he'd spell it out so I knew right where to go.

"You're not ready for the things that dwell here. *They* are." His tone was hard.

"I thought I was waiting to transition, and now that I have, I could move here, have a little more freedom. Was that all a lie?" Or was that why they'd kept me from the door?

"Eventually you will. But you're not ready." His gaze wandered over me. "You wouldn't last two minutes here right now, or at least I don't believe so, and until I'm sure of where you stand, we're going to leave it as is."

Burning adrenaline fueled by one insult too many drove me to straighten. There was a limit to the amount of crap I'd take in a day. "What do you think I am? Some sort of spy?"

"I don't know what you are, and you can't seem to enlighten me. I do know nothing is adding up. You might be as ignorant as you act, but that doesn't mean it's not a setup."

"You're saying my gram put me in here to spy on you with zero clue as to what I'm doing? A spy that continually wants to leave?"

The words nearly stunned me. He thought I was planted here to watch him? I swallowed, not even sure how to reply.

"Until I know more, I'm not ruling anything out."

"As much as I enjoyed this pleasant morning with you and your *lovely* friend, I think we both know where we stand. I'm ready to go."

I walked out of the bedroom and headed downstairs, ready to find the door back to the outpost whether or not Kaden followed me.

CHAPTER FIFTEEN

Kaden followed me out of his place. We didn't talk on our way to the outpost. He opened the door for me when we got there. I didn't say goodbye, and neither did he.

I stepped into the lounge and felt myself unwind a hair. Could it be that I was actually relieved to be here?

The rest of the gang looked up and nodded their acknowledgments. I went into the kitchen and made myself a coffee from this nice little latte setup they had. I went back to the lounge, dropping onto the couch where Cookie was sitting, across from Dice and Conner, feeling like I'd gone ten rounds in a no-holds-barred cage fight.

Cookie sucked on her lollipop, making a loud noise when she plucked it out. "You look a little better than you did last night. That doesn't say much, considering how bad you looked last night."

"Yeah, I'm good. Thanks. I guess. I'm definitely better anyway." I rambled, belatedly realizing she hadn't actually asked how I was doing.

Connor was eyeing me up in between flipping through

a motorcycle magazine. Dice was cleaning another gun, making me wonder how many of them he had.

"Want a lollipop?" She used her own to point to the jar sitting on the coffee table. "Just got some grape in. Dice hasn't managed to eat them all yet."

Dice threw her a glare but remained silent. I didn't want to get involved in their bickering, but I had noticed him going hard on the strawberry the other day.

"For someone who just came out the other side of transitioning in the most painful way ever, you should look a little more relieved. And yet..." Cookie hummed.

"She looks slightly out of sorts," Dice said, nodding and smiling, as if there were some inside joke I didn't know.

"It wasn't Monday or Thursday date night, but I'm still guessing she met the twat," Connor said, laughing as he kept reading his magazine.

"She *definitely* met the twat," Cookie said. "There's only one soul-sucking asshole who can make blue skies turn gray, and that is, drumroll, please..."

"The *twat*," all three of them said in unison.

"You mean Antoinette?" I'd always hated the word *twat*. Maybe even despised it. But nothing about my meeting Antoinette had filled me with motivation to defend her.

"Yes, *her*," Cookie said.

They were all waiting for me to confirm it.

"She did happen to be there this morning." If they asked me for details, they weren't getting any. The details had been humiliating enough the first time they were said.

"Oh yeah, finding that you'd stayed overnight? That must've burned her up," Dice said. "I would've paid to be there for that introduction."

Cookie handed me a lollipop. "Take it. You deserve it."

I shook my head. "Thanks, but I'm good. I'm not much of a lollipop person."

"That's because you've never had Nowhere lollipops. Trust me."

I took it just to not argue. My last twenty-four hours hadn't left much energy to do anything but agree. I leaned over, willing to take any kind of lift I could get, even if it were a sugar high.

I sucked on the lollipop, and it was like sucking on heaven. These things might become addictive. I looked at it, trying to see whatever magic was used to create such a glorious candy.

"Where do you get these? This is next level," I asked.

"I know, right? Good shit," Cookie said. "There's a place on the corner of Purgatory and Main that sells them. Little retired leprechaun cranks them out. Don't tell him you know he used to be a leprechaun. Word is he sold off all his gold on the exchange because of gambling debts. Made things difficult for him back home. Lost all street cred after that. Pisses him off something fierce, and no one needs a pissed leprechaun on their hands. They can be nasty little shits on a good day."

Purgatory and Main? Pissed-off leprechaun? There were so many odd things about what she'd said that it was hard to know where to begin.

"Too much info?" she asked, probably because of the dazed look on my face. "You'll get used to it eventually. So what did you think of the twat? No one but Kaden likes her."

Understandable, considering the interaction I'd had with her.

"Oh," I said, not sure what else to say.

145

"What did she say to you? She can't open her mouth without insults flying out," Cookie said.

"I didn't talk to her much."

"Yeah, I'd try to keep it that way. She's not what you'd call a girl's girl, like me."

If she hadn't nodded, reinforcing her words, I might've taken it for a joke. Cookie was a girl's girl? I mean...I *guess* I could see that, if I put a lot of work into it. She had been the only one to tell me Nowhere wouldn't kill me and defended my right to make my own choice. In retrospect, feeling as banged up and wiped out as I did right now, a few more details might've been helpful, but it didn't negate the intent.

"Is Antionette a tinker or does she work with Kaden?"

Connor laughed to himself while he read. Dice rolled his eyes.

Cookie scoffed. "She *wishes* she were a tinker. That woman has zero skills outside the bedroom, from what I can see, other than politically. She's so cold that I have my doubts about in bed as well, except that Kaden isn't exactly desperate, so I imagine she must have something.

"He'd never mess with anyone who works for him. He doesn't even like to mess around with anyone he does regular business with. Says it 'muddies the waters.'" She laughed hard before she added, "Considering how many jaded women he's left behind, it's a good thing, because he'd be standing in a mud pit by now."

Habitual womanizer. Just another thing to add to my long list of reasons not to like the man. He was attractive enough, if you liked the cold, too-much-testosterone type.

"Politics? Wait, I thought Nowhere had no rules?"

"Rules or not, there's no place in the universe that

doesn't have politics," Dice said, holding up his gun and squinting down the barrel.

"I wouldn't feel bad about the twat disliking you," Connor said.

"Yeah," Cookie added. "She universally dislikes anyone that takes any of Kaden's time. She hates all of us because we work with him, and his work takes his time. She's definitely going to hate you the most. She might even despise you at the moment, but you'll eventually fall into just bland disdain." Then she leaned forward, and it looked like she was counting lollipops by color.

"How long have they been together?" I asked, since everyone seemed eager enough to gossip.

"If by together you mean hanging around and waiting for whatever crumbs he has left to give her?" Cookie asked, writing down numbers on a scrap of paper while she talked. "A year or so? Eventually she might tire of it and move on like the rest. Some stick around longer than others."

"Does it bother him that his relationships fail over and over again?" I asked.

"Who, Kaden?" Dice laughed. "If he did, he might try a little harder. He hasn't yet, and has never seemed overly upset."

"You need to understand something about Kaden," Cookie said, pocketing the scrap of paper with the numbers. "He doesn't get into relationships because he cares. It's more about convenience. The only long-term commitment that man has ever made is this place."

I sank another inch into the couch, kicking my feet up on the table and letting the sugar do its job. For some reason, hearing about Kaden's escapades only annoyed me more, probably because it showed what a bastard he was.

"At least you can start getting on with things too," Cookie said. "Get some real freedom and move on with your life."

Move on? I wasn't moving forward. I was going back home. Ignoring Kaden's rules, being able to go into Nowhere, was one step closer to being able to navigate this world on my own, learn its rules and how to get myself out of this place.

It was one more step closer back to my life that felt like it was slipping away. As it was, my phone had barely rung this last week. Johnny used to call me every day after work. He hadn't called me in days.

"What's wrong? That should make you happy, and you look like you lost your dog," Cookie said, shifting close enough that her arm brushed mine.

I was ready to buy her a box of hair dye. I moved over a couple of inches as casually as possible before answering.

"This is a nice place and all, but I'm not completely convinced that this is where I should be. I understand it might not be easy to undo this, but that doesn't mean it can't be done." I wasn't giving up until there wasn't a shred of my life left to return to. My entire life, I'd worked toward having some stability, a normal existence. This place? I might as well be a kid again, moving from place to place, never knowing what would come next.

"Why are you so set on getting back? This isn't a bad gig," Connor said, tossing his magazine on the table, bored enough to participate in the conversation.

Dice squinted. "What'd you leave behind? You upset about a guy?"

"No, not *just* a guy," I said. "I have plans. I'd finished an accounting degree and was interviewing. I also have a mother that depends on me, and yes, a boyfriend who I'm pretty serious with."

"Let's see him," Cookie said, blowing past all the other details.

I dug my phone out of my pocket and flipped to a picture of Johnny and me from his last birthday. We'd gone out with a bunch of friends and then danced until our feet hurt. He'd told me he loved me that night, when we were sitting in his car later on. It had been a slow burn with him, but he became my rock.

"His name's Johnny," I said, showing Cookie. Connor and Dice leaned in, and I turned the phone to them.

There was a look that passed between the three of them, as if I were blind to facial expressions.

"He's cute," Cookie said with a flat tone.

"Oh. Well, yeah, I can understand that," Dice said, sounding as if he didn't at all.

There was that look again. I could handle judgment toward me, but I'd always been more sensitive when something derogatory was directed at someone I cared for.

Not just cared for. *Loved.* It wasn't his fault he wasn't thinking about me. It was whatever voodoo happened with this place.

"What was that look for?" I asked, pausing to look at each one of them, trying to determine who'd be the weak link and talk first.

"Huh?" Cookie asked.

"What are you talking about?" Dice asked, going back to his guns.

Connor said nothing, but that was par for the course. He was always more inclined to silence.

"I saw the look you guys gave each other. What was it for?" I asked.

"It was just a look. Let it go," Cookie said.

Connor nodded, as if that were good advice.

"Some things you're better off not knowing," Dice said.

"Except I'm not one of those people. I want to know." They might not realize it, or maybe they did, but I wasn't going to drop this until I found out what that look was about.

"If you really—"

"Don't do it," Dice said, looking at Cookie as he cut her off.

Connor shook his head and then picked up his magazine again so he could bury his head in it.

Cookie waved her lollipop at Dice. "She wants to know. I'm not going to bullshit her. She's a big girl. She can handle the truth."

"It's pointless," Dice said, leaning forward. "Why upset her? She's not going back anyway. No one goes back alive."

"*I'm* making it back alive, so I suggest you tell me," I said.

Connor's head, buried in the magazine, was shaking.

Cookie stared at Dice. "I'm telling her, and you're not stopping me." She turned toward me, as if dismissing Dice once and for all. "Chickee, I hate to break this to you, but you got yourself a bad apple there."

"You're saying Johnny is a bad apple? Because why? You didn't like his shirt in the picture? The part of his hair?" They didn't know him. They might imagine that they knew everything about everyone, but *I knew* him.

"We can tell certain things even from a picture. He's a bad apple. You don't want to believe it, that's your choice. You asked what the look was, and that's what it was. We all saw it." She shrugged and went back to sucking on her lollipop.

She was right. I'd asked. I couldn't get mad that she'd told me something I didn't like, and definitely disagreed with.

"Thank you for telling me the truth." I wanted to get up and leave. This day was already too much, and this was the last straw, but I wasn't going to skulk off, so I sat, sucking on my lollipop.

The silence spread until Dice stood. "I got a thing I gotta get to."

Connor stood. "I'll help you out with that."

"Yeah, I've got a thing to do," Cookie said, getting up.

They all bailed on me. My heaviness must've been spreading outward. I sat there for a few minutes, staring at my phone, which didn't ring. Then it hit me. Kaden wasn't rushing back in here, and I'd scared the rest of them off. For the first time since I'd been here, I had the place to myself, and I wasn't going to waste this gift.

CHAPTER SIXTEEN

As far as I was concerned, Kaden's pronouncement this morning that I was a possible spy had drawn a line, a big, ugly line. Before today, there had been no trust but a thin layer of civility. After that conversation, there was no doubt we were fully on opposite sides. Another small movement or two from either side and it would be an all-out war. As far as I was concerned, the enemy didn't deserve any loyalties, and this morning, that was what he'd declared himself to be.

I walked around the lounge first, checking every drawer and shelf. That search only turned up a bunch of old-style phones, a video store's worth of DVDs, and more remotes than made sense for a single television.

I continued down the hall, toward my bull's-eye. There was no way Kaden would leave the door to his office unlocked. I'd have to find a screwdriver or something to jimmy it open. If that didn't work, there were probably videos of how to pick a lock. You could find a video on how to perform heart surgery these days.

I grasped the handle, and it turned. Well, this was interesting. I swung the door open, and then jumped back, waiting for some sort of trap that would spring out.

Nothing. I tossed my phone a foot into the room, seeing if something would get triggered. Still no ax swinging down, so I jumped in headfirst, grabbing the first folder on the nearest shelf.

Flipping it open, I saw the pages were empty. I went through the entire folder, not finding anything but blank pages. I grabbed another, and more empty pages. Another file, and more nothing. None of these folders had anything in them. What kind of sham was this? I went through every single piece of paper in there and couldn't find a single line of writing.

There were papers sitting on his desk, but they were all blank. The drawers had papers that were blank. I combed every inch of the room and only found blanks. As far as gathering an arsenal of information against him, things weren't going well.

I was about to abandon the office to see where else I could search when my phone lit up with the landlord's number. I leapt for where I'd left the phone on the floor.

"Jose? This is Billie from your rental on 222 Franklin."

As soon as I was greeted with dead air, I knew exactly how this conversation was going to go.

"Billie?" he said. "I don't have a renter named Billie over there. I've got Georgina, and her mother who died. Who are you?"

How many times had I met this man? Seen him as he bubblegummed something together in my house? Wanted to vomit as he stared at my ass? Yet he'd completely forgotten me already. It was pointless to remind him when he might just forget me in a few minutes.

"I misspoke. I meant my mother rents your house. I

need to take care of the rent there for…" I had a bag full of money, more than I'd need, since right now, I had no bills. "I'm going to send you rent payment for the next six months, all right? It'll go out today."

"You are?" he asked, stunned enough that it was clear this wasn't a typical thing for him.

"Yes. All I ask is that you don't send the rent statement to the house, okay?"

"Where do you want me to send it?"

The door to Nowhere was opening.

"The garbage."

I hit end and slid my phone in my pocket as Kaden walked in, finding me in the hall, the door to his office open.

He stopped beside me. "How'd that work out for you?" he asked, tilting his head toward his ransacked office.

"Not very well. You think you'd bother to fill out a few of those papers just in case," I said. If he could insinuate I was a spy, I wasn't above calling him a con artist.

He laughed.

"I'm glad you find getting caught in your charade so amusing."

He laughed more. "Come. I'd like to show you some of the fake files you're talking about. Just so you know, I don't lock this room because I don't need to." He waved his hand toward the walls lined with files. "Go ahead, grab any one you would like. If I pulled it for you, I'm sure you'd say that was a setup too."

I didn't bother telling him I'd gone through nearly every file. I eyed up the wall, grabbing a folder and flipping it open. The pages were filled with writing, the top had a name, date of birth, and then paragraphs of—

He took it before I could read it. "You can glance at whatever file you want, but no in-depth reading."

I grabbed another folder, finding it filled with writing, and then another. "How is this possible?"

"I allowed you access, which I'll be revoking again."

"No way."

"Then look again," he said, motioning to the file in my hand.

I flipped it open, and the words were gone. I grabbed another file, one I'd just looked at, and it was the same. I was starting to hate this place more and more.

"I'm assuming no one else is here?" he asked.

"Just me." I didn't want to tell him that a picture of my boyfriend scared them all away this morning and they hadn't been seen since.

"Come with me. I want to check something," he said, heading down the hall.

He obviously wouldn't be doing whatever it was he had planned if the others were around. They were his people. What would he hide from them?

"See what?" I called after him.

He was already halfway down the hall. "Come and you'll see," he said. "Hurry up. I don't have all night."

I chewed on my lip, lasting another half a second before following him. There was no way around it. I wanted to know what he was doing that he didn't want anyone else to know.

The door to the aptitude-testing room was open, and he stood beside the chair that measured aptitude, tablet in his hand. "Take a seat."

I did, too curious not to.

He tapped on the tablet.

"Well?" I asked.

"You're still not reading," he said, tapping a few more times before putting the tablet down and pointing to the transition scale. "Let's try this again."

This, I knew, would be good. After all, I had transitioned. It should light up, right?

I got on and waited as he flipped the switch. One bulb lit. The test bulb.

Nothing else.

"Do it again," I said.

He stared at me for a second.

"You dragged me in here. Do it again," I said.

He turned it off and on again. Same result. One bulb.

I got off the scale and pointed to it. "It's your scale. Your equipment is broken."

"It's not the scale," he said.

"It has to be. I transitioned. I was in Nowhere walking around without any pain this morning."

"That's the problem. If your reading had been correct the last time, your transition should've been worse, and lasted longer. You don't go from barely transitioned to done that fast. The scale isn't able to read you."

"Then your scale is broken."

He looked at the scale and then me again. "There's something wrong, but it's not the scale."

"Maybe it's because I'm not supposed to be here."

He ignored my suggestion as he stared at the scale, but his attention wasn't anywhere in this room.

His attention focused back to me with laser intensity. "Don't mention this to anyone, not even the crew," he said. "Do you understand?"

He watched me, paying attention to every flicker of emotion. Yeah, I got it. There was something very wrong about me, and he was trying to keep it under wraps until he could gauge whether it would benefit him.

"Sure." I didn't want the few people I saw every day looking at me cross-eyed. He wanted me not to talk? That was the easiest request he'd had so far.

"I'm bringing you to a job tomorrow at eight. You'll need a cocktail dress. Ask one of the crew for whatever."

He left.

I walked past his office and didn't bother going in. Getting a latte from the kitchen machine would be more gratifying.

CHAPTER SEVENTEEN

It was seven o'clock, and I was supposed to be ready for a cocktail party at eight. That I was showered was about all I could say for myself.

Why he'd want to bring a spy with him didn't make any sense, other than he figured I'd be useful somehow. He'd use me up until he found a way to kill me. I dropped onto the couch, ignoring the rest of them as I silently stewed.

Cookie eyed up my shorts and t-shirt. "Don't you have a thing to go to?"

I shrugged.

"I think she's still deciding," Dice said, laughing.

I could refuse, but what if Kaden tried to kick me out of here? Could he do that? Probably. My mother had looked startled when I walked in the house. My boyfriend wasn't answering my calls. If they were forgetting about me, I didn't have any hope for anyone else. I had a bag of cash, but it was technically Kaden's cash.

"Cookie, do you have something you could lend me for tonight?" I asked.

"Wise choice," Connor said softly from his chair.

"Your ass is never fitting into anything I have," Cookie said. "We don't have time to shop, so you'll have to pick something from the closet." She stood up, stretching like she hadn't gotten off the couch in a couple hours. "I saw another couple of racks rolled in the other day. Kaden must've gotten it stocked for you."

"Gotten what stocked?" I asked, following her.

"The closet. I prefer to do my own shopping, but it'll do when you're in a pinch." She walked to the door that typically brought you to the bridge and flipped a switch on the right-hand side.

"Are we going Topside? I thought you said there was a closet?"

"Hit the switch and it *is* the closet. It's climate controlled, humidity or some mumbo jumbo. I don't know. Keeps the clothes good or something. I don't bother with it most of the time, so I can't tell you specifics."

She opened the door, and I walked into heaven. There were crystal chandeliers, plush carpets, tufted velvet benches, but that wasn't the beauty of the place. There were racks and racks of clothing, shelves of shoes and bags. The center had several islands with accessories, scarves, and jewelry...

I touched a pair of drop diamond earrings that sparkled like nothing I'd ever seen in person. "Are these real?"

"Yeah." She yawned, then shuddered, as she looked about. "I hate this place. It feels so sterile. I wouldn't let the designer touch the lounge, not after I saw what he did here. I picked out every inch of that room."

Suddenly a few things were making sense.

"Yeah, it's...comfortable there," I said.

"*Exactly*. Not like this. There's no place to kick up your

boots without worrying you're staining something. Yuck. Okay, well, have at it."

"Wait, is there makeup?"

She pointed to the vanity set up on the side. "Whatever you need."

I walked along the racks, running my hands over every color, every designer imaginable. There was dress after dress in my size. Any style I could imagine was here.

The plan hadn't been to look good enough to impress anyone. I was going to dress just well enough to get by, maybe be slightly dowdy, but there was no way I could resist some of these dresses.

I slipped on a slinky silver number. It was long, with a slit up the side. Nothing would be displayed, but it followed every curve of my body. After the dress, it was hard not to wear a decent pair of heels, and then I had to accessorize. By the time I realized I'd put in too much effort, it was too late to scale it back.

Connor let out a low whistle as I walked back into the lounge.

Cookie nodded. "Not my style, but you wear it well."

"She does do that," Dice said.

Kaden approached from the hall, dressed in a black suit, looking so handsome that it was hard not to stare.

He was silent when he saw me, but his perusal was slow enough to make my skin flush.

He stopped in front of the door beside me, flipping the switch. "For some reason, I was expecting you to be wearing sweatpants when I arrived,"

"You did say it was a cocktail party." Sweatpants had been a possibility, not that he'd be informed.

He hummed. "You got sucked in by the closet," he said.

"Maybe."

161

The light over the door was green as he opened it. We stepped out onto the bridge, but we weren't in Florida anymore. The New York City skyline glittered to the right, as Hank, the toll bridge guy, nodded to us.

"How did Hank get here?" After Nowhere, showing up in New York didn't shock me at all, but how was the same toll guy here? Did he work every bridge? Did he get advanced warning?

"That's not Hank. That's Frank." Kaden opened the passenger door of the Lamborghini parked along the side.

I wondered what these people saw instead of this car that they merged around it, no one blowing their horn.

"They see construction," Kaden said.

I belatedly realized I'd thought aloud.

"Where are we going?" I asked once we were on our way.

"A party not far from here. There's a gentleman there that needs some tinkering, and there's not much time left to do it," he said. "Some cases are more difficult than others. Not all tinkers are compatible with different subjects. Trying to narrow down if you have a specific niche."

"I thought my aptitude was spying?"

He looked at me as if to silently ask, *Is this how the night is going to go?*

I replied with a noncommittal shrug, a silent *We'd see.*

Kaden turned off the highway, slowing the car down as my heart started racing. Did I still have a heart? Something was pounding in my chest, even if it didn't serve a purpose.

Were we really going here? It was clearly a private event.

Kaden pulled the car to the curb, and the valet opened my door.

"Who am I supposed to be if someone asks?" I whispered as soon as Kaden was in earshot.

"No one will ask. They'll know on some level you're supposed to be here and won't question you. Part of the way our thing works."

Our thing, and I was being included in the *our*. It was getting so every moment that passed, my real life slipped away and I became part of their world.

We walked into the private party, surrounded by beautiful people smiling and smelling intoxicating. Kaden's hand was at my back as he guided us to the bar, the heat of his touch sending a sizzling awareness through me. I'd never felt this kind of sensation with Johnny. I wouldn't put it past Kaden to be manipulating me somehow.

The bar was packed, but as soon as Kaden raised a hand, it was as if we were the only ones there. The bartender rushed over.

"What would you like?" Kaden asked.

"Glenlivet, neat."

He tilted his head slightly as if I'd surprised him. He turned back to the bartender. "Make it two."

I could barely wait to get my hands around the drink, hoping the burn would smooth out the nerves. The place Cookie had taken us was open to the public. This place I was keeping one eye on the security dressed in suits by the door, expecting to get tossed at any moment.

Was that a holster I just saw under the guy's jacket?

"Can I die?" I asked, and then took a sip.

"Yes, but it would have to be very violent." Kaden's hand was at my back again as he leaned closer. "We've got company headed this way. Don't say anything more than you need to."

"Company? You mean like people who are going to know who we are?" I asked.

"Yes. Now stop talking."

"But I don't under—"

He wrapped an arm around my waist, pulling me slightly to him. The intimate hold threw me off my game long enough for our company to descend upon us, as I was sure he'd planned.

I'd never been the jealous type with other women. Maybe watching my father with his new family had burned that out of me. When he had a daughter with his new wife, she'd been everything he wanted, while I was the frumpy kid with the crazy mother he couldn't wait to get away from. The fight had been over before it even began.

But if I *were* the jealous type? I'd be greener than spring grass after a week of rain. The legs, the curves, the hair—the *face*. Antionette was beautiful, but this woman was walking sex appeal. It felt like I'd seen more stunning women up close and personal in the last week than in my entire previous life. I didn't believe people could look like this without filters.

"Kaden," the woman said, her voice almost a purr.

I didn't glance his way, wanting to avoid the lust that would surely be there. It was bad enough I appeared to be his date, let alone one he'd like to swap out.

"Catherine," he said, sounding almost bored.

I looked his way. Was he so used to attractive women drooling over him that he was immune? Hard to not to take the obvious invitation this woman was offering. I wasn't inclined toward women, and even I struggled to keep my eyes from her.

I shifted my gaze to the crowd meandering around, attempting not to gawk at Catherine.

"Who's this gorgeous creature?" a man asked.

"She's none of your concern, Alec," Kaden said, his hand back to my waist.

I turned, finding an attractive man smiling at me. He wasn't quite as pretty as Kaden, but he was close enough that it was flattering.

I glanced around again. No one else had shown up, and Alec was still staring at me.

"Wait, were you asking about me?" I said, sounding about as uncouth as a person could get.

"But of course," he said, letting an appreciative eye run over me and then turning his attention to Kaden. "How about this: give me a little time with your friend and I'll even stay out of tonight's festivities."

Wait a second! Did he think I was some sort of prostitute?

I was about to ask him exactly that when Kaden pulled me into his side again.

Yeah, yeah, I know the drill. Don't talk too much.

"I don't need you to stay out of my way. I'll win regardless," Kaden said.

"Only because I'm too bored to put up much of a fight. I guess I've grown comfortable in my situation," Alec said, his eyes wandering back to me.

"Soft, just as you like it," Kaden said.

Kaden was many things, but I couldn't imagine anyone ever accusing *him* of being soft in any way. He was all hard surfaces and sharp angles. Maybe that didn't give you the same comforting feel as a warm Sunday morning, but I had to say, if things got ugly, I'd much rather have him watching my flank.

Watching my flank? Who was I becoming? I was an accountant. Maybe not at this very second, but I would be.

"Well, you won't get any competition from me—not here for that one anyway. I'm here for a different person," Catherine said, having moved her attention from Kaden to the crowd.

Who were these people? Were they from a competing organization? Were they from Nowhere?

"Enjoy the party. I believe we'll retire early tonight."

"You're leaving?" Alec said.

"Yes. Consider it a gift," Kaden said.

CHAPTER EIGHTEEN

I didn't ask any questions as we left the party, not willing to slow down our departure for even a few seconds. It wasn't until we were back in the car, the scenery flying past, that I weighed whether I wanted to know who those people were. Well, of course I *wanted* to know, but should I ask? Knowledge was power, but sleep counted for something too, and I was too tired to find out something else bad.

It would be nice not to hear anything disconcerting for at least a day, so I toyed with the idea of remaining silent. Except I couldn't take that liberty, good or bad, if I wanted to get out of this. All I wanted to do was sleep for a solid day, but I had to ask anyway.

"Who were those two people at the party? Competing organizations?"

That might've been leading the witness. Would he lie to me? It surely wouldn't be the first time. Probably not the second, or third...

"Those two work for a couple of different gods. Sometimes we have competing interests." He looked at his sleeve as he said this. "Dammit. I liked this jacket. I knew I felt something spill on me when we were walking out."

Gods? Not even one god, but multiple? Of all the times he had to be forthcoming with answers, this was the one time that a lie would've been preferable. This new situation, job, whatever it was, was swimming in a cesspool of danger.

"Can you see that?" Kaden asked, holding out his arm. "This designer is long dead. I can't get another."

"Doesn't that cause a problem? Do you want to be in direct competition with gods?" I asked, hoping my tone of voice imparted the level of seriousness this subject deserved.

If I was associated with his organization, this wasn't good. I wasn't going to war with gods for these people. I didn't want to have beef with some random deities that might be able to strike me down with lightning.

He smirked, as if I'd amused him enough to soften the blow of losing his favorite jacket.

"They're not overly powerful ones. Tonight wasn't a big enough target for anyone to get their feathers ruffled. Everyone knows the game."

Everyone but me. This was another day of work for him. I wouldn't be sleeping tonight, again.

"And nobody gets upset about that?" I asked.

"They don't care that much. This is a game to them. You saw them. Did either appear that interested? They've got another billion people lined up to play with."

If they weren't that big of a deal, why didn't we do the job? Why did he walk away?

"Or did you have another goal in mind?" This hadn't

been about seeing whom *I* could tinker but getting a read on whether they'd met me before. To see if I was a spy for one of their organizations?

"Perhaps," he said, confessing enough to confirm my guess.

"Did I pass?" I asked, knowing I had, or he probably would've dumped me in a river already. How was I supposed to navigate a world in which my only allies were also potential enemies?

"You're still here, aren't you?" he asked.

He sounded as if he were kidding, but for all I knew, he might make jokes right before he pushed his victims off a cliff. I wasn't taking anything for granted.

He swerved the car over to the side when we got to the bridge. Frank was heading over, or it might be Hank now. Who could tell?

Frank wasn't smiling. "Sir, we have a slight problem right now. I can't put you through to the outpost. I can only open up to Nowhere."

"Why is that?" Kaden asked, and it didn't sound like this was a usual occurrence.

"Technical issues," Frank said.

"That's fine. Just open up directly to Nowhere."

"Very good, sir," Frank said, and turned, heading toward a little house on the side of the bridge.

Kaden turned to me. "I'll bring you to the outpost through the back route in Nowhere."

Frank stopped walking and turned back around, retracing the few steps. "Sir, that might be an issue. We've had to close off that route while we assess the issue."

"You closed that door as well? For how long?" he asked, sounding like someone who wasn't used to being told no.

"Hard to say, but we're expecting it to be until morning." Frank weathered Kaden's displeasure with a shrug.

"*Morning.*"

"Yes. Very sorry for the inconvenience."

Frank didn't sound remorseful at all. Or appear as if he had any regrets as he headed back to the booth.

"Damn unions," Kaden said.

"You have union workers?" I asked, looking back to Frank and then Kaden.

"Not even Nowhere has been able to dodge unions. They work a little differently, but the gist is the same."

A few seconds lapsed as the reality of staying at Kaden's hit. Would he be getting company again?

I looked around, wondering if they could get me a bridge somewhere else. "I can always just go to a hotel, or my mother's if Frank could get me back to Florida."

The way it was going lately, my mother might think I was an intruder and hit me over the head once I walked in the door. A hotel was a safer bet. Good thing I'd stuck some hundreds in my little purse.

"I have a feeling a bridge to Florida isn't going to be available either."

We stood there waiting another few minutes, and I had this strange feeling that Frank wasn't trying to open a broken bridge, but breaking a working one.

Another few minutes stretched by before Kaden broke the silence. "Why were you surprised Alec was interested in you?"

It was pretty obvious, but if he needed it spelled out... "Because I was standing beside Catherine?"

"And?"

He sounded so convincing, as if he really didn't understand. Maybe he didn't like blondes? Some guys were like that, so set in their preferences they couldn't see beyond them.

"She might not be your type, but she's blindingly stunning. Surely you noticed that?"

He turned and looked at me, his eyes narrowing a little, as if he couldn't make heads nor tails of something. "Do you find yourself unattractive?"

Compared to Catherine? Who wouldn't?

I'd never considered myself ugly, but I'd never be a head turner. I was one of those girls that found a boyfriend because all the better-looking girls were either taken or out of their league. I was average, decent, run of the mill, and I was fine with that. What wasn't okay was being played for a fool. Was he having a good time at my expense?

"I'm average. Everyone who looks at me knows I'm average, and it's fine to be average."

The bridge opened, and I walked through before he could continue this awkward conversation.

I glanced back at Frank right before I crossed, and he was grinning. Why would he be happy that I was stuck in Nowhere? These guys were weird.

Kaden didn't try to broach the subject as we headed back to his place.

"I'll get you something to sleep in. Antoinette keeps some things here." He was walking away when I rushed to stop him.

"You know, I don't really like her stuff. Do you have a long t-shirt or something I can use? That'll be more comfortable."

He froze, but then shrugged. "Sure."

He returned to me a few minutes later with a few different t-shirts and laid them on the back of the couch.

"I'm assuming you remember where the guest bedroom is?" he asked.

There was something heavy, nearly awkward hanging in the air, like we were two teenagers on the fringe of getting in trouble.

"I'm fine." I grabbed the shirts and headed toward the stairs.

"Billie," he said, stopping me before I had a chance to make my getaway.

"Yes?"

There was a long pause before he said, "Never mind."

He walked away.

I got up the next morning and padded down the stairs in bare feet, poking around, looking for coffee.

He walked in the front door a short time later, his gaze running the length of me.

His t-shirt fell to mid-thigh. I had shorts that were shorter, but I felt as if I should've put pants on before I came downstairs.

He continued inside, throwing some sort of newspaper on the table.

"They have newspapers here?"

"Why wouldn't we?"

Because the place was named Nowhere? I didn't bother replying. If he wanted to think this was normal, I wouldn't burst his bubble. He took out another mug, helping himself to the coffee I'd made, and then groaned.

"This is atrocious."

"What do you mean? It's great coffee."

"That you don't realize it's bad is alarming," he said. But he continued to drink it as he made his way to the table.

"Does that thing have a crossword?"

He pulled out an interior sheet and slid it toward me.

I looked around, but before I could ask, he leaned over toward a breakfront and grabbed a pen out of it.

"I don't have pencils."

"That's fine. I prefer a pen."

"And here I thought you always took the safe route," he said, his tone flat but a glimmer of humor in his eyes.

"There's nothing wrong with the safe route. Some of us like comfy and secure. Not everyone likes to live on the edge. Some of us appreciate things that are calm, broken in. You know just what you're getting."

"I'm sure, like a pair of used slippers," he said. "Sounds like a fabulous way to go through life."

"Don't underestimate old slippers."

He let out a soft laugh.

The door sounded, followed by heels clacking on stone. My options for escape disappeared before I lifted my head and saw her.

Antoinette walked in dressed in a pantsuit that showcased every feminine line. Her hair was perfect, as if she'd just walked out of the salon. I glanced at the clock. It was seven thirty in the morning. Who got up and dressed like this every day?

She stopped short as she spotted me in the kitchen, doing a crossword, wearing Kaden's shirt.

She walked over, and he got to his feet. She put a hand on his chest and glided it up to his shoulder. She leaned in for a kiss on his lips that seemed a little too showy for someone who wasn't trying to prove something.

I went back to drinking my coffee before the second act started.

"Just came by to tell you I'll be a little late for the company gathering on Saturday night."

"No problem," he said in the clipped tone of someone looking to shift the conversation.

"You're not upset that something has come up, are you?" she asked, keeping her voice loud enough to ensure I could hear every word.

"Not at all. I said it's fine."

He didn't ask why she was going to be late. Why was she going to be late? Was it a legitimate reason, or was it a ploy to make him jealous?

"It's just I have to meet some people and finalize that deal I've been brokering."

"I told you, it's not a problem," he said. He moved away from her, putting his mug in the sink.

She walked over and stood behind him, putting her hands on his shoulders then smoothing the fabric of his jacket. "What time are you planning to go? I know you don't like to get to these company parties too early."

Company gathering. Of course Kaden didn't want to talk about it.

"I'll let you know later on," he said, but it felt like he wanted to say something else, or something more.

"It's too bad you aren't coming to this one. You aren't, right?" Antoinette was looking at me while leaving a possessive hand on Kaden. Her mouth should've had a warning label, declaring sharp objects inside.

Kaden visibly stiffened and then answered for me. "No. She won't be. It's a bit much for this early on. She won't feel comfortable there."

I wouldn't? I kept my face blank, my annoyance buried. I wouldn't give this woman an inch.

"It's a yearly thing where all the tinkers get together. It's fun, but I understand why you wouldn't be quite up to it yet. If you're still around, maybe next year you'll get to meet everyone." She parted her red lips, flashing perfect teeth.

I didn't doubt that if something bad did happen to me, her smile would be genuine.

CHAPTER NINETEEN

I stood in front of the door to Topside the next day, staring at it.

Dice walked up beside me, pointed to a switch on the wall, then flipped it up. The light near the door turned green.

"That's it?" I asked.

"Yep. That's it."

He seemed amazed by my bewilderment. He'd lived with this stuff for decades. Maybe even centuries? Of course it was old hat to him. To me? This sort of shit shouldn't happen.

"What about a car?" I asked.

"I usually request one ahead of time, but ask Hank and he'll get you something." Dice walked over to settle himself on the couch in the lounge area.

Hank would get me something? Me? There was a strong possibility of a bus pass in my future.

I opened the door and was slightly speechless when I walked out onto the bridge without anyone else helping me.

Hank gave me a nod as he headed my way. His face seemed especially blank of all emotion, which was an improvement from the usual annoyed look.

"Hi," I said as he stopped beside me, and I wondered the best way to broach the car situation.

"Heard you might've annoyed someone over in Nowhere?" Hank asked, rocking back on his heels, arms crossed.

There was only one place this was going: Antoinette. She was going to be more problematic than I originally figured. I was doomed for a bus pass now.

I wasn't rolling over and saying it was my fault. There was a limit to how much crap I'd take because of that woman.

"I believe the person you're referring to hated me at first sight. Not much to be done about it." I'd taken the bus before, and if my memory was correct, there was a stop not far from here.

The straight line of his mouth softened a little. "Well, if you're not getting along with her, that's okay. We aren't all meant to get along with everyone, after all. I mean, take us bridge people, for instance." He pointed to himself, looking more animated than I'd ever seen him. "*Some* might not think we're essential to business, might think we're even beneath them, but without us, tinkers wouldn't be able to tinker at all. They'd be lost half the time, landing in all sorts of crazy places. We're extremely important to the structure."

It looked like Antoinette had made more enemies than I might've imagined. I hated people who shit on the little guy. *I* was the little guy, or had been, and when someone trod all over you without even noticing, or caring, you never forgot that feeling.

"I can see it. Since I've been here, I've noticed you work harder than anyone else I've met." It was true. He was always on this damned bridge, when the crew was laid out on the couches watching DVDs half the time.

He shrugged. "It's not just me. There's a lot of us bridge folk holding the line, making sure everything runs smoothly. I can't take all the credit. You know, you should come meet the gang at some point. We get together from time to time down at The Deep."

"I would love to. Just let me know when."

"Are you looking for a car? I've got some really nice inventory today. I can hook you up."

"You will? I'd really appreciate it."

"Don't worry. I'll take care of you." He winked at me, and a few moments later, there was a Bentley in front of me.

I couldn't even speak or move. He couldn't mean I was going to get to drive *this*.

"Keys are in the ignition. You're good to go."

I pointed to the car wordlessly.

He nodded.

My hands shook as I took the wheel.

I was standing in my favorite coffee shop a few hours later, waiting for a chai latte. I'd already dropped off a money order to the landlord, who had no clue who I was. After that, I'd run past my mother's, dropping off bags of groceries.

It had taken her ten minutes to recognize me, and it wasn't the booze. Would it take an hour next week? Would she not recognize me at all in a month?

As fun as it had been to drive the Bentley, have a huge

new wardrobe of clothes and jewelry to wear, I had no one I trusted to talk to. No one to vent my concerns to, or just plain old vent. I was surrounded by people but felt like I was on an island by myself.

"Chai latte for Billie," the barista called out, placing a cup on the counter.

"Thanks," I said, smiling.

This guy used to know me, smile and nod in recognition. There wasn't a drop of familiarity now.

I took my chai and headed outside to the park across the street, walking to the large oak my grandmother had loved, wondering if I'd hear from her. A month ago, hearing from the dead would've been an absurd thought. Not anymore. Or maybe I was so desperate to speak to someone I knew cared about me that I'd believe anything at this point.

I took out my phone, dialing Johnny. It went to voicemail—again. I didn't bother leaving a message.

"Billie?"

I spun, startled to hear anyone calling my name at this point. A man who appeared a little older than I was walked briskly toward me.

A childhood friend? It couldn't be. They'd never remember me at this point. This man with his height and tawny hair wouldn't be someone I'd forget easily.

"I'm sorry, do I know you?" I asked as he caught up to me.

He smiled, laughing a little. "No, you don't, but I've heard of you and was hoping we could talk for a moment."

Heard of me? No one had ever *heard of me*. I was in debt, had no job, no prospects. Plus I was pretty much invisible on top of that.

Wait. I wasn't even fully a person anymore. I couldn't even claim *that*.

"Can I walk with you? I'll only take a moment of your time," he said.

I closed my mouth, realizing I'd been standing there confused and gaping. "Uh, yeah, okay."

The park was fairly busy today. How much harm could there be?

I walked. He walked.

Please be someone normal. Anything *normal*. I was maxed out on crazy.

"I know you've recently taken a position with Kaden's organization."

Nope. Not normal. More crazy, which was the last thing my life needed. I was on an overload of crazy. I sighed, feeling there was no way around hearing him out.

"Who are you, exactly?"

He dug into his pocket and pulled out a card. "My name is Alaric. I have a competing organization."

"Oh. That's very nice." I took the card and put it in my pocket. It was politer than tossing it in the garbage pail we passed.

"Thank you. I'm hoping it's even nicer for you, as I wanted to offer you a place with my team."

"You did?" Every part of me was groaning. *No.* No more teams or crews or whatever they wanted to call them. I wanted none of this.

"Of course. This is a very competitive market, and good tinkers are hard to come by."

"I'm not sure what you heard, but my skills are mediocre at best, and I don't plan on being in this business long." I picked up my pace, and he did the same, smoothing back his thick hair, as if that made a difference.

"I happened to have a man in the area at a recent tinker you performed. We know this was a particularly difficult subject. You shouldn't undersell yourself."

The concert. I felt bad for some kids, and now look, it was screwing me left and right. I still thought that Kaden would've have helped me get out of his crew if he hadn't discovered my usefulness. Now I had a new person wanting me.

"Even if I was spectacular, which I'm not, this isn't my cup of tea," I said, realizing how far I'd walked from the car and that he'd trail me back the whole way.

I spun, and as suspected, he dogged my steps.

"I can understand your resistance to talking, but let me fill you in on a few of the finer points of this situation, in case not all of these matters were explained thoroughly. I've heard you're new to Kaden's organization. Just because you joined them doesn't mean you have to stay with your current employer. I would suggest to anyone in your situation to explore all their options. Maybe his crew isn't a good fit, but mine might be. I can offer you a highly sought-after recruitment package."

There were other options? My pace slowed a hair. If I did end up stuck...

"What kind of package are you talking about?"

"Well, let's start with the family plan. If you come with me, your family could be lotto winners after signing with me. Parents, cousins, extended family, and friends will all be taken care of." He smiled and shrugged. "I can also offer them long lives. I don't like to brag, but I do have connections in other departments."

Other departments? He was going to extend their lives? Weren't we meddling enough? How far did these people take it, and how many of these tinkers were there?

"That's just the family bonus. You'll be set up hand-somely as well." I stopped, sipping the last of my chai as I listened. He held out a travel cup toward me. "I took the liberty of ordering you another before I came."

"Oh, well, thank you," I said, taking the hot refill. He motioned for my empty, took it, and tossed it. It landed in the trash can fifty feet behind him.

"As I was saying, top-of-the line penthouse in Nowhere, or a rural estate if you prefer. Houses wherever else you would like. Retirement package is amazing as well. When and if you do decide to stop working, or you want to retire Topside for a while, you'll have your choice of options: CEO, artist, filthy rich and doing nothing? It can all be arranged. I don't know what your current plan is, but I assure you I can match and go above anything Kaden has offered."

Kaden hadn't offered anything, not that I'd tell him. One, it was embarrassing now that I was hearing this offer, and two, I didn't want this guy to know how cheap I'd come. They'd stuck me in a broom closet.

Still, as he stared at me, waiting for some response, my head was going to fall off my shoulders from the weight of it all.

"I need some time to think this over."

"Of course. You have my card. It has my contact details on the back. Hope to hear from you soon."

He smiled and nodded to me before leaving.

I dug his card out and flipped it over. *Dial Alaric.*

I walked into the outpost lounge, and Kaden was there, talking to Dice. Kaden turned to me. Dice looked in my direction, his eyes owlish, and shook his head in the universal message of *you're going to get it now.* Then he took off into Nowhere.

What had I done this time? Kaden walked over calmly, but the tendons in his neck looked stretched to breaking.

"How was your afternoon stroll? Did you enjoy the sun and your tea?" he asked.

"How did you know where I was? What I was drinking? And you accuse *me* of being a spy?" Now we were both strung tight enough to break.

"Earth is an easily trackable place when you don't know how to hide your trail," he said. "How do you suppose Alaric found you?"

Note to self: learn how to hide my trail, and fast. Too bad there weren't instruction manuals for this stuff. How many people were watching my every move? Was there nowhere safe to go?

"What did you say when he offered you a position in his organization?" Kaden asked.

Kaden might be intuitive, but mind reader he wasn't, or he'd know I wasn't a spy. This place seemed frighteningly like the corporate world, where stealing talent was par for the course.

"I told him I'd think about it, and I am. Not like you mentioned a family plan. You and your people were ready to dump my body into the river and then stuck me in a broom closet. Far from loyalty inspiring."

"Did you not realize that you can do your own family plan at this point? You're a tinker. That's what tinkers do."

One of my biggest pet peeves in life was when I didn't notice the obvious, like now. I hadn't thought of that at all. If I was going to tinker other people's lives, why not help out my mother? How to go about it, though? First I needed to get her sober. Then what? I'd figure it out, because the last thing I'd do was ask Kaden how to do it.

"You're going on assignment with me tomorrow night. It's at a club, so dress appropriately," he said, turning to leave.

"More tests to see if I'm a spy?" I called out as he walked away.

"See you at ten."

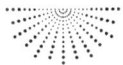

CHAPTER TWENTY

A waitress came over to our cordoned-off booth in the corner of the Miami nightclub. She poured us both a glass of champagne, smiling outrageously at Kaden in front of me. What if I was his date? Thinking of date night, hadn't Dice mentioned something about that?

"It's Monday. Won't Antoinette be upset you're missing date night?" I crossed my leather-clad legs, sipping from my flute.

"She's fine. She knows work comes first." He smiled, as if there were something amusing in that statement.

I tried not to focus too much on him. Since he'd arrived in a black button-down shirt, hair perfect, smelling like heaven, he'd been even more unsettling than normal.

"You're such a romantic. I don't know how she can stand it." I sipped more champagne, reminding myself of how unattractive he was in spite of his allure.

He did have good taste, though. Whatever he'd ordered was mighty tasty. I had to admit, if I was going to be stuck in a miserable situation, it was nicer than being poor in the same situation. The clothing I'd picked out for tonight would've paid for a month of my schooling. I couldn't imagine how much the diamond hoops I was wearing were worth.

I scanned the crowd, wondering whom we were here for. Kaden kept staring at the same empty spot.

"Is the person not here yet, or was that a pretense again?" I asked, finding I didn't mind being out, even if the night ran long. I'd been sitting cooped up in that outpost so much that hanging out here, listening to the music, was a nice change.

"We have to leave." Kaden put his glass down and got to his feet.

"What are you talking about? We've got a job to do. Or testing me out?" I might not have been a tinker for long, but no one would ever accuse me of having a bad work ethic. Plus, we just got here. I hadn't even finished my champagne.

"Billie," he said, "this is not a request. Get up."

I stood, but only because it was easier to stand my ground on my feet. "You can't micromanage every moment of my life. I won't live like that. I want to stay a little longer. I'll make my way back to the bridge on my own."

"We're going," he said as if I hadn't spoken at all, grabbing my arm and pulling me after him.

"Let me go," I said, yanking at my arm.

A large man stepped in our way. The guy had to be close to seven feet tall. I'd heard that this was a hot spot for celebrities, and there was something familiar about this man's face. I had this strong sense I might've seen him playing football.

He clearly had an ego and something to back it up to get in Kaden's way, because no one got in Kaden's way. He didn't have to have a recognizable face to be recognizable as dangerous. There was just something that lurked under the surface, something that made sense the moment you met him, that let you know he wasn't one to be messed with. Just because I regularly did it anyway didn't mean I didn't see what a sane person would.

"Miss, do you need some help?" the big footballer said, speaking to me over Kaden's shoulder.

"Get out of my way." Kaden didn't budge.

"Not until the lady tells me to."

Great. Now I'd have to defend Kaden and pretend I was happy about getting dragged out of a club like a rag doll. It was that or he might hurt the big man. If a fight broke out, my money was on Kaden.

"It's fine. I'm—"

"Move," Kaden said, his voice deep and reverberating. The man moved, keeping his eyes on Kaden the entire time as he stepped off to the side.

I hadn't seen Kaden lay a hand on the guy. It was just as he'd done to me, tinkering without even touching him? It was a cool trick I'd like in my back pocket for sure.

I was getting dragged past the man as I said, "Really, I'm fine!"

A second later, the sound of bullets let loose and screams erupted. All of a sudden, bodies were stampeding toward us.

Kaden grabbed me around the waist, pulling me into him as he started to steer us with the crowd.

"What the hell is going on?" I asked. He'd known something bad was about to happen. That was why he'd wanted to leave.

The crowd was shoving this way and that, making it hard to move through the room. Instead of getting out of the building, he opened a closet and pulled me out of the fray. We were shut in a small, dark place, surrounded by stacked chairs that took up most of the space. Our bodies grazed each other's in the tight space.

The bullets were still flying in the club. Kaden shifted so that his body was between me and the door.

"What's happening?" I whispered, hearing the screams.

He pressed his fingers to my mouth. I could see him shake his head in the small sliver of light that entered through the tiniest crack in the doorframe.

The bullets continued, along with screams of pure terror. I'd thought the yelling and crying, the stampeding, knowing that people were fleeing for their lives, was the worst thing I'd ever heard or experienced.

I was wrong. What came next was way worse. The screams grew muffled, almost like I was hearing them underwater. People were all right beyond the door, rushing past in a panicked horde, their feet thudding so hard it shook the ground, but something else was filling the air, buffering the noise or focusing my attention so swiftly that everything else faded to the background. It oozed forward, filling even the tiny closet.

Even if I hadn't been huddled in this closet, if the guns hadn't been going off, I didn't need any other thing to signal that I should be terrified of what was approaching now. I felt it on a primordial level, the remnants of my ancestors now warning me I needed to do one of two things, run or hide, unless I wanted to cease to exist. And even hiding didn't seem good enough.

My heart was beating so loudly that I was afraid its pounding would give away our location. I tried to breathe softly but found that a struggle, as a shaking overtook my entire body.

I tried to swallow back the urge to flee, or scream—or

both. It didn't work. I moved, trying to reach for the knob to get out of this place, to run for my life before I was slaughtered in this closet.

Kaden wrapped his hand around my wrist, pulling it away from the door. He flattened it on his chest, covering it with his own.

He cupped my face, and I could feel the intensity of his eyes, even in the dark, trying to infuse some of his calm into me.

More bullets, louder screams, and I shook my head, trying to fight the urge to run. He curved his arm around my back, pulling me snugly into him, then rubbed gently up and down.

I let myself form to him.

He'd get us out of here, and away from whatever this thing was. He would, but I had to stay calm. I couldn't unravel.

I found myself gripping the fabric of his shirt, pressing my cheek to his chest, curling into him, listening to his heart, letting his scent surround me. He continued to rub my back with one hand as he cupped my head with the other, slowly massaging my scalp. He was doing whatever was needed to keep me together, and I was letting him because I would've been screaming otherwise.

The running faded, and more importantly, so did that strange, horrible feeling that had scared me worse than being thrown into the river. I'd thought I was meeting my death. This thing, this feeling, had seemed a fate worse than dying.

Kaden's hands stilled as he tilted his head toward the door, listening to or seeing something.

"We have to leave," he said.

I stood frozen, like I was literally immobilized. The fear

coursing through my veins had robbed my body of strength.

I was an accountant. This wasn't where I should be. My life was supposed to be calculators and numbers, calm and orderly. That hadn't been a whim. I'd chosen my profession with a good deal of thought. I liked orderly, calm, and neat. I'd never been good under duress. Tax season was about as bad as my life should've gotten.

He lifted my chin up, our eyes met, and then his flitted to my mouth.

The door banged like someone had fallen into it before footsteps sounded off in the distance.

"We're going to leave," he said, his gaze shifting from my lips. "Don't look around. Keep your eyes on me and don't let go of my hand. Do you understand?"

I swallowed, debating how long I could stay in the closet. After what I'd heard, that *feeling*, the last place I wanted to go was out there.

I didn't have a choice, as Kaden did not wait for me to answer. He gripped my hand and tugged me after him into the room. I followed, trying to keep my eyes on his back as we made our way through the huge room. It was silent now, everyone who could escape having done so. Those who hadn't been able to...

Just watch his back. Don't look anywhere else.

I slipped. His quick reflexes and grip kept me from falling, but it didn't stop me from seeing what had caused my almost-fall. There was a pool of blood. I followed the trail back to the body lying facedown.

I began shaking so fiercely that there was no moving or walking anymore. Kaden had me in his arms the next second and we were back on track as he carried me out of the place. There was a crowd forming around the building, people who had escaped and curious onlookers drawn to the scene. Police sirens blared in the distance.

He didn't put me down until we were blocks away and at the car.

We crossed a small bridge, and then a larger bridge, all of it a blur until I found myself in the outpost. Kaden's hand was on my lower back, steering me as if he thought I'd get lost if he didn't. I might have.

"What happened to her?" Dice said from where he was reclining on the couch, his boots propped up on the coffee table.

I jerked my gaze in his direction, startled, still feeling numb.

"Chaos," Kaden said.

Dice nodded. "Oh yeah, that'll do it. First time seeing Chaos is always a bit jarring. Still remember my first time. Don't think I'll ever forget."

Cookie walked in from the kitchen, carrying a bag of chips. "What happened to you?"

"Chaos," Dice answered.

"Oh. Got it." She dropped down on the other couch.

Kaden steered me forward, and my body followed his lead. I was too stunned to want to think on my own. Plus, he'd gotten us out of there. That had earned him some trust, even if only for tonight.

He urged me toward the couch in my suite. All I needed was a little nudge to take a seat.

He disappeared into the bedroom, then came back with a blanket that he draped over my shoulders.

I clung to it, pulling it tight around me.

"Whatever that was, can it get here? To this place?" I asked, following his movements.

"No. It can't happen here. Outposts aren't here or there,

so to speak, but a space in between—a buffer zone, if you will."

He went to the sidebar that I hadn't touched since I moved in. He carried back a glass, handing it to me.

"Here, drink it. It'll help."

Help? That was all I needed to hear. I took a long gulp, struggling to keep it down, hating the taste but liking the warmth when I felt like I was an iceberg.

I kicked off my shoes, wondering if they had blood on them, and tucked my legs to my chest, curing into a ball under the blanket, wondering if Kaden was going to stay or leave.

I scrambled for a way to keep him here, the man I usually tried to avoid, and yet was ready to tackle if he took a step toward the door. He said it couldn't come here, but right now, after having felt it, nothing made me feel confident.

"What was that, exactly? You called it Chaos, but it didn't sound like you meant that as a generic term." I looked up at him, wishing his arms were around me again.

"It's not generic. Chaos is a thing that happens at times." He topped off my glass with a bottle I hadn't realized he'd brought over.

He took a seat on the other side of the sofa. I wanted to crawl on top of him but restrained myself, feeling like sanity was creeping back in time for me not to make an absolute ass of myself. It had been close, though.

"But what is it?" It was a legitimate question, but I would've asked him about the flooring, or the light fixtures, if it would keep him here for a little while longer.

"Have you ever heard of the chaos theory?" he asked, reclining and resting his arm on the back of the couch.

"No," I said, and all I could think of was that he didn't look like he was leaving in the next couple minutes.

"Butterfly effect?" he asked.

"Yes. I've heard of that." I rolled into a ball on my side, waiting for him to continue.

"They're basically the same thing. It's the theory that a small change can ripple out and cause a larger effect."

A heavy dread filled me as the logical cause of the initial change hit me.

"That was because of something a tinker did." I hadn't thought it possible to be more shaken.

He took a sip of his drink, making me wonder if tonight had affected him as well, even as he seemed to be as calm as ever.

"Might not have been a tinker. There was a change that had a greater effect down the road. Things had to be realigned. That's when this Chaos happens." He shrugged, as if accepting tonight as the way it was.

"You *knew* something was going to go wrong."

"I didn't know, but I've been at this business long enough to sense ebbs in the energy, feeling a hint of it coming." He put his glass down, looking like he was going to stand.

I shrugged off the blanket, getting to my feet. "I have some brownies in the kitchen. I should've gotten you something to eat," I said, as if he were a guest and I was a normal person in the regular world.

Shit. I didn't have a kitchen in my suite. Where were those brownies? Didn't I bring some of them in here the other night when I was having a pity party? I scanned the room, searching for something to give him.

"Billie, you don't need to get me—"

"I have..."

195

He was in front of me, grabbing my shoulders, before I took off looking for anything to stall his departure.

"Billie, sit. I'll stay."

I froze, my cheeks warming as he stared at me like he could read every cowardly thought in my head.

"It's okay. Everyone reacts the way you did. It's normal," he said, letting go of me and sitting down again.

I went back to my seat on the couch and buried myself under the blanket, trying not to stare at him like he was going to try to make an escape. "The brownies are really good. You know, if you're interested." It was a pathetic attempt to cover my crazy behavior and probably failed.

"I'm sure they are."

He leaned back, doing something on his phone, not looking like he was going anywhere.

Curling on to my side, I kept my eyes forward, even if I kept Kaden constantly in my peripheral vision.

CHAPTER TWENTY-ONE

The door to my suite swung open and Cookie walked in. She stared down at where I was lying on the couch, popping chips into my mouth. *The Matrix* was playing on the TV and I hadn't changed out of the sweatpants I'd put on last night after I woke in my bed alone.

She made a swirling motion over me. "Is this because of your brush with Chaos?"

"No," I lied. "Just tired, is all." I flicked a couple crumbs off my shirt.

"You know that's a once-in-a-decade phenomenon at most, right? It's not like you're going to be dodging it every time you leave this place."

I nodded, as if I'd known. Once every ten years? That was better than waiting for it to hit every time I went for coffee. It wasn't like it had hurt me or anything. It just felt…

I shivered, trying to push the feeling from my mind, as I'd done fifty times already and failed.

"You know what? You need to get your ass up and start

getting ready. Go pick out some tacky outfit out of that closet you seem to love so much and get moving. We leave soon, and you can't go like this." She was pointing at the crumbs still clinging to my t-shirt, while making a face like I smelled.

I didn't. I might not have showered, but I would've noticed an odor.

"For what?" I popped another chip in my mouth, having no intention of going anywhere.

"There's the annual tinker party tonight. *All* the tinkers go. It's, like, the thing. You can't miss it."

It was as if the close call with Chaos had wiped my brain clean of anything else, including any annoyance at being left out. I popped two chips in rapid succession.

"Yeah, I'm pretty sure I'm not invited." I wasn't just sure, I was positive. Kaden and Antoinette's conversation had spelled that out pretty well.

Cookie looked at me like I was dumber than dirt. "What are you talking about? There's no formal invite list. It's the same time every year, and if you're a tinker, you're automatically invited. That's how it works. And you can't go like that."

"Yeah, you can't go like that," Dice said as he walked into the suite, looking at my sweats and t-shirt, complete with oil stains.

Cookie turned to him and said, "She wasn't planning on going. Can you even believe this shit?" She threw her hands in the air.

Dice shook his head at me. "You've got to go. All the tinkers go. If you don't show up, it'll look weird, like we're hiding you."

The two of them were staring at me and not budging. If

they'd been willing to throw me in a river, dragging me to a party against my will wasn't going to faze them.

"I'm not quite sure I'm supposed—"

"To go?" Cookie asked. "Are you not listening? *All* tinkers go. And don't tell anyone you're a reservation when you get there, either. They'll really think something is wrong with you. No one wants a reservation on their team."

"How do I say I ended up here?" Maybe Kaden was right. I wasn't ready for this loony bin.

Cookie glanced at Dice.

He pointed to me, as if he'd had some stroke of brilliance. "Lie and say I recruited you," he said. "Now come on. Get going. We're going to be late."

I was only halfway through the first *Matrix* and now I was going to have to get up and go to a party that at least one person didn't want me to go to. Kaden was going to be pissed when he saw me walk in, I *knew* it, and I wasn't in the mood for a fight tonight. This was a lick-my-wounds kind of night. Not to mention Antoinette…

I got off the couch, finally finding my motivation.

"Give me twenty minutes," I said, thinking Alaric would surely be there too. He might be an untapped well of knowledge. Why hadn't I asked him if he knew a way out of this situation?

"Wear something that shows off your ass, too," Cookie yelled as I walked out of the room.

"Yeah, I don't want people saying our new crew member is dumpy," Dice screamed. "Then I'll have to make Connor kick someone's ass, and he really doesn't know his own strength."

"Fine. Nothing dumpy. Now please shut up so I can get ready," I yelled back, heading for the shower.

. . .

They'd all said I should go. Said it would be fine—no, *required*. Yet as I walked into the crowded room at the place called The Deep, right on a bustling corner of Nowhere, I couldn't help feeling like I was doing something wrong. The place would've looked like any regular bar or restaurant Topside if it didn't have gaslights and some of its customers didn't have scales, or leather, or —*fangs*. I'd assumed all tinkers looked human, but maybe not.

"I'll be right back," Cookie said, then waved to someone and melted into the crowd.

The place was packed, and yet as I scanned the room, taking in all the different-looking people, I spotted Kaden almost immediately. His gaze had already been locked on me, as if he'd spotted me the second I walked in. He was standing near the bar with a group of people I didn't recognize, but his attention was solely focused on me.

He hadn't wanted me here. I'd convinced myself otherwise, that maybe he was really worried I'd be uncomfortable, but his cool gaze told me otherwise. If his attention had felt chilly, Antoinette, who was standing beside him, was arctic. I nodded, and then inched my chin up higher. I was a tinker now. I had every right to be here too, even if I felt like I was going to get dragged out by a bouncer at any moment.

Dice leaned in, drawing my attention to him. "Don't forget, anyone asks, you tell them I recruited you. No mentioning that other word."

"Don't worry. I got it," I said, wishing I wasn't here at all. "Where's Connor?"

There were only a handful of people I knew. One was glaring at me. One had disappeared already and another hadn't even shown up yet. I needed some numbers.

"He's getting laid, but he'll get here," Dice said.

The entire place seemed to be realizing someone new was in their midst. It felt like every single set of eyes was on me in judging perusal.

Why had I come? Because Kaden hurt my feelings when Antoinette talked about the party? So here I was, in a room where I wasn't wanted, and for what? To prove I could? I was the sideshow attraction at the circus. All I needed was a beard and a third eye.

Kaden wasn't the only one who'd caught sight of me fast. Alaric was heading across the room, straight for me.

"I was hoping to see you here," he said. "You didn't call, but I'm hoping you're still considering my offer."

"Unlikely to happen, buddy," Dice said, smiling. "She's quite happy with her current position in our organization."

The warmth in Alaric's smile chilled as it was turned toward Dice. "I'm glad she's got you by her side to express her every thought. How convenient to not have to speak."

"She'll tell you herself if you don't believe me. She's not shy," Dice said.

Dice was right. I wasn't shy, but I *was* preoccupied. The attention in the room seemed centered solely on me. Kaden's glare was burning a hole in my back.

"That's a great idea. She can tell me as I show her the fountains." Alaric took my hand, putting it in the crook of his arm.

Dice puffed out his chest as I raised my other hand in his direction. "I'm fine. It's good if we talk for a moment," I said, letting Dice take that as he would.

I would've let Alaric take me on a tour of the dumpsters if that got me away from all the eyes.

Alaric steered me through the room, and it was becoming almost as painful as staying and letting everyone look their fill. Having the competition walking me through the room was drawing even more attention. By the time we made it to the outdoor area, breathing was becoming a labor.

I dragged in a deep breath of the crisp air outside. There were people outside as well, but only stragglers compared to the crush inside. The fountains he'd spoken of were all around the grounds, and the water wasn't normal but glittering, as if liquid diamonds ran through it. Other than that, it looked like any garden I might've found Topside, with scattered benches and tables intermingled between the trees and bushes.

I walked closer to the nearest fountain, reaching out toward the glittering water.

Alaric grabbed me. "You don't want to do that. It's highly intoxicating." His fingers lingered on my wrist a few seconds too long before he let go.

"Even just touching it?"

"Yes. Somebody should be showing you around a little better so that you know these things." He smiled, as if offering himself up for the job.

I was beginning to wonder if the job he was pushing would come with more than just a boss.

"I had a question about that offer. With your organization, is there an option to live Topside?"

"Oh, of course. You can live anywhere you want. A lot of tinkers don't because it gets a little lonely, but—"

"Lonely? You mean because no one knows you?"

"Well, yes, no one there, that is."

"There's no way around that?"

"Only recycling fixes that. You know, getting put back in as a baby? Starting from scratch?"

I nodded, trying to not let on that everything he said felt like a stab wound in my soul.

"Alaric." His name rang across the enclosed garden.

I turned to see Kaden walking toward us.

"I was just getting to know the newest tinker a bit better. She's quite lovely," Alaric said.

"Yes, I heard you've been trying to do that quite a bit," Kaden replied.

For someone who hadn't seemed to want me in his crew, he was acting a bit territorial. Or maybe it was the nature of these two's history that was causing them to stare off the way they were.

"You never know when a situation might change," Alaric said, winking in my direction.

Kaden nodded stiffly. "I wouldn't try too hard. It'll just make you look more desperate than usual, and I'm not sure you can afford to take another hit to your reputation."

Watching these two go at each other, I could see there was some bad blood somewhere in their past. I wasn't getting dragged into whatever had happened.

I never thought I'd be happy to see Antoinette, but when she came outside, sniffing after Kaden like a bloodhound on a trail, I took a breath of relief.

"There you are," she said. "Raulo is opening up a bottle for us but is waiting for you."

"I'm coming now," Kaden said. He nodded in Alaric's direction and then gave me a glare, perhaps warning me to behave myself.

Whatever gratitude I'd had toward him for staying with me the other night after Chaos was quickly getting worn away.

"May I give you a piece of personal advice?" Alaric said once we were alone again.

"Sure. I can't guarantee I'll take it, but I always listen."

Alaric took two glasses of wine from a passing waiter and handed me one. "I don't know what your situation is, but getting involved with Kaden on a deeper level might not be a good idea. He's broken every heart in Nowhere and doesn't even realize it as he wades through the corpses."

"Trust me, I'm in no threat of losing my heart to him." I laughed because Kaden was about as far from the type of man I'd get mixed up with as could be. He was everything I avoided. I knew a walking, talking broken heart when I saw one. "Actually I'm in..." I was about to say in a relationship, but that was a hard thing to call my current state of affairs.

Alaric was looking at me, waiting for me to finish, when an older gentleman approached him.

"Alaric, do you have a minute?" the man asked.

"I'm sorry. Do you mind? This is one of my people, and I've been waiting on some news."

"Of course not." I turned to stroll around the numerous fountains, not having any urge to head back to the crush of the party, or all the eyes on me.

The largest of the fountains was in front of me, and so breathtakingly large, standing a good twenty feet high, that it was more like a waterfall. It drew my full attention away from where I was for a moment, and I just marveled in the creation.

I leaned my head back, staring at the top. There were various creatures carved into the stone that the sparkling liquid flowed over, partially obscuring their forms so only a fin or a tail were visible. Or was that a mermaid? I was in the midst of trying to figure it out when someone bumped into me. My shins hit the front of the fountain that was only a foot or so high, and I broke my fall with my hands flat in the lower pool with a great splash.

By the time I got up, no one was anywhere near me, but Alaric was rushing over, and I saw several people standing by the doors pointing and talking.

"What happened? Are you all right?" Alaric asked, looking down at the dripping fountain water that was coating the front of my dress and dripping down my arms.

"Someone bumped me and I tripped."

He grabbed a tablecloth off one of the few setups outside and used it to dry off my arms and hands, careful not to get it on himself.

"You have to get that dress off, and now." He continued to pat me down.

"You think?" I ran a hand along it. Stripping out of my dress seemed a bit silly, but if he thought so... I giggled at the thought of running around here in my underwear.

Maybe that stuff didn't work on me, though, because I felt fine. Better than fine. Actually, I was starting to feel absolutely fantastic.

"Billie, you need to get that off fast."

He motioned to a corner, where some potted plants formed a small alcove, then steered me in that direction. He shrugged out of his suit jacket, holding it up in front of me.

"You really think I should?" I asked, giggling.

"Yes, and fast. Tell me when you have it off," he said, keeping his eyes averted.

I dropped my dress on the ground. "Okay," I said. "I'm undressed."

Alaric's jacket was draped over my shoulders. It came to mid-thigh, and the fabric was so soft that I couldn't stop running my fingers over it.

"Put your arms in the sleeves," he said, trying to maneuver it while I spun around.

"Oh, this isn't bad," I said, doing a twirl and spotting Kaden heading back toward us. I looked up at Alaric. "You know, I don't think he likes you very much."

"Yes, I know, and this isn't going to help."

The intensity of Kaden's gaze was chilling, or maybe that was the breeze with this jacket on?

Kaden's expression grew darker, and my laughter built. He looked like he wanted to kill me, or Alaric. I wasn't sure who. Maybe a double homicide kind of night? If he did try to kill me, I might die of laughter first. The whole evening seemed a little absurd when you thought about it. Who fell into a magic fountain?

By the time Kaden got to us, his eyes were flashing like he no longer cared if there were witnesses to his crimes.

His eyes went to the front of Alaric's jacket, which was gaping wide. He tugged it closed and then took my hand and clamped it over the spot.

"What is going on? What happened to her?" Kaden asked, stepping uncomfortably close to Alaric.

"As much as I'm sure you'd like to blame me, I stepped away, and when I came back she was covered in fountain water," he said.

"Billie, what happened?"

"I got bumped, and then I *swish*," I said, trying to reenact the falling movement, moving my hands out.

As soon as I did, Kaden grabbed the jacket, pulling it closed again and keeping his hand there.

"She got bumped?" Kaden asked, turning back to Alaric.

"I got bumped," I said. He wasn't hearing very well tonight.

"Stay away from her," Kaden said. His one hand was

holding the jacket closed as the other wrapped around my waist, pulling me close to him.

"She's your employee," Alaric said. "She can choose to leave whenever she wants."

Kaden ignored him, leading me back toward the doors that led to the main room.

CHAPTER TWENTY-TWO

W e walked into the main room and all eyes were on us, including Antionette's, which were about to set me on fire. I giggled.

"What happened to her?" she asked, looking me over with thinly veiled contempt. "You were right to tell her not to come. She obviously can't handle herself."

Kaden turned to deal with Antoinette while everyone watched.

I threw my hands up, smiling and then doing a twirl for them. If they were looking for a show, the least I could do was give it to them. They looked so shocked that there wasn't much else to do but laugh.

Kaden's hand was out, gripping the jacket closed again and leaving his hand there so I couldn't keep spinning, or go anywhere else, for that matter.

I was trying to get his hand free while he was leaning closer to Antoinette, saying something I couldn't hear. They continued talking quietly to each other as I tried to unclench his outstretched hand from my borrowed jacket.

When he turned his attention back to me, Antoinette

walked off. He removed his belt and wrapped it around my waist to try to keep the jacket closed.

"How much did you get on you?" he asked.

"I don't know. Why are you so angry looking?" I ran my finger across his forehead.

"You're leaving, now." His voice was soft but as steely as his grip on the belt about my waist. He looked about the room even as his hand felt like a steel trap.

"Why? I like the party. I want to stay," I said, raising my hands and trying to dance in spite of his hold. They were playing a song from the eighties that made me want to jump up and down. Actually, the words even instructed you to jump, and the killjoy was holding me down.

"What the hell." Dice rubbed his goatee as he stared at me. "I only left her alone for a little bit. Who knew how quickly she'd get into trouble? She made the most of her time."

"You brought her. You take her home," Kaden said, dragging me closer to Dice.

"I don't want to go home. I want to stay at the party," I said.

"You've partied enough for the evening," Kaden said before ignoring any further protests I might make and turning to Dice. "Get her back, and don't leave her alone until she's passed out in her bed."

"You got it," Dice said, sounding as bummed as I was to be leaving early.

Dice grabbed my arm, tugging me after him like a kid sister he was dragging out of a frat party that was just getting going.

"Bye," I said as we walked through the crowd. Everyone watched on, clearly sad I was leaving. "I'm sorry, but they're making me leave." I waved.

"Where are you going?" Cookie asked, catching up to us by the door.

"She's a hot mess, and I'm stuck bringing her home." Dice sounded a little sulky about the situation, like he'd gotten grounded too.

Cookie took a look at me and laughed. "Yeah, I caught some of the show." She moved and opened the door. "Come on. I'll go too. You're taking the best entertainment with you anyway."

I stumbled on my way out the door, and they both locked arms with me as we made our way outside.

"How much of that fountain did you get into?" Cookie asked.

"I don't know, exactly. I fell… I think." Did I fall? I kind of remember being bumped, but things were getting a little hazier for some reason.

"Okay, party girl. Time for bed." Cookie walked to the outpost door and held it open for me.

I walked forward, giving up any fight to return to the party. They all followed the killjoy's orders, so I tried to walk through into the outpost. Then I bounced off the opening and fell back into Dice.

Cookie and Dice looked at each other before she walked through the door and back with no issue.

"What's the problem?" I asked, trying to straighten up and struggling.

"You're too drunk to go through," Cookie said. "It happens on occasion to make sure drunken idiots don't wander into our outpost by accident. Still, it should've let *you* in. The bridge guys must've upped the calibration on it or something."

"Call Hank," Dice said.

Cookie waved the phone in her hand. "What does it

look like I was about to do?" She dialed and then waited. "Hank, we're having a problem with the outpost door. Did you do something to it? Call me when you get this." She put the phone back in her pocket. "He's not answering."

"Really? I hadn't figured that out," Dice said.

Cookie rolled her eyes then looked around. "Now what do we do with her? She's tanked. We could be waiting for hours for a bridge guy to fix this."

"I'm not tanked. I feel *good*," I said.

"Maybe some coffee? I could go fetch a jug of it from down the street," Cookie said, ignoring me.

"I don't want coffee," I said.

Dice raised me an inch with his grip around my waist. "You think coffee is going to fix this?"

"I'm messaging Kaden." She dug her phone back out of her pocket and started typing.

"Oh great," I said. "Now he's going to come and ruin more fun."

"What fun do you think you're having now?" Dice asked.

I looked around. "I don't know, but it's not going to happen. That's for sure."

"Great. He's bringing her," Cookie said.

Dice and I turned as one to see Kaden approaching, Antoinette with him.

"What's the issue?" Kaden asked.

"I'm trying to get her home, but she's too drunk. She can't get through the door," Dice said, shrugging.

Antoinette glared at me. I was so sick of her looking at me that I wanted to smack her face. Considering I couldn't seem to lose Dice, who was stuck to my side, I settled for sticking my tongue out.

Kaden looked like he was going to laugh.

Antoinette took a step toward me. "You little—"

"Antoinette, she's clearly drunk. No need to get that offended," Kaden said.

Cookie cleared her throat, and Dice was making jerking movements.

"Go. I'll take her home with me," Kaden said.

"Kaden, I'm sure she'll be fine soon and would rather be in her own bed," Antoinette said, stepping closer.

"It could take hours before she can make it through. She's slept in the guest suite enough times to be comfortable." Before Antionette could say anything else, Kaden picked me up.

"Now she can't walk either?" Antionette asked.

"She'll never make it the whole way without falling. Maybe you should go home tonight. I don't want to ruin your evening dealing with this."

I didn't know whether to laugh in Antoinette's face or scowl at Kaden for how he'd implied I was a "this" to be dealt with.

Every line in her body seemed to stiffen as she said, "If you think that's a good idea."

Kaden had already moved his attention to Dice and Cookie. "Don't forget to swing by and get that delivery in the morning if I run late." He turned around with me in his arms, giving Antoinette a nod. "Sorry about this. I'll talk to you tomorrow," he said, and then began walking with me.

I glanced over his shoulder, seeing Cookie and Dice disappear into the outpost door. Antionette watched us walk away, her eyes glued to me. There was pure hatred shining there, as if her single wish at that moment was my death, and not a clean one, either. Maybe something long and drawn out, with plenty of torture before the end.

I giggled again before turning my attention to the

people passing us, nodding.

"Should I pretend to be dead again?" I asked, remembering the first time he'd carried me to his place.

"It's too late after tonight. Everyone already knows who you are." I could feel the muscles in his shoulders tense.

"Oh."

He carried me up the steps and then kicked closed the door to his home, a place that was getting to be almost as familiar as the outpost.

"You can't afford to get like this in public," he said as he carried me upstairs.

I groaned. Here came the lecture and rules. "I didn't do it on purpose."

"You need to be more careful, be more aware of your surroundings here. This isn't Topside," he said, and then dropped me onto the bed in the guest room.

"Do you know how bossy you are? It's very irritating," I said, pushing up and then wobbling to my feet.

"I have a vague idea." He dug in a dresser drawer and pulled out one of his t-shirts that I'd used last time I was here, as if he'd known I'd be back.

"Maybe you should try to work on that," I said.

"Why would I do that? It doesn't bother me," he said, dropping the shirt next to me on the bed.

"Well, you're not the boss of me, just so you know." I got off the bed.

"Actually, I am, and I'm telling you to watch yourself, especially around Alaric."

"Why? I like him. I think he's *nice*. And *cute*, too," I said, just so he knew he wasn't the only attractive tinker around.

"Billie, you have no idea what you're doing. Don't push me on this."

He wanted to lay down the law? I didn't think so. I

wasn't here to take his orders. I'd do what I wanted. I smiled and then *literally* pushed him. Or tried. The attempt was there, even if it threw me more off balance than him.

"Time for bed." He pushed me slightly, and I landed back on the bed.

I went to get up again but was thwarted by a hand on my shoulder. "You're just mad because you didn't want me to come to your stinking party."

"I didn't want you to come because I didn't think you were ready to deal with all of them. Clearly you weren't." He knelt down and pulled off my shoes before grabbing my legs and swinging them onto the bed.

I leaned up on my forearms, the jacket falling off one shoulder. "You won't let me have any fun. You were mean to Alaric because he likes me. You just want to keep me locked away, slaving over whatever you want."

His gaze flickered down to the flesh of my shoulder and the swell of my breast peeking out right above it.

"Maybe you're right. Maybe I don't want you to have fun with him." His attention shifted to my lips and stayed there. My breath froze in my chest, nearly burning. It felt like we were on the edge of something I couldn't quite put into words. Or something that didn't need words at all.

"Why is that?" I asked, taunting him.

"It doesn't matter why," he said. He knelt on the bed, our gazes fixed on each other as he leaned over me. My lungs ceased to function as he paused like that for a second. Then he pulled the corner of the blanket, wrapping it over me.

He brushed the hair from my face, his gaze dropping to my lips for another second. "Go to sleep, Billie."

He got up and walked out of the room, closing the door softly behind him.

CHAPTER TWENTY-THREE

I heard footsteps coming to where I was sprawled out on the couch in the lounge. I lifted the ugly yellow pillow from my head.

Dice stared down at me. "Feeling it today, huh?"

He was compounding the concern that I'd made an utter ass of myself last night. I'd woken up in Kaden's guest room this morning, my head foggy and pounding. My memory of the prior evening was near nonexistent. It felt akin to an abstract painting where I got a general sense of a mood but the details were all a blur of blues and grays.

Kaden had walked me back in the morning but barely uttered more than a couple of words. I hadn't had the nerve to ask him what went down.

"Don't give me details, but was it as bad as I fear?" My entire body tensed as I waited for the verdict. Maybe I shouldn't have asked. What possible good would come from having what I feared confirmed?

"You didn't have time to be *too* bad. Couple of spins for the crowd, a little bit of stumbling, quite a bit of giggling, and some flashing. Other than that, you were fine. Kaden got you out of there as soon as it started hitting the skids."

"Flashing?" I sat up, hoping I'd heard wrong.

"Yeah, when you were doing all those spins?" He made a little twirling motion with his finger. "The jacket you were wearing would flap open. Everything was hanging out."

I dropped my head into my hands and groaned. I thought I'd felt bad ten minutes ago.

"I don't know why you're reacting like this," Dice said. "I've had dates that were more of a scene on your average Monday night. At least you've got nice tits and, if you don't mind me saying, a killer ass."

My skin was so hot that I must've looked like an apple. "I'm an accountant. I don't get drunk and make scenes and flash my..." I planted my palms on my eyes, groaning again.

I didn't want to ask any more questions, but there was one I had to know. How had I ended up at Kaden's? Had I thrown myself at him? *Please tell me I didn't come on to him. Anything but that.*

"Do you know why I was at Kaden's place? Why didn't I come back here?" I tried to sound as casual as possible. Last thing I needed was Dice to know what I feared. He'd tell Cookie and Connor, and I doubted I'd hear the end of it.

Dice laughed, each guffaw upping the temperature of my cheeks.

He leaned on the back of the couch, looking for support until he stopped laughing. "That was the funniest. You were too drunk to pass through the outpost door, so Kaden ended up taking you home. You should've seen Antoinette's face. It was priceless. You don't remember any of this?"

I was too relieved to care if he laughed some more. At least I hadn't come on to Kaden.

Cookie walked in. "Hey, the good-time girl is here! You feeling like death warmed over or what?"

I said in a deathly serious tone, "I'd rather not talk about it."

She let out a belly laugh. "Yeah, considering last night, I can see your point. Or see your *points* might be more accurate." She laughed some more, taking a second to wipe a tear from her eye.

I couldn't take it anymore. I needed something…

I eyed the jar of lollipops. There was a purple left. They were the best by far. As if Cookie and Dice were psychic, they both turned as my hand approached the jar. I paused, not having committed the crime yet. These people really liked their purples. Did I dare?

There was a gasp from Dice.

Screw it. I grabbed it, not caring if there were going to be repercussions. Last night I'd gotten drunk on fountain water and proceeded to flash everyone in my prospective field of business. I *needed* the purple lollipop.

They gaped at me as I unwrapped it and popped it in my mouth.

"That's right. I took the purple, and I'm not sorry." And it was oh so worth it. This thing was like sucking on candy heaven. Another few of these and I might get through this day of regrets and humiliation.

"Fine. You're on pick-up rotation now, just so you know. And it's not pleasant to go. That's all I'm saying." Cookie looked at Dice. "Someone is going to have to go with her the first time."

"Why can't I go alone?" I asked.

"You need a recommendation from a currently

approved purchaser before you're allowed to buy," Dice said, settling onto the other couch and grabbing a machete from the side table to pick under his nails. "I'll bring you. It was my turn to go anyway, but I can't do it today. I have a really bad assignment."

"Why so bad?" I asked.

"Real old guy, over a hundred. The centenarians are always a pain in the ass. There's a reason they lived so long. Too stubborn to die."

Cookie leapt over the back of the chair and dropped into it. "Want me to come?"

"Yeah, why not? Day wasn't going to suck enough if I went on my own." He got to his feet. "Gotta leave now, though."

"I'm driving," she said, and got to her feet.

"Hell you are." Dice ran after her.

They both ran through the door like ten-year-old siblings trying to get the best seat. I dropped back on the couch, closing my eyes, appreciating the silence that filled the room.

When the ancient yellow phone rang, I nearly jumped out of my skin. In all the days I'd been here, and they were starting to add up, that thing had never rung. I rolled over, dragging the pillow over my head, waiting for it to stop.

By the thirtieth ring, I began to lose faith it would ever stop. Who was calling? Demons and weird gods invaded my thoughts.

What if it was for me, and that was why it kept ringing? What if it was an emergency from one of the crew? No one had ever said *not* to answer it. I went and picked it up.

"Hello?" I kept my eyes on the various doors as I answered, feeling a little like a criminal, simply for answering a phone. I'd been here too long. It was getting that normal actions were questionable, while the regular was absurd. My entire life had become topsy-turvy.

"Billie?"

I nearly dropped the phone. My voice was gone. I didn't have any air left to speak with. *It couldn't be.*

"Billie, are you there?"

"Gram?" Saying her name, even imagining it was her on the other end, made it feel like I'd finally lost my last bit of sanity. I gripped the phone like someone was going to rip it from my hand.

"We have to meet and talk," she said. Every word, hearing her voice, made me want to cry.

I'd never truly believed I'd hear from her again. If it *was* her. That this could be some imposter made my heart want to shrivel up and die, but that didn't mean I could be an idiot about things.

"How do I know it's you?"

"*Billie*, it's me." She exaggerated my name the way she had thousands of times before.

There was no way this was Gram, was there? If it was Gram, she'd respect me for what I said next, or this was a fraud.

"I need proof that it's you," I said.

"When you were ten, I was the one that sat with you the entire time you were down with the flu. I'm also the one that told you countless times to let your drunk of a mother sleep it off. That she wasn't your responsibility." She paused a few seconds. "She might've been my daughter, but what a waste of a life. She wasn't special like us, though. I always told you that."

It was her. There was no way a fraud would've been able to copy the inflection in her voice that perfectly, could they? Well, maybe, but I was going to make a leap of faith on this one.

"Gram," I said, that single word carrying weeks of mourning and missing her, and decades of love.

"I told you we'd talk again," she said. "But we can't do it over this line. We have to meet."

"Where? The house? I can be there in a half an hour."

"No. Not there. There's a place in Nowhere called The Deep. Can you go there yet?"

"In Nowhere? Yes." At least, I thought I could. I'd chance it to see Gram again, give her a hug, and get some answers.

"I need a little time to get back. Meet me there after dusk on Wednesday night. I might not look like myself, so I'll find you. Don't tell anyone."

"I'll be there."

I hung up, my hands still shaking when Connor walked in from Nowhere.

"Hey, heard you had a rough night. Sorry I missed you at the party. Got there late but heard you were a real hit." He held out a cup. "Brought this for you. Latte from the same place we get the lollipops. Thought you might need it."

I took it, trying to act calm, hoping he didn't see that I was shaking worse than a shack in a hurricane.

"Thanks. It's great," I said, afraid caffeine on top of nerves might take me down, except that I needed a distraction.

"I wasn't sure you'd be here. Figured you might be with Kaden," he said, walking over and dropping onto the couch, remote already in hand.

"Why would I be with him?" I asked. Had he seen Kaden? Did he already know I'd gotten a call? Said he was coming back here? Gram had said she couldn't talk on that line. Was it tapped?

"He said he was going to your house," Connor added. He kicked his boots up, yawning. "I might need a nap. I'm wiped."

I stared at Connor, no longer caring about the party, what an idiot I'd looked like, or what I'd flashed. I might care about that tomorrow, but not now. Was Kaden going to my house to try to find my gram?

"*My* house? You mean where I lived Topside?"

"Think so." He squinted at the television.

"Why?"

"I don't know." Of course he didn't.

I grabbed my phone and my bag and hightailed it out of there.

By the time I pulled up, Kaden looked like he was saying goodbye to my mother on the stoop in front of my house. She didn't seem to be wobbling or holding on to anything to stay upright. It was only three. She tended to not be too bad until closer to six. He probably smelled the booze on her, but at least she wasn't falling down.

Kaden had a thing for high-end sedans, and in this neighborhood, his stuck out like a sore thumb. With the overgrown hedges, my mother didn't see me as I made my way to his car and slid into the passenger seat. Even if she had, she might not recognize me anyway.

I watched from the window as he headed over. He got in the car and didn't so much as blink at my presence. He put the car in drive and pulled away from my house.

My voice was as calm as I could manage when I said, "Why were you talking to my mother?"

Please, don't let it be about Gram. If he picked up on nerves, he'd think it was because he was here at all, not that I had something to hide. If I wasn't worried about Gram, I might be furious, so it wasn't a stretch to think I'd be out of sorts.

"There's a lot of unanswered questions. Do you really need to ask why I'd want to speak to someone who knew your grandmother?"

He didn't say anything about Gram calling. He probably would've said something about that if he had. So that just left him coming here and snooping without so much as a heads-up.

"You didn't think maybe you should have spoken to me before coming here?" Had he seen the bottles? Probably. More often than not, Mom would leave them scattered around the house. I used to clean them up, but now that I wasn't there…

"No. I didn't."

"Did your snooping pay off?" I asked, fury replacing the nerves.

"Other than finding you had a penchant for stubbornness right out of the womb? No. Your mother didn't seem to know much at all."

He said it like it was a joke she'd made, as if she hadn't said it in her snide way. He spoke like he'd had a normal chat with a regular parent.

I could hear her in my head still, the way she'd always carried on about how I thought I knew best, right before she took another swig of her vodka and passed out on the couch.

"I'm surprised she remembered," I said, wishing she'd forgotten for a change. "Pull over here. I left my car back there."

"Hank will get it," he said.

"Pull over. I want to get it myself."

He did as I asked.

"Billie, I…"

I turned back to him before I shut the car door, waiting for him to finish.

"We have a job in two days," he said.

"Fine." I shut the door, feeling like that wasn't what he'd meant to say, and headed back toward my house.

Mom was standing in front of the kitchen window when I got back, staring outside. Her gaze wandered over me and she squinted, as if she thought she might recognize me.

I didn't bother going inside.

CHAPTER TWENTY-FOUR

This morning, I'd broken down and sent out a message to everyone I knew. Every. Single. Contact.

That was hours ago, and there hadn't been any replies. Not one. My old life was slipping away, and there was nothing I could do.

"Oh shit. I double-booked," Cookie said as she stared at the calendar on her phone on the other couch.

I hummed, sensing she wanted some sort of reply, and I was the only other person there.

I caught her looking up from her phone, staring at me, and alarms blared in my mind. Was it too late to run into my suite, lock the door, and pretend not to have heard her?

It was worth a shot. I leaned forward, ready to make a run for it. She looked straight at me, catching me in her visual snare before escape was possible.

"Billie, your schedule is wide open, right?" She smiled, as if she knew she had me.

After what had happened the other night with Chaos...

I got to my feet, getting ready to run for it, and to hell with who got insulted. "I'm not sure if––"

She grabbed my arm, locking on to it like a steel vise. "Look, just go to this address and find Callie Pritchard. Make her…" She stared up at the ceiling. "You know, I can't remember what was supposed to be fixed, but it'll kick in when you get there. It always does."

I tried to tug away from her. "I'm not sure if I'm cleared to do jobs on my own. I think we'd have to talk to Kaden."

"What are you talking about? Of course you are. Plus, you're a natural." She grabbed a piece of paper out of her pocket and shoved it into my hand. "Go here. It's the last day before it's too late. It *has* to get done. This is really important, and you can name your price."

Did she really mean that? All I could think of was my mother standing in that kitchen window, drinking herself to death, alone. If I could tinker her, convince her to quit drinking, and get her a house in a community where she could maybe meet some people…

I took the paper and held it as I thought this through. "Can you give me an example of what I could ask for?"

"I told you. Name your price. What do you want?" Cookie asked, tucking her phone in her pocket and grabbing her bag off the table, as if this was already settled.

"There's a house I've been looking at buying for—"

"Done. I'll show you how to put the details in after the job is completed. Talk to you later!" She was out the door before I could ask anything else.

"That's it? And I get a house for my mother?" I said to no one.

This could work. I could do this.

No. I *was* doing this.

I looked up the address she'd given and found out it was a motor vehicle agency. At least I didn't have to worry about changing, since I didn't have very long to get there.

Jeans and a sweater were perfect. I'd get in, get out, and be done.

I went to the door and headed Topside. If I was going to be a tinker, I'd tinker and at least reap the benefits.

Hank smiled when he saw me, and it didn't look like he was used to that expression.

"What do you feel like driving today?" he asked, keeping the painful expression on his face.

"I'm going to a motor vehicle agency, so nothing too fancy. Anything you have is fine."

He pulled his phone out of his pocket and texted something. A few seconds later, a Porsche Carrera pulled up with a phantom driver.

This was a non-fancy car?

I didn't move for a few seconds.

"What's wrong? Do you not like silver? I could call up a black one," Hank said.

"No, it's great. But are you sure? It might get dinged in the parking lot."

"Don't worry about that. You deserve it." He reached out and then awkwardly patted my back, as if he'd never initiated physical contact with someone before.

"Thanks, Hank," I said, and then patted him back. I was as stiff as he was, like the awkwardness was catching. "I'm just going to..." I motioned to the car, knowing I had to get out of here before this escalated into hugging or something equally disastrous.

"Take care now," he said, waving to me like he was my well-wishing grandpa or something.

I stripped the gears in my rush to get out of there.

The agency parking lot was packed, and I was getting a sneaking suspicion that my getting this job had nothing to do with Cookie being double-booked. There weren't any conflicting appointments. This place was a hellhole. It might take hours to find this Callie person. Still, it *was* for a house.

People were spilling out the back door, and I had to weave my way in. This building had three floors. Might as well start on the highest and work my way down until I found my target, and then hope instinct kicked in to tell me what exactly to do. So far, there was nothing.

The seats in the waiting area were full and the lines long. I barely avoided getting my feet trampled by a herd of teenagers passing by.

No one caught my eye. This was technically my job. Cookie said I'd know what to do, so I'd probably spot the target, right? Just to be safe, checking some nametags would be safe. I was new to this tinkering business.

I tried to move closer to the front of one of the lines, ignoring all the warning glares from people who thought I was trying to cut.

"Just grabbing a tissue," I said, trying to keep the mob happy, because after waiting an hour or two, these people were primed for violence.

The worker glanced at me, looking as unhappy as her customer. Her nametag said "Diana." Nope. Not her. What if it wasn't a worker?

I weaved around the room, trying to locate my job, hoping something would hit me when I was close. That was when I felt it.

My lungs seized. My heart beat double time and my limbs felt like mush. It was coming again. No. It was already here.

How? Cookie had said people brushed against Chaos once a decade at most.

There wasn't enough time to get out. I had to move. I

had to hide. I spun around but couldn't find a closet. I ran and squatted under the nearest desk. The workers looked at me.

"You can't be behind here. You need to leave," a young female employee said.

"Run," I yelled at her. "Run," I screamed at the others joining her.

They started to laugh at me, the insane girl huddled under their desk. But it only lasted a second before the noises started and their expressions changed.

It sounded like a tornado touching down on the building. I cowered under the metal desk, covering my head with my knees to my chest as hell let loose around me.

The wind whipped through the building, things flying all around, and I squeezed my eyes shut. It was howling like a rabid animal through the building, tearing up everything around me as I stayed crouched, waiting to be ripped apart. I was going to die. This was it. I was dead.

Tears rolled down my face as pure terror shot through me. I'd never get to meet Gram, help my mother, get back to my life...

Things flew into the desk as that horrible feeling sucked all the joy out of me. The building shook, parts of the floor caving in. I stayed balled up in a corner, the desk somehow staying in place.

At first I thought I was imagining the wind and howling dying down. Then it weakened to the point that there was no mistaking it. That horrible, dreadful feeling began to fade with it.

I stayed down, afraid to move an inch. It was gone. It was definitely gone, and yet my muscles refused to unclench. I had to move. I needed to get to my feet and move, dammit.

I'd take five deep breaths and then move. Breathe in and out. I could do this.

I opened my eyes, and the picture around me stole all the air I'd forced into my lungs. The cinder-block walls were intact, but that was all. The floor was almost completely gone, other than the small spot that I'd huddled on, with the desk. I leaned forward, and beneath me, there were limbs and bloodied bodies mixed in with piles of debris. The worst part was that there wasn't a moan, a cry, a twitch. This place had been filled with people, and it didn't sound like a single one was still alive, other than me.

I didn't know how to get out if I wanted, perched on a pedestal of some sort. I could hear the sounds of sirens in the distance. They'd get me down, but how would I explain this? Who would I say I was?

"Billie," Kaden yelled from somewhere in the building. "Billie!"

"Kaden," I called, unsure whether he'd hear me.

He appeared two floors below, climbing over mounds of rubble. He looked up, and a flash of relief crossed his face.

"You're going to have to trust me," he said, walking until he was right underneath me. "I know trust isn't a big thing with us, but you need to take a literal leap of faith."

He was already lifting his arms, as if to wave me down. That lunatic wanted me to jump?

I plastered my back against the side of the desk. "Oh no. I'm not doing it. No, no, no."

"Billie, look at me," he said calmly.

I didn't look.

"Billie, we don't have time for this. There are going to be people swarming in here any second."

He was right. I leaned forward, just a hair, peeking over the edge, hoping he had a better idea than jumping.

He stared at me, looking much calmer than I felt.

"I don't know what is keeping that landing you're on upright, but it should've crumbled with the rest of this place," he said. "I can't come to you. You need to come to me."

"You want me to jump two floors down. No way. Go get a ladder." I pointed in a vague direction.

"We don't have time. Now you need to jump." He had his hands out as if he were capable of catching me.

"You're trying to kill me. That's what this is." I sounded hysterical. There was no way other to describe my voice.

"You're not going to die. Now you need to jump," he yelled.

"I'm *not* jumping."

"I promise I will be standing here to catch you. The worst that will happen is you'll use me to break your fall."

That actually didn't sound too horrific. I leaned over, wondering if he *would* be enough to break my fall.

"Give me your word you won't move," I said.

"I give you my word that my feet won't leave this spot. Now I need you to jump."

I could hear the sirens growing louder, and I really didn't want to explain how I ended up on this little piece of floor, the sole survivor.

I got into a squatting position, back just far enough to clear my little landing. I closed my eyes and took a leap of faith.

He caught me in his arms as if I was no heavier than a ball and immediately started to move. He leapt over the rubble and had me out a back door and several buildings away before he set me on my feet.

He swung his jacket over my shoulders and began pulling me after him toward a car parked at the curb.

Kaden drove as crazy as Cookie, almost as if he thought Chaos itself were following us.

Hank saw us coming and said, "We're having technical—"

"We're not going to the outpost. We're going to Nowhere. I'm *assuming* that's fine?" Kaden asked.

"Craziest thing, but that doesn't seem to be having any issues." Hank shrugged as if he couldn't understand it himself.

Kaden opened the door to his place and then walked me to the couch and pushed me onto the seat. It didn't take much effort to get me to sit, as a gentle breeze would've knocked me over. I could barely think straight, let alone put up a fight.

He walked back over with a glass of water, a double shot of whiskey, and a box of first-aid supplies.

I went straight for the hard stuff.

"You need to tell me what happened," he said, while the warmth was spreading down my throat. He was wetting gauze with a flask filled with a concoction of black, gooey stuff that smelled a bit like licorice.

"What is that?"

"It's for the cuts. Now tell me exactly what happened. Leave nothing out, not even the most minute detail."

He was leaning close enough that I could smell his scent over the gooey stuff as he dabbed at the tiniest scratches. I was barely nicked, so there had to be something else he feared.

Instead of asking, I drank more whiskey and tried to

relay every detail of what happened. There wasn't much to say, other than mundane details of walking through a DMV.

I took another sip of whiskey. "I was trying to find the target, but it was so quick I couldn't do anything but duck and hope I lived."

He pushed his jacket off my shoulders and dabbed at a scrape on my neck. "And what happened then?"

"By the time I felt it, it was already almost there. I didn't know what to do, so I simply tucked into a ball." The last thing I'd seen were their terrified faces as I yelled for them to run. That young girl was standing there, healthy, her whole life in front of her, was now buried in rubble.

I took another sip, closing my eyes, trying to force her face from my mind. "I could hear the destruction, the screaming, and I kept my head buried in my hands, praying it would pass."

My hands shook so badly that he took the glass from me and put it on the table. "Billie, you can't tell anyone what happened today. If anyone asks if you did that job, you say no, that I called you off at the last minute—right before you were about to go in, I got a hold of you. We were outside the building when the blast went off, but you didn't go in."

I nodded, having a hard time finding my voice.

He cupped my face, dragging my gaze to his. "Billie, I need you to say you hear me. That means *no one*."

"I hear you." I sat back, crossing my arms, trying to pull myself together. The way Kaden was staring at me so intently wasn't helping.

"No one," he said. "This isn't something that we can risk being overheard. You can't be immune to Chaos and live in Nowhere."

"What do you mean immune?"

"No one survives Chaos twice, not like this. It carved out the space around you but left you virtually untouched. It's not natural." He got to his feet, leaned an arm on the mantel, and looked out the window, appearing as jarred as I was.

"If word got out"—he shook his head—"you would be hunted down and killed by every creature who lives and breathes. Being immune to Chaos means you are beyond the rules of what balances everything in the universe. It makes you a threat to not only Topside, but Nowhere and beyond." He turned and looked at me. "Do you under-stand? Because you need to."

I picked up the glass and drained the last few drops.

He walked back over to refill the glass, but didn't ask if I understood again. He might've guessed speaking was now beyond me for the moment.

This was all so outlandish that it was hard to believe. My whole life at this point was hard to believe. Not only was I a freak, but I was the biggest freak in a world of oddities?

"If what you're saying is true, then you should want to..." I stopped talking. I wasn't sure why I'd even said that in the first place. My life felt like it was dangling by a single thread.

It didn't matter. I could tell he'd filled in the blanks.

"I'm not so set in my dogma to believe everything outside of the realm of normal is bad," he said. "Some things can even be useful."

So that was it. He was going to use me somehow, but I still didn't know what for. As long as I was useful to him, though, he'd keep me alive, and that was all I needed right now.

"How did you know Chaos was there? How did you know to come and get me?" I asked.

"I'm more sensitive to its flow than most." He tilted his head toward the stairs. "You'll stay here tonight, and I'll take you back in the morning."

There was no point in arguing, since the last thing I wanted was to go to the outpost. He'd said the outpost was safe from Chaos, but I'd also been told people didn't have constant brushes with it. At least if I was near Kaden, he'd sense it coming. Having a walking and talking early warning system was definitely reassuring at the moment.

The first time I got close to Chaos, it had severely rocked me. This time? I wasn't sure I'd sleep for a week.

CHAPTER TWENTY-FIVE

The front door opened. I glanced up, expecting to see Kaden, since the house had been empty when I awoke.

It was *her*.

"Why are you here?" Antoinette asked, staring at me where I sat at the table. The way she glared, it was as if I'd climbed in through an unlocked window like a beggar.

"The bridge was down last night. I couldn't get back to the outpost." I wasn't going to tell her that Hank and the bridge workers all seemed to be conspiring to get me to Nowhere, most likely because of her. She was the one that had pissed them off so bad. It was her own fault if they found a way to aggravate her.

"Actually, I'm glad you're here. I wanted to chat with you." She motioned toward a chair at the table.

As if I could refuse her a seat at her boyfriend's table. Her fake manners were threatening to bring up my morning oatmeal.

I waved as if I didn't mind. As if I didn't want to drink

my coffee alone. As if I didn't absolutely dread being in this woman's presence, even for a few minutes.

"Would you like some coffee?" I offered, not because I wanted to but because if we were going to feign politeness, there was some inner instinct to go along with it.

"No. Thank you." She situated herself on the seat with too much care to be normal, smoothing down the fabric of her dress and crossing her ankles as if there were a rule book she was following.

She probably didn't drink coffee, the way she didn't eat croissants. Too beneath her for reasons I'd be too uncouth to understand. I folded my legs up on the seat, sitting cross-legged, instead of the elegant way Antoinette crossed her ankles and folded her finely manicured fingers.

"Kaden seems to have an interest in you," she said. "You might not have noticed it, since it's not an overwhelming one, but more of what you'd have for a casual oddity."

"You don't say," I replied, as if I had any interest in what this woman thought of anything.

I continued to drink my coffee, wishing she'd leave, or someone would come hit me over the head and knock me out. Anything before she continued.

"He gets this way when he thinks someone might be useful to him. I didn't want you to misconstrue it into something it wasn't. A lot of women find him attractive. In the past, there's been some awkward instances where he might be kind to someone, as he tends to when they're down on their luck, and they've misunderstood. I wouldn't want you to embarrass yourself in that way."

First off, were we talking about the same man? Although I guess not making me sleep on the street would strike her as generous if my hunch on her standards and ethics was accurate.

"Yes, well, I wouldn't worry yourself over that. We work together. That's all. I wouldn't be so foolish to think he'd ever want me," I said. I would've declared myself a troll if it got rid of her. Plus, it was true. I might not always like Kaden, but I knew when someone was out of my league. He'd never want me. Why would he? I might actually look like a troll standing next to Antionette.

She smiled, eyeing me up as if she didn't quite believe me. As far as I saw things, that was her problem, not mine.

Kaden walked into the house and nodded to me before giving Antionette a kiss hello.

"How old's the coffee?" he asked, clearly speaking to me, since she was too good for coffee.

"About twenty minutes."

He was already on his way over to the coffee pot.

"I'm glad we had a chance to get better acquainted," Antoinette said, faking it so well that she almost sounded genuine.

"This coffee is horrible," Kaden said.

"What's wrong with it? It's the way I like it," I said.

He sat in the chair beside me, instead of her, with his newspaper in hand.

I shouldn't have cared that he sat by me, but I had to swallow back a smile then drink coffee to hide it. It wasn't as if he liked me better. He didn't. I didn't want him to, either, or I shouldn't. I had enough issues right now.

"Your coffee tastes like dirty water. You don't use enough grounds." He slipped the crossword out of the middle of the paper and slid it to me.

"I use the perfect amount of grounds for the way I prefer it." I took the sheet, perusing the first couple of clues. Oh! I knew a few of these.

"Next time I'm pre-measuring it and leaving it out for you," he said.

"Fine. And then I'll take what you leave and fix it," I replied. I glanced up, looking for a pen. He already had one in his hand for me. I took it and went to work filling in my spots.

"My, how cozy you two are getting," Antionette said.

I'd somehow forgotten for a few moments that she was still sitting here. There was flash of pure hatred in her eyes right before Kaden looked up.

"Just like a pair of used slippers," Kaden said, repeating my words from a different morning.

Antionette's spine softened slightly. She clearly thought he'd insulted me. I should be grateful she misunderstood. I should rather her think I was taking a hit to the ego than deal with the fallout from her realizing it was an inside joke with me and her boyfriend. But in truth, it burned a little because of how easily she believed it. I was the old, banged-up shoe in this scenario. The only reason he was probably playing around with me in front of her was because I was so obviously not a threat.

This was a perfect time to make my exit.

"Well, I'll be seeing myself out."

Kaden's attention zeroed in on me, already getting to his feet. "You sure you don't want me to see you to the outpost?"

"I think I can manage it."

"Kaden, she's a big girl. She can see herself back." Antoinette leaned forward, laying her hand on his.

I got out of there while I could.

I'd barely gotten a half a block away from Kaden when I saw Alaric heading toward me.

"Didn't expect to see you out and about on your own.

Thought Kaden was keeping you under close surveillance," he said, as if he'd just happened to run into me. I'd never been suspicious in nature until recently, but somehow everyone knew where I went at all times now.

"And yet here I am," I said.

"Here you are." He fell into step with me as I continued walking.

"You know, the way you happened to stumble upon me alone just now makes me wonder if you're the one keeping tabs," I said.

He smiled, clearly not offended. "What if I am? I know a valuable commodity when I see one."

Was I going to have people stalking my every step? It was bad enough Kaden was doing it. Now him too?

Although if he was going to stalk me, I'd get something out of this.

"I heard the craziest story the other day. Is it true that Chaos wipes out everything in its path? Can nothing stop it?" I kept my tone light, as if nothing about Chaos sent me into a panic.

"It's true. As to stopping it, why would anyone try? It's a re-balancing, a necessary evil, so to speak. If someone did figure out a way to stop it, I don't think things would go very well for them." He laughed.

"Not even if that person was you? You're telling me you couldn't figure something out?"

"I would never try, and if I did, I'd expect to be hunted. It's keeping the equilibrium."

I'd gone from casually walking beside this man, thinking he wasn't such a bad guy, to wanting to run. I hadn't stopped Chaos, but I'd definitely been untouched. Would he be among the first to try to kill me if he knew that? I wouldn't be finding out.

The door to the outpost loomed a few feet ahead.

"Well, this is my stop. I'll see you around," I said, trying to keep it light, like I wasn't hiding a thing.

"Tell me, Billie, what can I do to entice you over to my organization?" he asked as we neared the door.

"I don't think it's going to happen. I'm starting to get settled and all. I'm sorry." I inched closer to the door, as if he'd be able to read the guilt on me at any second.

"I respect your wishes, but I won't disappear completely. I don't believe in taking no for an answer." He took a step back, making a show of giving me space, and bowed his head.

I walked into my mother's house—*my* house—a little while later, wondering what type of reception I'd get. She screamed and grabbed a pan off the counter.

"Who are you? Get out!"

I guess that was settled.

"Mom, what are you doing? It's me," I said.

She squinted, staring at me, pan still raised.

Recognition seemed to flash before she dropped the pan an inch. "You look familiar. Who are you?"

"It's me. Billie."

"Billie?" She lowered the pan slowly. "I don't know why, but you looked so weird for a minute."

"I cut my hair differently," I said, giving her a lie to hang on to. I'd known being forgotten by my mother was going to hurt, but somehow it still felt like I'd been sucker-punched. She wasn't perfect, but she'd loved me. Probably still did when she remembered me.

I pushed the door to my room open, to find it barren. "Where's my stuff? My room is empty."

She walked over, glancing at the room that held nothing but the metal frame where my bed used to be and a scarf I'd never liked hanging on the doorknob.

"Oh. I was clearing out a little. I didn't think you were coming back for some reason."

Clearing out? "Sold everything" was probably a truer statement. "Why didn't you call me first?" I knew why, but that didn't seem to stop the words from coming or the hurt from building up inside. It wasn't her fault. It was the transition. Everything was disappearing, and I couldn't stop it. It was like trying to stop water from flowing through my fingers.

My head spun and my stomach swirled. I left my room, the emptiness feeling claustrophobic, and dropped onto a kitchen chair.

"What's the matter? With your new job you can buy some more stuff. You did get a new job, right?" She pushed a few greasy strands out of her face. She didn't look like she'd showered in a week. I used to nudge her along, but now she was truly alone.

"Why do you look so bad?" she asked, her voice getting that edge. "You've got everything. You didn't have a man steal your youth, abandoning you with a baby. You had a charmed life. Not like mine."

I'd heard this one too many times to listen to it again. It wasn't a big hit the first hundred times. But it wasn't only that. I was beginning to feel like a ghost, and this place only reminded me of that. I'd come here for one purpose. I needed to do that and get out.

I gave her a hug, for tinkering purposes. Then I couldn't seem to let go, holding on a little tighter and longer. How much longer did I have before she didn't recognize me at all? Would I be completely gone?

"What's wrong with you?" she said, pulling back.

I blinked several times, trying to keep the tears in check and not let go. I needed this to work. If I couldn't get back, this was the best I could do for her.

"You know, you're not that old. I bet if you stopped drinking, things might turn around. You might meet someone really nice and maybe even get a new home."

"You think?" she asked, looking a little dazed.

I didn't know if the tinkering was working or she'd already drunk too much.

"Yeah, I do. You know, I remember you telling me how you don't even like alcohol."

How would I take care of her when she didn't know me? This had to work. Had to.

"I've got to go. Call me if you need me," I said as I walked out the door, knowing she'd probably forget she had a daughter by next week.

"Okay," she said.

I lifted a hand, giving her a wave as I kept my back to her, not wanting to have to explain why I was crying.

CHAPTER TWENTY-SIX

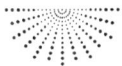

It was Wednesday, the day I was going to meet Gram. My entire life I'd been a rule follower, but if I wanted to survive in this new world, I'd have to change. I'd have to push the boundaries, discover the truth on my own.

I went back to my room, rifling through my drawers, not finding anything that would work. The people in Nowhere didn't dress in furry sweaters and pastels, at least not the ones I'd seen coming in and out of The Deep. They were edgier, harder, the way I'd have to be.

Letting other people determine my life wasn't an option. This wasn't the world I'd grown up in, where following rules was perhaps a good thing. I was living in the Wild West, and if I didn't adapt, I'd get stampeded by horses and have my gold stolen.

I went to the big closet, the space that was one of my happy places here, and scanned the racks of clothing until I found thin leather pants. A bustier? Yeah, why not. A pair of knee-high boots and a sleek jacket? All good.

I slicked my hair into a high pony, applied more makeup than was my norm, and stood back, admiring my handiwork. I looked nothing like my usual self. I looked like someone who belonged in Nowhere.

I made my way to the door that led to Nowhere, looking hotter than I'd thought possible. Mentally? I felt like a kid playing dress-up who was about to get snagged for smoking.

Heads turned as my boots hit the street. I didn't look at them or away. I acted like I was right where I should be. I'd passed by The Deep before and knew right where to go.

There were two bouncers at the door as I approached. They eyed me as I neared, but neither made a move to stop me as I walked in.

The music was some otherworldly blend of disco and pop. The entire place was eyeing me, from the patrons dancing and grinding on the floor, to the ones drinking, to the staff. Some of them I recognized, but most were faces I'd never seen.

They tracked my steps as I made my way to the bar, realizing suddenly I didn't know what currency they used to pay for a drink. Or what to order in this place. I could ask for a water, but would they charge me? And how would I tip? I swerved away from the bar at the last second, finding a stool in the corner. Maybe I'd avoid the bar until I found Gram. Or more likely, until she found me.

A man approached me and leaned his shoulder against the wall beside me. Was this Gram? A bit bigger and burlier than I thought she'd go for, but all bets were off when you were switching bodies. Somehow, I assumed she'd opt for a frame like Grandpa's, lean and wiry, like a runner's. What if you didn't get a choice?

"Haven't seen you before." Big and Burly smiled, his eyes dropping to my chest.

This man might be a lot of people, but he was *not* Gram.

"I'm meeting someone."

"I think you just met them." He grinned like a cat with a bowl of cream and kept glancing down at my chest.

I wanted to poke him in the eyes so he'd stop staring at my breasts, and then scrub myself down. I couldn't afford a scene, but I wasn't going to leave. Gram was coming. That left getting rid of this guy, and trying to put some space between us, while I waited.

"No, I'm sure I haven't." I got up from my stool, inching away.

"How can you know until you give it a whirl?"

He'd taken a step to follow me when Kaden filled the space between us.

"Because she's here to meet me," Kaden said.

Big and Burly backed away with a nod. "Sorry. I didn't know she was with you," he said, his grin gone, and he pointedly avoided looking in my direction as he walked away.

Kaden smiled, almost looking charming, as if he *were* meeting me for a date.

With his back to the crowd, he asked, "What the hell are you doing here?"

Up close, the fury was nearly palpable. There was a smirk on his face but the threat of murder in his eyes.

"Just wanted to check the place out," I said, trying to appear as casual as he was.

"I thought we'd established rules. You aren't supposed to be in Nowhere alone." He smirked, keeping up appearances.

"I believe you made some requests, but I don't recall signing away my every choice in blood." I smiled wide.

He planted his hand on the wall behind me, leaning in

slightly. From a distance, he might've appeared to be flirting. They couldn't see the glower. His jaw shifted.

"I get word that an individual I have issues with, someone that hasn't been seen in Nowhere in decades, is heading *here*, on the one day you decide you want to check this particular place out? If you're looking to convince me you're not a spy, this isn't the way."

I kept my face soft and relaxed, while the possibility of Gram being his enemy niggled away at my brain and, worse, roiled around my gut. The one lesson I'd learned was that pretty much anything could be true. But she was the one who'd made my reservation with Kaden. It didn't add up. But I couldn't deny the timing seemed suspect.

He inched closer. "My greatest desire at this very moment is to drag you out of here and torture the truth out of you. But I won't."

"And why is that?" I asked, not even slightly alarmed. His gaze kept flickering to my lips, and every time it did, I stopped breathing. The fury I'd felt seemed to be mingling with something hotter.

"If I did, it would look like there's a rift between us, one wide enough to invite all sorts of vultures to swoop down into my business and start nosing around. I'm going to give you the benefit of the doubt that you're not betraying me and continue to protect you. But mark my words, you're treading a dangerous path."

"I hate to break it to you, but I don't need protection at the moment. I'm doing quite fine." The only thing I might need protection from was getting involved with him. Letting him kiss me. Worse, my bridging the gap and kissing *him*.

"Glance over my left shoulder to the thing staring from the shadows, eyeing you up like you're an appetizer."

I broke my gaze from him and did as he suggested. All I could see were yellow eyes glimmering in a dark shadow. Or was that shadow part of the thing I was looking at? A shiver shot down my spine. "What—"

"We don't ask. And if we do know, we don't repeat. Some things are better left unsaid. He seems to have zeroed in on you. You sure you want to walk out of here alone?"

I glanced back at the corner, my skin crawling as the thing met my gaze with a greediness in its eyes. I looked away from it, waiting to hear what Kaden was going to want.

"Good choice. Now, you are going to drape your arms around my neck and curve into me like death is right behind you and I'm the only one who can save you. And if you can convince everyone in this room that you're so into me, you wouldn't possibly betray me, I will get you out of here in one piece."

"I'll play your game," I said, giving him a flirty smile, falling into the act. "But what about your girlfriend? You think this is a good idea?"

"Antoinette isn't your problem."

She wasn't? Did he realize I was stuck in Nowhere all the time because of Antoinette? Obviously not. Or he didn't want to know.

I gave him a look like the only thing I wanted was to kiss him and draped an arm around his neck. Faking it came a little too easily.

He dropped his hand to the curve of my waist and dipped his mouth toward my ear, like a lover whispering secrets.

"In a few minutes, after everyone's gotten a good look, we'll make our way to the door."

He pressed me close enough that I could feel his body all along mine. I was finding that the longer we stayed like this, the less I cared who was paying attention. Our bodies sizzled everywhere they touched.

We had to leave, and now. I had enough problems. He wasn't getting added to the list. I was about to tell him I was ready to get out of there when he beat me to it.

"I'm going to lead the way out of here now."

Shit. Gram. With everything going on, my reason for being here had been obliterated from my mind for a few seconds.

He threaded his hand through my hair. "Is there a problem?"

Was there? His eyes were on my lips, and it didn't seem as if it was because he was waiting for my answer.

"No. We should get going," I said. For his sake and mine. This farce had to end before it became more real than I could handle. Gram would understand that sometimes you had to change up your plans. If she was here somewhere, she'd been watching and didn't want to approach. She'd get me another message. That was better than what would happen if we kept playing pretend.

Or was it pretend?

With a hand on the small of my back, Kaden steered me out the door.

He hadn't specified whether we were going to his place or the outpost. As we continued to walk, it became clear it was his place.

His hand stayed glued to me until we were in his house, door closed. I walked toward the fireplace, and he stayed on the other side of the room, as if neither of us trusted being close together and alone.

"Why did you go to Nowhere tonight?" He gripped the

chair in front of him, his knuckles white as his fingers pierced the fabric.

"I told you. I wanted to get a better sense of the area, what goes on there. Whatever it is you think I am, I'm not a spy," I said, trying to force him to see that truth, which was the only one that mattered. He didn't need to know anything else.

"I think *you* believe what you're saying. What I'm unclear on is whether it's the truth."

I jerked, having expected anything but that.

"What, then? You think I'm brainwashed? That I don't know what I'm doing?"

He turned his head, cracking his neck both ways before putting his hand behind it, rubbing, as if everything about tonight had grated on his last ounce of control.

"Let's look at the situation, shall we?" he asked. "You say your grandmother got you a reservation but you have no idea how, why, *or* what she might've been. You have no aptitude, according to testing. Not only that, you test negative for transitioning even after you have." He nonchalantly waved toward where I was standing. "Then there's the issue that Chaos seems be to following you, yet you survive. And again, no answers for any of it. You think that there isn't something strange about all of this?" He narrowed his eyes, daring me to disagree.

Was he right? When he put it like that, he made me wonder if I'd somehow been manipulated. What was I? He wouldn't be the person I'd ask, not if there was a possibility he was right.

"Now what? Should I leave the outpost?"

I mentally catalogued my belongings. I still had the money. That would feed and shelter me for a while Topside. It would be hard to get a job if people kept forgetting who I was and I had no identity left, but maybe I could get some kind of work in Nowhere.

"Now nothing. We're both going to continue to play this out. If I didn't think you might be useful to me, you'd already be dead."

"Is that a threat?" I asked, stiffening.

"No. That's reality. I wouldn't have had to lift a finger. You would've died several times over by now from your own stupidity. Things aren't as simple as they might seem, and you're going to have to make a choice. Either decide that you're with me, on my team, and give me a reason to trust you, or we sever ties. You go your own way. You can't straddle the wall. It's one or the other. You're either with me or not."

Handing him my blind loyalty? No. That wouldn't work. Alaric wasn't an option either. If he knew about Chaos, he might be the first to kill me. What could I do? The choices were impossible. If I'd gotten to talk to Gram tonight, I might have some idea of what was going on.

I needed time. My grandmother was where I'd gotten my stubbornness. She'd show.

"What if I can't decide?" I asked.

"Then I'll decide for you."

Which meant I'd be out. I'd be flying in the wind on my own in this strange world. The idea was utterly terrifying, but I wouldn't make my choice based on fear. I just needed to buy myself some time.

I walked toward the door, planning on walking to the outpost, but he grabbed me.

"What are you doing?"

"I'm trying to leave," I said.

"So you can make your meeting? No. I might not believe you are intentionally spying, but I still don't trust your reasons about tonight." His eyes roved over me, almost hungrily. "Although I can see you certainly made an effort to please whoever your company was going to be," he said, sounding angrier than he had all night.

I found my back arching without thought, some part of me glowing from his perusal. Was he jealous? Over me? The thought was so stunning, I found myself throwing an accusation at him before I thought better of it.

"You're acting like a—"

"Man with a vested interest that you don't meet with my enemies."

Enemies. There was that sticky word. Would it apply to Gram? I hoped not. This was not the man you wanted to fight with.

He still had a hold on my arm when Antoinette appeared in the doorway. Oh, just what I needed to make my evening complete. The jealously I sensed somehow had dulled my anger over his wanting me to stay, but with her here? This wasn't going to go well.

"Kaden, what's going on? I thought you had to run out for some emergency, and yet I got a call you were at The Deep, with her." Her eyes were glued to the place Kaden and I were connected.

"It was an emergency, and it's handled," Kaden said, letting go of me, although I didn't think it was because of her glare.

She smiled. "Why is Billie here? Is she staying the night —again?" she asked, her voice sounding brittle enough to crack.

"Yes, she'll be staying," he said.

This was definitely where I needed to exit. If I couldn't get out of the house, I'd at least get out of the vicinity, to avoid any shrapnel.

"I'll just give you guys a..."

Kaden walked into the dining area, and she stared at me as if the sound of my voice was going to make her snap.

I exited to the stairs.

I'd barely made it to the upstairs hallway when her screaming filled the air.

"I want her gone!"

Kaden's voice was more of a hum, completely indiscernible. He wasn't much of a screamer, unfortunately for me, since I'd have to try to fill in the blanks. My guess was he said no, simply because I'd already tried to leave on my own.

"Why can't you get rid of her?" she yelled. "You're not trying hard enough."

I had to agree with her on this one. I felt like he hadn't tried hard enough either. Seemed to me that Antoinette and I had finally come to something we could agree upon.

"If you don't get rid of her, I'm leaving," she yelled.

More muffled noise.

"I see the way you look at her."

She did? And how was he looking at me, exactly? Had there been more looks like the ones tonight? Had I been bumbling around, such a mess, that I'd missed them?

More muffled talking.

"You're going to regret this," she said. "I was the best thing you ever had." Her voice was louder and clearer, as if she were moving closer to the front of the house, where the sound traveled easier.

I edged as close as I could get without being seen.

"I'm sorry that you feel that way. I never meant to hurt you," Kaden said.

His calmness in the face of her wrath was a code every woman alive could break: *I'm sorry I hurt you, but I'm fine with the way things went down, and if they happen to end, I won't be devastated.* Or more bluntly, *I didn't give a shit about us. You were nothing but a good time.*

"Can I walk you out?" he said.

The blows just kept on coming.

"No. I'm fine on my own," she replied.

Not a bad comeback. It would've been better if she hadn't hung on like a desperado for that last... How long had she been with him? Plus, of course, the scene tonight was hard to come back from.

She slammed the door so loudly that it nearly shook the house.

CHAPTER TWENTY-SEVEN

L avender? It had never been my color, but maybe I hadn't given it enough of a chance. This dress, its silky smoothness, the way it wound over one shoulder and with almost carved-out flesh here and there, was enough to brave the pastel world. It was enough without being too much. It was elegance and sexiness without looking like I tried too hard. Plus, it would go spectacularly well with the new pair of heels I'd spotted.

My cell rang from the lounge area, and I jumped. Was someone calling me?

"Hello?" I answered, breathless from my run out of the closet room. It wouldn't do anyone any good to know how much time I was spending in there. As it was, they might've been catching on. There might've been a comment or two dropped about my *happy place* recently.

"I need you to be ready to go to a party in two hours," Kaden said.

"What kind?" I asked. Would it be appropriate for that dress?

"Cocktail attire."

I hummed, as if I weren't already half sold. That lavender dress was getting its day.

"What am I getting paid?" I asked, cutting to the more important issues. It couldn't all be about the clothes.

There was a pause, as if he hadn't expected me to ask. Well, if I was going to be stuck working here for a while, I was going to set myself up, and others. I still needed that house for my mother. It wasn't like I could collect after the building had blown up.

"What do you want?" he asked, sounding slightly amused.

"There's a house I'm looking at. I think it's receiving multiple offers, so I can't give you an exact price yet, but I need to get a bid in soon."

"Done. Text me the address and it will be handled. I'll be there at nine."

I stared at the phone. That had gone way easier than expected, and I had just the dress.

He pulled the car up in front of a mansion in the Hollywood Hills. The moon was low on the horizon, and warm lights spilled from the squared lines of the home, the glass windows showing right through to the back of the house. The two-story entrance teased at my brain as if it were something long forgotten. I'd seen so much architecture like this that it was probably just familiarity.

The valet opened my door, and as I stood outside the house, people flowing in and out around me, that feeling of knowing this place grew even stronger. This wasn't a familiarity with an architectural style, but as if I knew this specific house.

Kaden walked over, laying his hand on my back.

"Where are we?" I asked, trying to sound as casual as possible, which was hard when I was nearly choking on the boulder lodged in my throat.

"Some musician's house. Our mark is going to be here tonight."

Breathe. Just keep breathing.

"Is our mark the musician?" There was no doubt that I still had a heart in my body, even if its only purpose was to pound away at my ribs.

"No. Some executive that's supposed to be in attendance." His gaze was intently focused.

When I was sixteen, I'd sat in my room while my mother slept one off, and watched a show on homes of the rich and famous. I hated home shows, but I'd watched for one reason: I wanted to see where my father lived. I'd watched as he, his wife, and his daughter gave a tour of their home. They'd laughed and made bad jokes as they moved from room to room. My sister's suite was bigger than the entire apartment we'd been living in at the time.

The final shot of the episode, the one that was forever scarred into my mind, was their saying goodbye from the front of this house. My father had one arm wrapped around my sister's shoulders and another around his wife's as the shot panned away. In that last second, right before the camera cut away from them, my father had looked at my sister like she was the crowning glory of his accomplishments. That was the very last time I'd watched anything about him.

My mother barely remembered me. My boyfriend didn't answer my calls. If my father, of all people, was here, he'd be the last to cling on to my memory. He'd been trying to forget about me since the day I was born.

"Is there an issue?" Kaden asked, his voice a little softer than I was used to.

My father was my past. He didn't deserve to have any sway over me or what I did.

"Not at all." I'd go in, do what I had to, and get out.

Kaden didn't look convinced.

I took the first steps toward the house, refusing to acknowledge there was a problem, because there wasn't.

The place was so packed that any worries of being discovered eased. It would be easy to disappear into this crowd. Still, I scanned it, looking for familiar faces to avoid. No reason to take any chances. If they were here, they didn't appear to be in this room.

Kaden nodded toward the bar area. "See that man standing in the corner, surrounded by beautiful women?"

I scanned the area he indicated and found an attractive man in his early forties. He looked as if he were holding court, deciding whom he'd bed tonight and then discard come morning.

"He's very wealthy, on the board of five different tech companies, each of which he helped start." He pointed across the room to an older lady, elegant gray hair piled upon her head and with cheekbones that would mark her as a beauty until the day she died.

Kaden leaned closer, talking softly. "That woman runs a cancer charity. The only reason she socializes at all is to encourage donors. That man needs to write her a substantial check by tonight."

"So I need to go tinker him?" I asked, trying to keep my focus on Kaden's words and not his nearness.

"No. They have to interact. You need to bring them together."

Two? I had to coordinate dual tinkering? Didn't he know I was a newbie?

"Why can't I just tinker him?"

"Because the job isn't just the donation. They have to interact. Someone, somewhere, obviously believes that this interaction will have a trickle-down effect. Why? I don't know. The IBA doesn't get that information."

I could feel my heartbeat ratcheting up. I wasn't ready for this. Two? This could be a mess. What if I tried to juggle them and they called me out as a fraud?

Kaden moved his fingers in a soothing gesture. It was probably all for show. No way he was trying to help me, right? It wasn't as if I'd told him I was uncomfortable.

"I do this, I get the house?" I asked, working my way up to heading over there.

He smiled slightly. "Already have the accountants handling it. We overbid. Cash deal. We waived inspections and contingencies. It'll be closed in a matter of days." He was scanning the crowd while I stared at him.

"You bought it already?" I asked, my voice sounding small even to my ears.

"Of course. Your terms were the house."

"I didn't hold up my end yet. What if I can't tinker them?"

"Then it'll be payment for a different job," he said, shrugging. "It's not that significant."

The house might not be a big deal to him, but it was life-changing for me, or at least someone I cared for.

"No. Of course not."

I nodded, stepping away and toward the mark, before I started acting like an idiot and profusely thanking him.

I grabbed a glass of wine off a passing waiter's tray, downed half of it, and worked my way in closer until I was at the mark's left-hand side. He glanced my way, causing a lag in the conversation as he tried to place me. The women surrounding him didn't seem to have any interest in doing anything other than kicking my ass out of their little group.

I needed flesh-to-flesh contact. Hand or face? Definitely hand. I laid my fingers on his wrist, making sure they touched his skin directly.

I could feel the connection instantly, see the attention shift as he suddenly didn't notice anyone in the room but me.

"Roger?" I said, having no idea where the name came from. "I'm so sorry to interrupt, but I believe we've met before."

He smiled warmly. "Have we? I can't imagine I'd forget a face like yours, but you do seem oddly familiar."

Reels and reels of images rushed through my head, nearly knocking me over. That hadn't happened before.

"The Bentley event a year ago?" I asked, going on a hunch.

His smile got wider. "I do remember you. You didn't have time for me because of that pesky date of yours." He glanced around the room. "I'm hoping you lost him?"

"Luckily, I came alone this time." I nodded toward the side of the room. "Do you have a moment? I'd love to introduce you to someone."

"For you? I'd walk through hell."

Hopefully that wasn't where he was heading.

He covered my hand with his, shifting it to the crook of his arm as he extricated himself from his group of admirers.

"Now who is this person you'd like me to meet?"

"She's right over here."

"She? You had me worried for a minute it might be a man. I'm not sure I'd handle that well at all."

Roger certainly didn't waste any time laying it on, and I didn't think it was the lure of being tinkered.

I brought him over to the woman, her name suddenly coming to mind as if I'd forgotten it, instead of never knowing it.

The lady glanced up at us as we neared her spot on a couch, and then squinted at me.

"Mrs. Felicia? It's me, Billie." I reached down with my free hand, hoping she'd shake it.

She did, thankfully.

"Oh, Billie! How are you?"

"I'm wonderful. May I introduce you to my friend?"

She let go of my hand. There was no casual way to keep a hold of both of them. I just had to hope the initial connection would persist.

She broke into a smile. "Of course. Please, take a seat. Join me."

We settled down, and I managed to get a seat between the two of them.

"Very nice to meet you," Roger said. "I've seen you at some of these functions before."

"Did you know Mrs. Felicia has her own cancer charity?" I leaned in slightly, squeezing his arm. I looked him straight in the eyes as I said, "Isn't it the most wonderful thing to give the way she does? To have the ability to make a difference like that? The legacy it leaves?"

He looked enthralled. He was right there. I was going to be able to get him to do this, but instead of doing it, he was staring at me.

Why wasn't he doing it?

I took his hand in mine, making sure I had a good connection, feeling the heat flowing from me to him.

"That would be amazing if you did that."

He stared at me and slowly started to nod. "It would."

"You should do it, now, tonight."

"I should." He nodded vigorously and finally turned to Mrs. Felicia. "I'm going to make a donation to your charity now, tonight."

"That would be wonderful," Mrs. Felicia said. "We're always looking for donors. I can get you in touch with my daughter. She helps me run the charity. Her husband just passed from cancer, and I know a large donation would really help her spirits. Make her feel like she's helping to do something."

He smiled at Mrs. Felicia and pulled out his phone. "Can you give me her contact information?"

"Here, take my spot so you two can work out the details," I said, slipping out from the center position.

"You don't understand the change this will make in so many lives," Mrs. Felicia said as I slipped away.

Job done. Time to make my exit and get out of this house.

I turned and walked toward Kaden, noticing a blond goddess who was heading in the same direction, focused on Kaden. Her slip dress shimmied over a lean body, breasts with the hint of nipple showing, and still she somehow looked classy and oozing money.

We ended up in front of Kaden at the same moment. Her eyes froze on me, her lips parting, and I suddenly realized who she was.

I'd only met her one time. *Once.* Everyone else was forgetting me, and yet this half-sister of mine, whom I'd met once nearly a decade ago, recognized me. There was no misunderstanding the anger burning in her gaze.

"What are you doing here? He's not your father. He didn't want you here before. You think he wants you here now?" she asked, as if she couldn't understand the nerve I had to trespass in her home.

"I…I was…" I couldn't speak. Just like that, I was the awkward fifteen-year-old with fat cheeks and clearance-rack clothes, feeling like an interloper.

Kaden wrapped his arm around my waist. "She's here with me. Is there a problem?"

My sister broke away and walked across the room, right to the person I feared seeing the most. She talked to him and then he looked my way.

"We should go," I said, keeping my back to my sister and father. I grabbed Kaden's arm, tugging him away from the bar, knowing we'd have to cross paths with them to get out of there but wanting to leave at all costs.

"What's going on?" Kaden asked.

"I…" I glanced behind me, and there stood my father, alongside my sister. He was smiling, probably to not cause a scene. When he made the settlement with my mother, a nondisclosure had been part of it. He wouldn't want anyone here to know who I was.

"Billie, I'm surprised to see you." There was no doubt about how distasteful he found this surprise, found *me*. I'd felt more warmth standing in the middle of a blizzard.

"I didn't realize when we were coming here it was your house," I said, wishing Chaos would kill me right now. "I'll be leaving."

"I think that's for the best," he said.

My sister smiled, her hand tucked into our father's arm.

"Excuse me, are you asking us to leave?" Kaden asked

the question in a tone dripping in arrogance. He typically sounded arrogant, but this was a notch beyond anything I'd ever heard.

"I'm sorry, have we met before?" my father asked, turning to Kaden.

"No, and you're going to wish we hadn't. Now, we'll be leaving, but only because I have no desire to remain anywhere near you." Kaden put his arm around my waist and steered me toward the door.

I glanced back at my father and could see his stare trained on Kaden's back, as if maybe he'd inadvertently stepped on the toes of someone he shouldn't have. He was probably safe. It wasn't like he'd kicked Kaden out of the house or that Kaden was actually my date.

I stood there, numb, in the driveway, as Kaden signaled for the valet to get the car. I willed myself to act normal, as if nothing as humiliating as having my father kick me out of his house had just happened. What kind of person got kicked out of their father's home?

I couldn't bring myself to look at Kaden, or even the valet. I stared off at the horizon, waiting to spot a car approaching, desperate for some sort of retreat. I turned and walked a couple of steps away, feigning interest in a potted plant as I wiped an errant tear that I hadn't been able to stop from escaping. There wouldn't be another.

Kaden laid his still-warm jacket over my shoulders.

"You looked cold," he said.

"Thanks," I said, hoping to continue with the silence. I didn't want to talk about what had happened, or why.

The minutes stretched out as guests meandered in and out of the house. Our car pulled up, and Kaden was the one to shut the door for me. I kept my face toward the window as he got in.

After a few minutes of awkward silence, I mustered up the will to say something.

"I'm sorry. I thought he wouldn't remember me, or I would've warned you. I don't understand why he did."

Kaden was suspiciously quiet. He wasn't much of a talker, but the way his lips were pressed into a flat line, the tense muscles of his forearm, he was clearly holding back on me.

"Are you upset?"

"Of course not. You wouldn't have expected him to recognize you." His knuckles were nearly white where he gripped the wheel.

"Do you know why he did?" I asked.

"It's normal for different feelings to last longer. Different intensities subside at different rates for different people. It happens."

I clasped my hands in my lap and went back to staring out the window, trying to keep my breathing even. In other words, my father hated me more than my mother loved me.

"Billie, no family is perfect," Kaden said. I could see him watching me out of the corner of my eye.

"Yeah, I know. I'm good. It was just a surprise."

Of course we got stuck at a traffic light on the way back to a bridge. I'd heard that Los Angeles traffic was bad, but this was not the time I wanted to discover it.

Kaden suddenly shut off the car. "Get out," he said.

For a second, I thought he was mad about the job. Until he got out and opened my door.

"It's coming," he said, pulling me out after him and running.

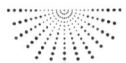

CHAPTER TWENTY-EIGHT

"How is this possible?" I asked, running beside Kaden. We'd stopped the car by a memorial park. There was nowhere to hide. No buildings close.

He grabbed my hand, pulling me with him through the gates. We ran until my lungs were burning acid and my muscles were screaming bloody murder. He kept going, running toward a mound of fresh dirt, and my stomach lurched into my throat.

"In the hole," he said. "The ground will help."

Oh no. I'd already be in a grave. This seemed like it would make it easier to kill me somehow.

"I'm not going—"

He leapt, pulling me with him. I fell and stumbled into him.

"In the corner."

He pushed me down, pressing me against the earth walls as he used his body to shield me.

"Don't speak, don't move, try not to even breathe loudly."

I nodded—barely, afraid to do even that. It wasn't only

Chaos that made it hard to breathe now but the feeling of being buried alive. This wasn't the way I wanted to go out.

Just as my heart was pounding out of my chest from the claustrophobic feeling of being tucked into the corner of a grave, the feeling of Chaos growing closer piled on top. A cold sweat coated my skin, a tremble growing and spreading until I bit down with all my strength so my teeth didn't chatter. Kaden tightened his arms around me, and instead of making me more claustrophobic, it calmed me slightly. I didn't know if he'd tinkered me or what, and I didn't care. As much as I'd said I never wanted him to make me do something against my will, without asking, not even sleep, right now all rules were thrown out, and the only thing left was survival.

The heaviness of it began soaking the air, filling it and charging it with dread. If I were capable of breathing, it would have stolen the air from my lungs as it spread over us, clung to the air all around, poking into every little crevice.

But it didn't see us. As I huddled under Kaden, it felt like its tentacles grazed over us, moving along the surface, as if we were part of the dirt and earth, nothing for it to see or sense at all.

It had passed, and yet we were still huddled. He leaned back slightly, and I pressed my head to his chest, my body seeming to instantly follow his. I gulped down deep breaths as if I hadn't breathed in the last few minutes, which I might not have.

Kaden grabbed my shoulders. "It's not completely gone. I can still feel it. We need to get out of here and to Nowhere, where it can't sense you."

I nodded. I would've agreed to anything that was away from that thing. He jumped out of the hole with no effort and then reached down, pulling me out behind him.

I turned to head back in the other direction, but he stopped me.

"No. The bridge is too far. We're going to have to take an unorthodox way." He raised his hands into the air, feeling for something I couldn't see. "Look for a sharp tool. Even a pointy stone will work."

There wasn't much in the way of choices other than a few items left near the machinery that must've been used to dig the grave.

"What about this?" I asked, holding up a pickaxe.

"That'll work." He took it from me and then motioned for me to move back.

I moved a few feet.

"Farther," he said.

I kept going until I was about twenty feet away, and he nodded.

"Stay there until I tell you. These openings aren't stable." There was something grave about his tone, and I took another step back, wondering if we should be doing this at all. Maybe we should've just run?

He was already at work, and interrupting didn't seem wise. He whispered words that I couldn't quite make out. The snippets I did catch didn't sound coherent, but they were doing something. There was a slight fizzling happening in the air, as if someone were holding up a few of those handheld sparklers.

Then he took the pickaxe and swung into the air.

It sounded like it hit a brick wall, with a loud smashing noise accompanied by the smell of burning.

A blast of light exploded from a tiny spot, bright enough I had to squint and turn away. When I looked back,

Kaden had shoved his hands into it, physically wrenching it open, Nowhere's night sky visible beyond him. He shoved his body into the opening, straining to force it bigger.

"Hurry. It won't stay open long." He was straddling the opening, but losing ground. There wasn't enough room for me to climb through. The only thing he was accomplishing was getting crushed.

In another few seconds, too short a time for us both to get through, it was going to kill him.

"Hurry," he said, as the hole shrank on him.

Chaos was coming for me. Not him.

I ran forward, as if I were going to aim for the too-small spot, and shoved him with all my might, dislodging him in his surprise. The last thing I saw before the hole closed was his shocked expression as he fell through it.

It closed up a second after, and I spun, pure panic surging through me. I was alone. I'd pushed Kaden to safety, and now I'd pay with my life.

Chaos was coming again. I could feel it circling back to me, getting closer. I jumped into the grave, curling into the same corner, closing my eyes and praying to Gram.

Chaos' presence grew again, swirling over the area. I remained still, reminding myself I'd survived the other times. Maybe it wouldn't touch me, the way it hadn't in the past.

I huddled there, waiting for death, waiting for it to rip me to shreds. It was like a tornado blowing around me but not striking.

Then there was a shift, and the dreadful feeling of Chaos started to subside again. As soon as it passed, the air went still, flat. A gentle breeze took its place, carrying the smell of marigolds. Marigolds had been Gram's favorites.

When she lived with Grandpa, they'd had marigolds everywhere. After he passed and she came to live with us, she'd still planted them everywhere she could, every place we went.

The smell of flowers intensified, and I could almost feel Gram's presence. I squeezed my eyes tight, wanting to cry from the feeling of her and the relief of still being alive.

"Gram? Are you here?"

A hand grazed my head, the same way my Gram's used to when I was a child in bed, sick. I was so scared to open my eyes and find myself alone that I stayed huddled, paralyzed. Maybe I was dead and Chaos had finally killed me.

"Billie, it's okay. I'm here."

I swallowed, hoping I wasn't imagining this, but opened my eyes and saw Gram kneeling beside me.

Or almost. She wasn't exactly Gram because I could see some of the dirt wall behind her.

"Gram?" I asked.

"You think I'd leave my special girl all alone?"

I leaned forward, wrapping my arms around her, not caring if she wasn't really there. To my surprise, my arms felt a force, some kind of the energy that probably didn't belong in this world. I leaned back again, scared that this was some sort of trick.

"Is it really you?" I asked.

"Yes. I'm having trouble in this realm, but let's not talk about that. I don't have that much time. Are you okay?" She reached out, holding my hands. Suddenly we were sitting on the grass above the grave.

"Gram, what the hell is going on? What did you get me into? Please tell me what's going on."

Her grip on my hand slackened, and I could visibly see her wanting to retreat from me.

"I need you to know I love you. You know that, right? That's the most important thing."

Tears ran down my face. "Of course. That might be one of the very few things I am sure of. But I *really* need you to tell me what's going on."

She nodded. "I know," she said, suddenly talking as if there were no urgency at all. "I would've told you all of this before, but I knew you wouldn't believe me. This is hard to tell you. Harder than I ever imagined. I know you think I'm this great person."

She smiled at me, as if she'd pulled the wool over my eyes all these years. I did love her. Did I think she was always a great person? Not really. She'd been great to me but a little lackluster in other departments, including my mother, my uncle, my cousins, my cousins' kids...

"I know you weren't perfect, but you couldn't have been a better grandmother to me." And only to me, but again, no need to drag it all out.

"So, like I said, I wasn't always so good in the..." She stared at the sky, tapping her finger to her chin. "I guess you could say good in the classical sense of the word. Maybe I played it a little free and loose with some of the rules? Did things maybe I shouldn't have? Sometimes." She waved a half-visible hand in the air, and I could see she was losing her opaqueness.

She was also stalling. What had she done? Was it that bad she couldn't even tell me? I'd spent the last month thinking if I could talk to Gram for five minutes, I could get a handle on what was going on and get out of this mess. Now I feared to hear what she was going to say. Didn't mean I didn't have to know.

"Why did you set up that reservation with Kaden?"

There was no way she was leaving without my getting some answers out of her.

"He was strong enough to help get you get settled until I got my situation straightened out," she said.

A small amount of the tension I'd been carrying since Kaden told me that eased. No sane person would send their granddaughter into the hands of their foe.

"So you're not the one he was talking about, right? He said, that night at the club, the timing was odd. But you wouldn't have sent me to your enemy."

She leaned back slightly and looked to the side. "Well, that gets a little more complicated. Let's just say we weren't exactly on the same side of the fight."

Oh no. This didn't sound good. This was not what I was hoping she'd say. Not even close.

"What fight?" That slight relief I'd felt boomeranged and magnified until it felt like I'd crack under the force of it.

"There might be some underlying conflicts going on, but I need more time to explain, and I don't have it. It's hard for me to stay here right now."

She didn't want to tell me. Whatever she'd gotten me mixed up in was so bad that she didn't even want to say it. I groaned. I couldn't help it.

She whipped her head in the direction of where Kaden had disappeared.

"I have to go. He's coming back for you. Don't say anything about me. Just stick with him and we'll iron things out later. You're a tough girl, just like I raised you. You'll figure it out until I'm back." She started fading.

"Wait? What about Chaos? Did you do something?" I said, reaching out and trying to keep her with me.

"I fixed that. You should be okay for a while." Her hand

turned into nothing as she faded into air, and as much as I'd been dying to see her, these few minutes weren't enough, almost adding to the grief.

A hole opened up next to me and a hand wrapped around my wrist, pulling me into it.

I crashed twenty feet down into an icy ocean, the shock of the cold ripping through me painfully. Panic struck as I tried to find the way to air in inky black water. Kaden grabbed me, pulling me up with him. My head broke the surface, and I coughed and gasped, treading water.

"Can you make it to the shore?" he asked, pointing to the city lights in the distance.

"Yes," I said, heading toward the rocky coast of Nowhere about a hundred feet away, the waves knocking me about every so often as we made our way.

I crawled out of the ocean a few minutes later, taking a second to get my wind. I got up before I was ready as Kaden stood beside me, hand out, ready to pull me to my feet.

We were walking on dry land a few minutes later and heading toward his townhouse. My shoes were long gone, my dress sopping wet. He was still in his evening clothes, but he'd manage to keep his shoes. We walked in, leaving a trail of water.

"I'm going to…" I motioned upstairs, and he nodded, as exhausted from the day as I was.

He was in fresh clothes when I came down, tending a fire he'd started. He put the poker down and leaned on the mantel.

"It's obviously following you. I can perform a cleansing spell or a masking spell, depending on what was done. I don't know how long it'll last, but I can keep redoing it until we figure out how to fix it permanently."

"I, uhm…" Gram had said not to tell him yet, but I couldn't live that much of a lie. To have him doing spells, thinking he was fixing things when she'd already done something?

He was waiting for me to finish. "What is it?" he asked.

"I don't think you need to do that," I said. I wouldn't tell him, but I didn't want to set myself up for a lie that would haunt me.

"Why is that?" He narrowed his eyes and took a step toward me.

What did I say now? Gram had had some sort of run-in with him. If I admitted to that, he'd kick me to the curb. Then what would I do? I didn't know if I wanted to stay, but I wasn't ready to leave.

I went with the closest version to the truth I could offer. "Because it came back. It swirled around me but didn't hurt me. This time I got a sense that something had changed. I think it's gone for now. I think it'll be okay for a bit."

"You might not realize how odd it is that you survived Chaos three times, but I can assure you, it's not normal. This doesn't just happen and then stop."

"Maybe it was just a fluke?" There was a glass on the table, probably his. I picked it up and took a nice, long gulp, wishing I could get my hands on some of that sparkling fountain water.

He watched me down his drink. "Every time something odd happens, it makes me wonder if you're some sort of evil mastermind. Then you say something like that and I realize you're not a skilled enough liar to have some grand scheme."

"And every time I think you might be, if not pleasant, at

least bearable, you say something like that." I toasted him with his own glass then finished it.

He laughed, but it didn't last long before he grew more serious. "You need to make a decision."

"I know. I just have a few things I need to work through." I curled my legs under me, too spent to talk about anything more tonight.

"Is this still about your old life? Why do you fight so hard to get back to the life you had? You can be so much more than what you were, have a life so few get to experience, yet you cling to that dismal existence."

"It was the life—"

"You chose? Did you, though? Did you choose to support your mother while she drinks herself to death? Go back to a man who hasn't asked for your hand and did little to help you in any way? What are you fighting so hard for? Or are you just afraid to change? Scared that you'll reach out, be found wanting, and rejected? Are you going to let that taint everything in your life?"

"You act like you know me because I've been here for, what? A month? You know nothing." Maybe parts of my life had been dreary, but it had been *my* life. He had no idea what it was like to have everything taken from you in a second.

"It's time to make a choice. I'll give you a few more days, but that's it. You're either with me or I need to cut you loose."

I swallowed, wondering why those words seemed to cut so deep. He took a step closer, and I thought he was going to keep going.

"Why do you smell like marigolds?" he asked.

"You know, I'm exhausted. I'm going to go lie down." I hurried upstairs, hoping he'd let it go.

CHAPTER TWENTY-NINE

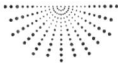

I wandered into the outpost kitchen. It was early in the morning, days past Chaos and seeing Gram, or some form of her, and time was running out. I had no life to return to, and yet I felt paralyzed.

I made a coffee and took a seat at the table, like I had for the last three mornings, looking at the newspaper the caterer had left.

Legendary Rock Singer Loses Family Home Due to Environmental Issues

Local officials discovered a rare bird nest on the property of singer William Viper and insisted the house and grounds be confiscated to be protected from human interference.

Viper refused to comment, even on the value placed on the house, which is less than a third of what most appraisers claim it's worth. The building is set to be demolished and the lot will permanently be declared a bird reserve.

. . .

There was a paparazzi picture of my father walking down the street, head down. Looking defeated.

Had Kaden done this? No. Why would he? Seemed extreme just for being asked to leave someone's house. But the timing was a bit odd, even if it brought me a little bit of peace. And maybe a little karma had been served.

I'd been eight the first time I met my father, in my best dress, which my mother got me on a Walmart clearance rack. Because it was brand new, not faded or stained, I'd thought it was special.

I'd walked up to him, and he looked like a god, tall, blond, and beautiful. I'd rehearsed everything I planned on saying, telling him how well I was doing in school and how I made my bed every day. I was going to smile and be happy. I wouldn't whine or complain. He'd see me and realize how much he wanted me.

"You're my father?" I'd asked.

"No. I'm not," he replied.

I could still remember how confused I was. I'd been told so many times he was my father.

"But everyone says you are."

He knelt down by my side and said, "This is going to be a hard lesson to learn, but some things are better to understand from the beginning so that there are no misunderstandings. Technically, I did *father* you. I slept with your mother once, many years ago, and she got pregnant. But you need to understand, being a father is a choice. I didn't choose to get her pregnant. It was an accident."

His eyes, so crystalline blue, had looked at me so coolly.

"But you got her pregnant?" I asked, still not understanding.

"But I didn't *mean* to," he said.

"But don't you support me because you're my daddy?" I asked.

He grimaced at the word. "I'm being made to pay for my mistake. The courts told me I had to, but you need to understand that I can't give you anything else. I have a family that I chose, and they need me."

"And I'm not your family?" I asked, still not grasping that I'd been thrown away like last night's leftovers.

"No. When you get older, you'll understand," he said, and then walked away.

I'd chased after him, and he motioned to some men that had come with him. They pried me off him as I cried.

Whatever understanding he'd referred to, it never came. The only thing clear was the fallout. It was still causing ripples throughout my life, my choices. Had Kaden been partially correct? Was I clinging to my old life because of my past? Maybe, but it didn't matter. My life was officially gone, and I had to accept that.

Dice walked into the kitchen with an espresso. He came near, reading over my shoulder before laughing.

"What's so funny?" I asked.

Dice pointed to the paper. "That. I don't know what that guy did, but he pissed Kaden off bad."

I dropped the paper. "What do you mean?"

"I was climbing a damned tree a few nights ago," he said, walking over and getting another espresso.

"You planted the nest there?" I asked.

"Yeah. Kaden sent me. He didn't say much, but man was he pissed off like I'd never seen. He sent Cookie over to the guy's label to get him booted. Do you know what this guy did?" He sipped his espresso.

"He didn't say?" I asked, playing stupid.

Note to self, don't ever ask Kaden to leave a party. Bit of an overreaction for what my father had done to him.

"Hey, I had a question. When you said Johnny was a bad apple, was there something specific you knew from seeing his picture?" I asked.

Dice leaned on the counter, thinking back to it. "No, but something jumped out about him, and we all picked up on it. The longer you do this job, the more that'll start to happen to you. Can't tell you exactly, but maybe murder or a crime nearly as bad."

"Murder?" No. That I wouldn't believe. Maybe Johnny did something, but not that.

Dice shook his head. "Don't ask me for details. I can't tell you because I don't know myself. Certain acts leave a bad mark on people, and that man is marked. I'd bet my existence on it, and if you look at my track record, you'll know that means something."

I nodded, not pressing him for more but knowing I'd have to know before I could move past it.

"What are you up to today? You've been kind of quiet the last couple of days," Dice said.

I leaned back in the chair. "Yeah, just figuring some stuff out. Coming to terms with other things."

"Getting ready to cut the cord to your old life?" he asked, as if he suspected more than what he'd let on.

I let the silence build for a little bit before answering. "Yeah. I guess I am."

"Well, you should do whatever you gotta do and just get on with it. If you're going to make the jump, staring at the drop doesn't change the distance." He turned, made another espresso, and then put it in front of me. "Drink up and just do what you have to."

"I know you're probably right."

"I usually am. The numbers in the betting book don't lie."

I waited outside Johnny's work, leaning against his car. There were a few things I was going to need to clean up Topside before I could move on. And it looked as if that's what I was going to have to do, whether I stayed with Kaden's group or not.

He walked out of the building, smiling at his coworkers and waving. He slowed down as he neared his car and saw me leaning there, arms crossed, waiting.

"Can I help you?" he asked, as polite as ever and without a drop of recognition.

"Yes. I've heard some things about you that I thought needed a discussion."

"Really? And what are they?"

The second he responded, I knew they were right. I didn't see it in his face the way they had. Maybe one day I would. But I could hear it. He was a monster. Was that why Gram never liked him? She'd known.

"First of all, I'd like to introduce myself. My name is Sabrina. I work for a nonprofit company. We're recruiting accountants and thought you would make a wonderful fit." I held out my hand, wanting to get a good hold of him before I attempted this tinker.

"Nice to meet you," he said, grasping my hand. "How did you hear—"

"You need to go to the police and turn yourself in." I gripped his hand hard with both of mine. "You know that what you did is wrong. You need to get in your car, drive there immediately, and confess."

His eyes glazed over, and then he began nodding.

I'd dated this monster for years. *Years.* Now I could barely keep my hand on him. I certainly didn't need any more closure. This was it.

"Go. Now."

I stepped away from his car, and he got in, still in a trance.

I didn't bother watching him drive away. I didn't want to see anything more of him. I got into the Tesla that Hank had hooked me up with and headed across town.

The house that I wanted to buy for my mother had somehow closed in a record of three days. The sun was shining on it like it was a fairytale cottage.

I parked across the street, a few houses down from her new home, and watched as she directed the movers. The sweepstakes she'd "won" had come with brand-new furniture. My mother, looking more lucid than I'd ever seen her, smiled as she pointed.

A neighbor from across the street pulled into his driveway then got out of his car and headed over. He held out his hand, introducing himself. I didn't see a flash of metal on his finger. Maybe she'd find company sooner than I'd hoped. Or maybe it would take a little while. Either way, I knew it would happen, because I'd make it happen. Was that necessarily right? Probably not. But if I was going to bend some moral rules, who else would I do it for?

CHAPTER THIRTY

I pulled the car to the curb, and Hank headed over, waving. I'd come a long way with the toll guy in a short time, and most of it not of my doing.

"Hey, Hank. Can you open up for me?" I asked.

Hank grimaced, shaking his head. "Sorry, Billie. We're having technical issues again."

"Again?" I'd thought those days were over. Hadn't they heard? The toll guys seemed pretty plugged in, but it could be possible. "She broke up with him. You know that, right?"

"We know, and your help in this matter is greatly appreciated by all of us." Hank smiled. He must've been practicing, because it didn't look anywhere near as painful this time.

"But I still can't go to the outpost?" I asked, laughing, finding this to be a fitting end to my day. I finally came to terms with what had to be done, and I still couldn't go back? "Before you answer, what if I tell you I was on my way to talk to Kaden?"

"You know what? I think it might've just come back online." He waved his hand in the direction of the opening.

"Thank you," I said, trying not to laugh. Did they think keeping me close to Kaden was like some sort of Antoinette repellant? Actually, maybe it was.

I walked into the outpost, only sparing Dice and Connor a cursory glance before searching the building for Kaden.

I walked back into the lounge and stopped in front of the television, blocking their view and getting some grunts in response. They tried to lean around me.

"Where's Kaden? I need to talk to him."

"Really?" Dice asked, his head popping up.

"He's at his place in Nowhere," Connor said, both of them watching me intently.

"Thanks."

"Good luck," they both yelled as I left.

I walked into Nowhere like I belonged there. Maybe I did? What if this was where I was meant to be? Either way, it was where I was *going* to be, and I'd make it work.

I walked up to Kaden's house and stood there, staring at the front door, wondering what exactly I'd say. How to say it. I wasn't ready to agree to his terms, but I needed him. There was no denying that.

The door opened while I was still staring at it, Kaden filling the space.

"You plan on coming in?" he asked.

I answered with a step in his direction, each one feeling heavier than the next.

He walked into his living room, and I followed, staring at the couch. Did I sit? What would that say? Probably that I was here to tell him I was staying on his team. That might not be the right thing to do. Sending the wrong signal might make this go harder. I should stay standing. But sitting might send a more cooperative signal. Or maybe it would broadcast weakness, like I was desperate? I was. That didn't mean I wanted him to know it.

I walked farther into the room, running a hand along the mantel. He took a seat, resting his hand along the back of the couch as he watched me fidget and then as I forced myself to be still.

I turned, taking in the man I was about to try to strike a deal with. He lifted an eyebrow as I sized him up. One look told you he was ruthless. If I hadn't had a reservation, he probably would've let them throw me in the river. If he hadn't found something to possibly gain from my existence, he might've let me die more than once. I couldn't even think about the conflict with Gram.

Yet, there were hints of a buried humanity, kindness, even. Was that a rationalization on my part to make it easier to do what I had to? I'd never dealt in delusions before, and hopefully I wasn't doing so now. No, I had to believe there was good in this man or it wouldn't work.

"Did you make a decision, or did you come by to say hello, but with a silent film sort of flair?"

"Are you trying to irritate me?" I asked. He had to know why I'd come. He wasn't an idiot.

"Maybe I'm curious to see what happens when you eventually say screw it and to hell with the rules." He smirked, the kind that made my stomach do a little flip-flop, as it was probably designed to do. He'd been managing and maneuvering people for ages, and it showed.

I made a show of looking at the fire so I could calm my heart and get on with this.

"I've made a decision, but I'm not taking either of the options you've laid out," I said. "I realize I'm not fully capable of navigating this world on my own, but I'm not willing to accept the existence you want to lay out before me. I don't want to be on your team. I want more autonomy." After my talk with Gram, having some distance might be the only way I might make it out of this alive. I didn't know what she was hiding, but if it was anything like this last secret, things might get ugly when it finally broke.

"Then what do you want?" he asked, looking slightly intrigued.

"Topside, they'd call me an independent contractor. We work together, a partnership of sorts. I'm going to move out of the outpost too, as soon as I find a place." I'd need somewhere secure I could hole up in if things went bad.

"Where do you plan on living? There are some obstacles to consider if you want to stay Topside."

"I'll be moving to Nowhere." Topside wasn't a possibility, not with the potential issue with Chaos. The outpost wouldn't be secure if he turned on me after finding out about Gram. The only option left was Nowhere.

"Sounds a little risky for someone who likes to play it safe. There are many things about this place you don't understand. I'm not sure you're quite ready to be here," he said, quietly, almost looking like a mentor.

"I'll survive." Unfortunately, I couldn't tell this mentor I had no other options.

"I'm not doubting you. You're a survivor," he said.

It might be one of the nicest things he'd ever said to me.

"Why are you being nice?" I said, almost aggressively, as if his compliment had been nothing but a tactic.

"It happens occasionally. It slips out when I'm not paying attention." He smirked again.

I was starting to hate those smirks. They were more lethal than his words.

"I will be fine, you know." I wasn't sure whom I was convincing, him or me.

"I know. I've met your family, remember?"

I didn't want to laugh but couldn't help myself. I would've laughed harder if I didn't think about Gram. He might've met her too, but he didn't know she was my grandmother yet.

"You want not so nice? How about this? I still don't trust you. How am I supposed to have you as a quasi-part of my team?"

"I could say the same. How do I work with you? But you have a lot more on me than I have on you. If you talked, if people knew what happened with Chaos, I'd be dead in a week. What do I have on you? Nothing. I'm surprised you'd be concerned at all." It was all so utterly true that I got a chill. He had the ability to have me hunted down by every single person in Nowhere. Would he one day decide to do that? I hoped not.

"You have nothing *now*. That might change."

Whatever he was hiding, I'd better find out, because if I didn't, I might not have any leverage to save myself. I was making a deal with someone who might be in direct conflict with one of the people I loved the most, and at her urging. This was insanity, and yet I felt myself moving along in the same direction. It was the only direction I had.

He stood and walked over to me, all the humor gone, nothing but cold lethality in his eyes.

"Are you giving me your word you won't act against me? Because that's binding," he said. "If you break your word, there will be ramifications."

"Same here," I said, bluffing. What possible revenge would I serve? But I wasn't going to stand here like a chump and not at least attempt to match him.

He smiled slowly. "Why do I have the feeling that you think I'm on the losing end of this bargain?" he asked.

"I know nothing other than what we've seen so far," I said, probably sounding a hair too defensive. "If you're saying that's too much to handle, beyond your capabilities..."

He leaned on the mantel, eyeing me up in a way that made me want to shiver, and said, "I wouldn't dream of bowing out now."

"So that's it? We have an agreement?" I asked, knowing I needed this more than him.

"We do."

Now, as long as good old Gram didn't have other plans, or Kaden didn't realize who Gram was, maybe I'd make it to next year.

CHAPTER THIRTY-ONE

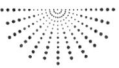

My phone was on the table in front of me—silent. It was eight o'clock and it hadn't buzzed with messages or rung all day. I thought I'd gotten used to this in the past couple of weeks, but somehow the silence burned deeper because of my birthday. This was officially my life now, and I was utterly alone.

The outpost was quiet, everyone off somewhere with something to do, except me, and it all felt a little surreal. I turned twenty-five today, and not even the woman who birthed me remembered. No amount of telling me that this was normal would take the sting out of this wound.

I picked up my phone, fighting the urge to call someone, and cracked. I dialed my mother.

The phone rang so many times that I thought it was going to go to voicemail.

"Hello?" she answered.

"Hey! It's me." I tried to tamp down the enthusiasm, the neediness she'd surely hear. Had she remembered? Had this date jarred her memory?

Silence spread, and all my hopes began to crash.

"Who is this?" she asked.

"It's Billie." And there were my emotions, a fiery explosion at the bottom of the cliff.

Dead silence greeted me, as if she were trying to jog her memory. She finally said, "Oh, Billie! Hey, what's going on?"

She spoke the way people caught unawares did. She had no idea who I was.

"Just seeing what you were up to. Haven't spoken to you for a little bit," I said, trying to fill the awkwardness.

Again, a long pause, and her thoughts were practically broadcast through the silence as she tried to figure out why not talking would be an issue.

"I've been really running crazy with the new house. I didn't realize you were expecting me to call."

Why wouldn't I? It was my *birthday*. Did I bother to say it? She wouldn't know why that would be an issue either.

"Billie?" she asked after a few more seconds of silence, this time my fault.

"Yeah, I'm here," I said, almost too forcefully so my voice didn't tremble.

"I'd love to catch up, but I'm actually meeting someone for a drink right now, so I have to get going."

"The neighbor?" I asked, finally finding a silver lining.

"Yes. How'd you know that?" she asked.

"That's good. That's really good. You sound like you're doing well." The sun had set, and there wasn't the telltale sign of a slur. She was sober and had found someone. As much as it killed me to lose my life, in the process, I'd been able to help her find hers. It wasn't all a loss.

"I don't want to hold you up," I said. "I hope you have a good time."

"Will do! Nice talking to you again. Good luck with...whatever."

She ended the call. I didn't have a mother anymore. I couldn't move or speak. I sat with my phone in my hand, realizing I was truly in this world now. There was no going back.

The TV played some mundane thing I'd thrown on an hour ago, but my mind was off, too busy drifting through the *could've beens* to pay attention.

It wasn't until someone was pounding on the door that I jerked back into reality.

"Billie? You awake in there?" Cookie yelled, making certain I was awake even if I had been sleeping. The locked door rattled.

"Yeah, I'm here." I got up and let her in before she broke the door to my suite.

She stood there, hands on hips. "I need you to referee something. I don't trust these jerks to keep the bets straight. Dice is trying to tell me I wrote a three in the book, but it's clearly a two with a long, messy loop, which is my nature. I need an impartial judge." She narrowed her eyes as she took a long look at me. "What's up with you? You look like someone took a dump in your Cheerios."

"I'm fine. Just a little tired today."

"Tired, huh? Heard the rumors floating around, you and Kaden getting a little touchy-feely at The Deep." She laughed.

Antionette had heard that night, so there wasn't anything surprising about this.

Connor poked his head in and asked, "Did you sleep with Kaden? We were all discussing it, and we're mostly thinking no, but"—he shrugged, his face scrunching up like a bulldog's—"word is you left The Deep looking like you were going to go get it in."

"I did not *get it in* with Kaden." I thought I'd outgrown blushing until I came to this place.

Dice's laughter rang out from the hall, and then his hand was palm up, in front of Connor. Connor reached into his back pocket, counted off several hundreds, and handed over the wad of cash to Dice, who handed half to Cookie.

"You bet on whether I'd slept with him?" I asked. Nothing was sacred with these people. "Thank you for giving me the benefit of the doubt that I didn't do it," I said to Cookie and Dice, who'd poked his head in enough that I could see him.

Cookie grimaced. "Uh, that wasn't the bet. We bet on whether you'd *say* you did or didn't."

"We tried to bet on *when* you'd sleep with him, but we couldn't nail down a date anyone was willing to agree upon," Dice said, and then walked back toward the lounge.

"I'm not going to sleep with him." I made sure I was loud enough that Dice heard.

"You sure about that?" Cookie asked.

"I'm positive. You said he didn't sleep with people he worked with," I said to her. Was I the only one here that was thinking logically?

"If that's the only thing stopping you then it's definitely happening."

"I didn't mean it like that. It's not. I don't want to sleep with him, and he certainly doesn't want to sleep with me." Although we both might've been on the brink of losing our senses last night.

"Yeah, I'm not so sure about that," Connor added.

"Either way, we need you to come look at the book," Cookie said.

I knew they kept a book with their bets. This was what my birthday had come down to.

I was about to tell them to fuck off, but it wasn't like I had anything else to do. Plus, anything that would get them off my situation with Kaden was welcome.

I followed her down the hall to the lounge and stopped cold. There was a cake. A *birthday* cake. The icing was chocolate, and it had my name written in pink with twenty-five candles burning. I hadn't even told them it was my birthday.

"Don't you dare get all weird, or we'll have to do something mean," Cookie said.

"You can get weird. We'll still get you a cake next year and we won't be mean," Dice said, and then stared at Cookie. "Will we?"

"Do you have to take everything so damn literally? It's exhausting."

Connor punched me in my arm and smiled.

I swallowed hard, like the kind of force you needed to keep your soul in your chest because it wanted to leap out and splatter everywhere, taking every tear you possessed with it.

Then they started singing "Happy Birthday." I hated being sung to, and yet I was about to make an epic scene, bawling at the gesture.

I blew out my candles and then wiped my face. "Smoke got in my eye," I said.

Cookie rolled her eyes but didn't say anything.

"Hey, we got you gifts too. We're not animals." Connor threw me a package.

It was a dagger with a beautifully engraved etchings on the handle and part of the blade.

"Sterling silver," Connor said. "That shit will kill more than you think, just in case you find yourself in an untinkerable position."

Cookie handed me a box and ripped the lid off. A pair of boots similar to hers were there. "I know you like fancy shoes, but you have to be ready to fight on occasion. I was trying to tinker this guy once, and his girlfriend did not appreciate me touching him. If I hadn't had these boots on when I kicked her in the crotch, things could've gotten messy." She lifted her foot, modeling them for me.

"This is from me," Dice said, handing me a jewelry box.

It was a beautiful strand of Tahitian pearls.

"These are so beautiful." I ran my hands over them. "What do they do?"

"Look good. I thought women liked that kind of shit?" Dice punched Connor in the arm. "I told you I should've gotten her a gun."

He reached for the box, and I yanked it to my chest. "No, I love them. I don't want a gun."

Connor was cutting up the cake already, and handed me a piece.

"Hey, how'd you all know it was my birthday?" I asked.

"Kaden mentioned it," Cookie said.

Kaden? There was no way he'd suggested doing something nice for me. If he had, he would've shown up. Kaden probably knew everyone's birthday, one of the tricky details he kept to use against people.

Connor elbowed me. "We got you a new-release movie to watch. That sci-fi thing you were talking about? I don't know. Whatever it was called." Connor turned to Dice. "Hey, get the movie on."

"The cake is from the leprechaun's place," Cookie said. "Try it."

I took a bite. "This is the best thing I've ever tasted in my life."

"Right?"

"Come on. It's starting," Connor said, sitting in his spot in the chair.

Dice and Cookie took their usual seats.

And I took mine. I had a *usual* seat. Maybe I didn't have nobody. Maybe I had these people. As gruff, obnoxious, and irritating as they could be, as much as I swore I never would, I actually liked these people.

We were only ten minutes into the movie when Kaden strolled in.

"Sorry I'm late," he said, and tossed me a small box. "Happy birthday." He walked over to the cake.

"Thanks." I tucked the gift beside me. I'd open his later, when I was alone.

Yeah, for better or worse, I had people.

Burning Bridges in Nowhere available now.

Use this QR code to sign up for new release notices from Donna Augustine. Don't worry! I won't flood your email box. You're more likely to wonder if you signed up correctly. Two emails in one month is my record.

Or, follow me on one of these platforms:
https://www.facebook.com/groups/223180598486878/
http://www.donnaaugustine.com
https://www.bookbub.com/authors/donna-augustine
https://twitter.com/DonnAugustine

ACKNOWLEDGMENTS

Every book comes with its own set of hurdles. Without these people, those hurdles would be a lot tougher to climb over. Lisa A., Lori H., Camilia J., Ashleigh Macleod, Michelle B., and Karen C., you turn my mountains into molehills.

A special thanks to Editing 720.

ALSO BY DONNA AUGUSTINE

Ollie Wit

A Step into the Dark

Walking in the Dark

Kissed by the Dark

The Keepers

The Keepers

Keepers and Killers

Shattered

Redemption

Karma

Karma

Jinxed

Fated

Dead Ink

The Wilds

The Wilds

The Hunt

The Dead

The Magic

Born Wild (Wilds Spinoff)

Wild One

Savage One

Wyrd Blood

Wyrd Blood

Full Blood

Blood Binds

Torn Worlds (Paranormal Romance)

Gut Deep

Visceral Reaction

River of Luck